The Unblushing Bride

Charity had not planned on finding herself in the same bedchamber as her noble husband on their wedding night, but there they were.

Charity would not have chosen the bedchamber to be the cramped quarters of a crude inn, but there it was.

Charity would have preferred to drop into the deepest of slumbers to escape the presence of the heartbreakingly handsome Lord Staunton, but she could not shut her eyes to him beside her in bed.

"Are you able to sleep?" he asked.

"No," she had to reply.

"I have no intention of asserting my conjugal rights by force," he said. "But if counting sheep does not achieve its purpose, I am willing to offer my services." His eyes met hers. "Do you wish to try it?"

Charity thought how far away was the dawn, and how close his lips.

"Yes," she said.

The Temporary Wife

by Mary Balogh

A SIGNET BOOK

SIGNET
Published by the Penguin Group
Penguin Books USA Inc., 375 Hudson Street,
New York, New York 10014, U.S.A.
Penguin Books Ltd, 27 Wrights Lane,
London W8 5TZ, England
Penguin Books Australia Ltd, Ringwood,
Victoria, Australia
Penguin Books Canada Ltd, 10 Alcorn Avenue,
Toronto, Ontario, Canada M4V 3B2
Penguin Books (N.Z.) Ltd, 182–190 Wairau Road,
Auckland 10, New Zealand

Penguin Books Ltd, Registered Offices:
Harmondsworth, Middlesex, England

First published by Signet, an imprint of Dutton Signet,
a division of Penguin Books USA Inc.

First Printing, May, 1997
10 9 8 7 6 5 4 3 2 1

Chapter 1

It being not quite the thing to advertise in the London papers for a wife, Anthony Earheart, Marquess of Staunton, eldest son and heir of the Duke of Withingsby, advertised instead for a governess.

He advertised in his own name, with the omission of his title and connections, to the decided amusement of his friends and acquaintances, who rose to the occasion with marvelous wit.

"How many children do you *have*, Staunton?" Harold Price asked him at White's the morning of the advertisement's first appearance. "Would it not be more appropriate to hire a schoolteacher? One capable of managing a full schoolroom?"

"What you should do, Staunton," Cuthbert Pyne added, "is hire a full staff. For a whole *school*, I mean. One would not wish to jeopardize the education of the budding scholars by crowding too many of them into one classroom."

"Are all their mamas to come and fetch them each afternoon, Tony?" Lord Rowling asked before inhaling the pinch of snuff he had placed on the back of one hand. "Do you have a salon large enough to hold them all while they wait? And will they wait amicably in company with one another?"

"Are you sure you wish to educate them *all*, Staunton?" Colonel Forsythe asked. "Do you have enough estates needing stewards and managers, old boy? Does *England* have enough estates?"

"You have forgotten Wales, Forsythe," Mr. Pyne said. "And Scotland."

"But it is hardly fair to everyone else's byblows if all the

positions are filled by Staunton's," the colonel said, speaking
with an exaggerated whine of complaint.

"I believe Tony is not in search of a governess at all," Sir
Bernard Shields said. "He is in search of a new mistress. I hear
you dismissed the delectable Anna just last week, Tony—with
rubies. You have decided to look elsewhere for her replacement than the green rooms of London? You have decided to
search for someone who can provide conversation as a diver-
sion while you are, ah, at work?"

"Or someone who can offer instruction," Lord Rowling
said. "It is said, you know, that one is never too knowledge-
able to stop learning. And who better to learn from than a governess? And in a schoolroom with all its desks and tabletops
on which to practice one's lessons. The mind boggles."

"I daresay," the very young and very earnest Lord Callaghan
said, "Staunton is hiring a governess for one or more of his
nieces and we are slandering him by imagining otherwise."

The Marquess of Staunton did not participate in the conversation beyond the occasional lifting of an eyebrow or pursing
of the lips. He looked on as if he were nothing more than a
mildly interested observer. He had no children as far as he
knew. He had no estates—yet. He had tired of Anna after only
six weeks and was in no hurry to employ a replacement. Mistresses, he was finding, were less and less able to satisfy his
jaded appetites. He knew all their tricks and skills and was
bored by them—Rowling was wrong about there being more
to learn. He had no dealings with any of his nieces—or
nephews either, for that matter.

No, he was not in search of either a governess or a mistress.
He was choosing himself a wife, as he made clear to Lord
Rowling when the two of them were strolling homeward later.

"Is that not usually done at Almack's or in someone's ballroom or drawing room?" Lord Rowling asked, chuckling as if
he believed the whole matter was a joke devised for his
amusement. "And without the necessity of an advertisement,
Tony? You are Staunton, after all, and will be Withingsby one
day. You are as rich as Croesus and have the looks to turn any

female head even if you were a pauper. Yet you have advertised for a wife in the guise of a governess? What am I missing, pray?" He twirled his cane and touched the brim of his hat to a lady whom they were passing.

"I cannot find what I am looking for at Almack's," the marquess said, no answering amusement in his face. He had the grace to continue when his friend merely looked at him with raised eyebrows. "She must be a gentlewoman—I'll not go lower than that, you see. She must also be impoverished, plain, demure, very ordinary, perhaps even prim. She must have all the personality of a—a quiet mouse."

"Dear me," Lord Rowling said rather faintly. "A quiet mouse, Tony? You? Do you feel such need to dominate the woman you will take to wife?"

"The Duke of Withingsby has summoned me home," the marquess said. "He claims to be ailing. He reminds me that Lady Marie Lucas, daughter of the Earl of Tillden, is now seventeen years old—old enough, in fact, for the match arranged for us by our families at her birth to be elevated to a formal betrothal. He informs me that the eight years of my absence from home have given me sufficient time in which to sow my wild oats."

Lord Rowling grimaced. "Your father is not displaying a great deal of wisdom," he said. "You have amassed a sizable fortune during those eight years, Tony." But he grinned suddenly. "As well as acquiring a well-deserved reputation as one of London's most prolific rakes. You plan to marry your quiet mouse merely in order to embarrass his grace, then?"

"Precisely," the marquess said without hesitation. "I did consider merely ignoring the summons, Perry, or answering it but refusing to wed the child who has been carefully chosen and groomed as the next Duchess of Withingsby. But this idea of mine will be infinitely better. If his grace is not already ailing in all truth, he soon will be. If he has not yet got the point of the past eight years, he soon will. Yes, I shall choose my wife very carefully indeed. I daresay there will be a number of applicants."

Lord Rowling looked aghast, perhaps only now understanding that his friend was in deadly earnest. "But, Tony," he said, "you cannot *marry* the dullest creature you can find merely to annoy your father."

"Why not?" Lord Staunton asked.

"Why not?" His friend made circular motions in the air with his cane. "Marriage is a life sentence, old chap. You will be stuck with the woman for the rest of your life. You would find the situation intolerable."

"I do not intend to spend the rest of my life with her," the marquess said. "Once she has served her purpose she will be pensioned off—a governess could hardly ask for a better fate, could she?"

"And she might live to the age of ninety," Lord Rowling pointed out. "Tony, you will want *heirs*. If you get them on her, she will wish—and quite reasonably so—to be a *mother* to them. She will wish to live in your home while they grow up."

"I have an heir," the marquess said. "My brother William, Perry. And he has sons—or so Marianne informs me. One can only hope that they are sturdy."

"But a man craves heirs of his own body," Lord Rowling said.

"Does he, by Jove?" The Marquess of Staunton looked surprised. "This man certainly does not, Perry. Shall we change the subject? This particular one grows tedious. Do you go to Tattersall's tomorrow? I have my eye on a promising-looking pair of grays."

Lord Rowling would have liked to continue the original conversation until he had talked some sense into his friend, but he was soon conversing about horses. After all, he had known the Marquess of Staunton long enough to understand that he had a will of iron, that he said and did exactly what he wished to say and do without reference to other people's preferences or to society's dictates. If he had decided to choose a wife in such an unconventional manner and for such a cynical, cold-blooded reason, then choose her he would, and marry her too.

The Marquess of Staunton meanwhile, although he talked

with enthusiasm about horses and then the races, inwardly contemplated with some satisfaction his return to Enfield Park in Wiltshire and the effect of that return on the Duke of Withingsby. It would be the final thumbing of the nose to the man who had begotten him and made his life miserable for the twenty years following his birth. For eight years, ever since he had left home after that final dreadful scene, he had lived independently of his father, refusing any financial support. He had made his own fortune, at first by gambling, then by reckless investments, and finally by more prudent investments and business ventures.

His father had clearly not got the point. But he would. He would understand that his eldest son was once and for all beyond his power and influence. Oh yes, marrying imprudently—and that would be an understatement for the marriage of the Duke of Withingsby's heir to an impoverished gentlewoman who had earned her living as a governess—would be the best possible thing he could do. He longed to see his father's face when he took his bride to Enfield.

And so he waited for replies to his advertisement, replies that began coming the very day after its first appearance in the London papers and kept coming for several days after that in even larger numbers than he had expected. He rejected several applicants, sight unseen—all those below the age of twenty or above the age of thirty, those with particularly impressive recommendations, and one young lady who so particularly wished to impress him with her knowledge of Latin that her letter was written in it.

He interviewed five candidates before discovering his quiet mouse in the sixth. Miss Charity Duncan had been shown into a downstairs salon and had chosen to stand in the part of the room that was not bathed in sunlight. For one moment after he had opened the door and stepped inside the room he thought she must have changed her mind and fled. But then he saw her, and it struck him that even her decision to stand just there was significant. In addition she was dressed from head to toe in drab brown and looked totally self-effacing and quietly dis-

ciplined. She was the quintessential governess—the sort of
employee even the most jealous of wives would not object to
having in the same house with her husband.

"Miss Duncan?" he asked.

"Yes, sir." Her voice was quiet and low-pitched. She curtsied
to him without once raising her eyes from the carpet before her
feet. She was on the low side of medium height, very slender,
perhaps even thin, though her cloak made it impossible to
know for sure. Her face looked pale and ordinary in the shadows. The brown of her hair blended so totally with the brown
of her bonnet that it was difficult to know where the one ended
and the other began. Her garments were decent and drab. He
was given the impression that they were not quite shabby but
very soon would be. They were genteel-shabby.

She was perfect. His father would be incensed.

"Please be seated," he said, indicating a chair close to where
she stood.

"Yes, sir," she said and sat down, as he expected, with a
straight spine that did not touch the back of her chair. She
folded her gloved hands in her lap and directed her gaze mod-
estly at her knees.

She was the picture of prim gentility. She was quite perfect!
He decided there and then that she would do, that his search
was at an end. He was looking at his future wife.

Charity Duncan sat close to the window in order to make
the best of the last of the daylight. It would not do to light the
candle one moment before it became absolutely necessary to
do so. Candles were expensive. She was mending an underarm
seam of one of her brother's shirts and noting with an inward
sigh that the cotton fabric had worn thin. The seam would hold
for a while, but there would be a hole more difficult to mend
sooner than that.

Her task was taking longer than it ought. Her eyes—and her
mind—kept straying to the newspaper that was open on the
table. Buying a paper each day was her one extravagance,
though it could not exactly be called that. She knew that Philip

liked to read it by candlelight after he got home from work, but in the main the purchase was for her own sake. She must find employment very soon. For almost a month she had been looking and applying and—all too rarely—attending interviews. She had even applied for a few situations more menial than a governess's or a companion's position.

No one wanted her. She was either too young or too old, too plain or too pretty, too high-born or too well-educated, or . . . Or prospective employers became too pointed in their questions.

But she would not give in and abandon the search. Her family—one sister three years younger than herself at home and three children considerably younger than that—was poor. Worse than poor. They were deeply in debt and had not even known it until the death of their father a little over a year ago. And so instead of being able to live a gentleman's life, Philip was compelled to work just to support his family. And she had insisted on working too, though there was precious little money a woman could earn that was sufficient to share with others or to pay off debts.

If only there were some way of making a huge fortune quickly. She had even considered some spectacular robbery—though not seriously, of course. She ought not to complain, she thought, her task at the shirt finished at last. At least they were not quite destitute. Not quite, but close enough. And there seemed to be no real light at the end of the proverbial tunnel.

But Philip was home, and she rose to smile her greeting, to kiss his cheek, to serve his supper, to ask about his day—and to draw his attention to the one advertisement in today's paper that looked like a possibility.

"It does not say how many children there are or what ages or genders they are," she said with a frown when they had progressed to that topic. "It does not say whether they live here in London or in the Outer Hebrides or at the tip of Cornwall. But it does say that there is a position available."

"You do not have to take employment at all, Charity,"

Philip Duncan said. It was his constant theme. Philip believed in taking full responsibility for his womenfolk.

"Oh yes, I do," she said firmly. "It is the only suitable position offered in today's paper, Phil. And there was nothing at all at the agency yesterday or this morning. I must try for it at least."

"You can go back home," Philip said, "and allow me to support you as I should. You can go back home where you are wanted and needed."

"You know I will not do that," she said, smiling at him. "You cannot possibly support us all, Phil, and you ought not. You ought to be able to live your own life. Agnes—"

"Agnes will wait," he said firmly. "Or she will tire of waiting and marry someone else. But it is unseemly for my sister to have to take employment."

"I need to feel that I am doing something too," she said. "It is not fair that I should sit at home working on my embroidery and cultivating a pretty garden just because I am a woman. And I *am* the eldest.

"I'll try for this one position," she said. "If I am unsuccessful then perhaps I will go back to the country. It is beginning to look as though I am unemployable, does it not?"

"Go back home, Charity," Philip urged. "I am a mere clerk now, but I will rise to a better position and earn more money. Perhaps I will even be wealthy someday. And indeed you are not cut out to be in service. You do not have the necessary spirit of subservience. You lost the last position because you could not keep your opinions to yourself."

"No," she said, grimacing. "I was of the opinion that the children's father ought not to be molesting the prettiest chambermaid against her express wishes and I said so—to both him and the children's mother. He really was horrid, Phil. If you had known him, you would have disliked him excessively."

"I have no doubt of it," he said. "But his behavior to another servant was not your concern, Charity. The girl had a tongue of her own, I daresay."

"But she was afraid to use it," she said, "lest she lose her position."

Philip merely looked at his sister. He did not need to say anything.

Charity laughed. "I had no wish to remain there anyway," she said. "But I do wish positions were more easily come by. Six interviews in the past month and nothing to show for them. Perhaps I had better hope that Mrs. Earheart and her children *do* live in the Outer Hebrides and that no one but me will be intrepid enough to join them there." She sighed. "Perhaps I should include in my letter of application my willingness to go to the ends of the earth. Perhaps they will pay more to compensate me for the remote situation."

"Charity," Philip said, "I wish you would go home. The children miss you. Penny says so in all her letters. You have been like a mother to them ever since Mama died."

"I shall not mention my willingness," she said as if she had not heard him. "I might sound overeager or groveling. And I shall try for this one last position. I shall probably not even receive a reply and all your wishes will be granted. But I shall feel such a helpless *woman*, Phil."

He sighed again.

But Charity was proved wrong in one thing. Five days after she sent her letter of application to Mr. Earheart, she received a reply, inviting her to attend an interview the following morning. She felt her heart begin to palpitate at the very thought. It was so difficult to endure being questioned, more as if one were a commodity than a person. But it was the only way to employment. How cruel it was, though, to actually have an interview, to be this close, only perhaps to have one's hopes dashed yet again.

"This will be the seventh," she said to Philip when he came home from work late in the evening. "Will this be the lucky one, do you suppose?"

"If you really want the position, Charity," he said with a sigh, "you must behave the part. Governesses, like other servants, you know, are to be seen and not heard."

She grimaced. Not that she was ever loud or vulgar. But she was a *lady*. She was accustomed to considering herself the equal of other ladies. It was hard to accustom herself to the knowledge that there was a despised class of shabby genteel people—of whom she was one, at least as long as she sought employment. It was something that had to be ignored or endured. "I must be demure then?" she said. "I may not offer my opinions or observations?"

"No," he said bluntly—and she realized with a sudden wave of pain that Philip must have had to learn the same lesson for himself. "You must convince the man, and his wife if she is present, that if they employ you, you will blend very nicely into the furniture of their home."

"How demeaning," she said and then bit her lip, wishing she had not said the words aloud.

"And, Charity"—he leaned across the table that separated them and took her hand in both his own—"do not accept the position even if it is offered if he—well, if he is a young man. Not that youth has anything to say in the matter. If he is—"

"Lecherous?" she suggested.

Her brother blushed. "If you suspect he might be," he said.

"I can look after myself, Phil," she said. "When my former employer glanced at me with that certain look in his eye during the early days of my employment, I looked right back and chilled my eyes and thinned my lips." She repeated the look so that her brother grinned despite himself.

"Be careful, Charity," he said.

"I shall be," she promised. "And demure. I shall be a veritable mouse. A quiet, drab, brown little mouse. I shall be so self-effacing that he will not even realize I am in the room with him. I shall be . . ."

But her brother was laughing out loud. She went around the table to stand behind his chair and wrap both arms about his shoulders. "Oh, you do that all too rarely these days, Phil," she said. "All will work out, you will see. We will be rich somehow and you will marry Agnes and live happily ever after."

"And you?" He raised a hand to pat her arm.

ᴵᵘ "And I shall live happily ever after too," she said. "Penny will be able to marry and I shall stay with the children until they are all grown and happily wed, and then I shall settle into a contented and eccentric spinsterhood."

He chuckled again as she lightly kissed the top of his head.

But for all that she was nervous the next morning when she arrived at the house on Upper Grosvenor Street to which she had been summoned for an interview. The hall was unostentatious but elegant. So was the servant who answered her knock on the door. So was the empty salon into which she was shown. She instinctively sought out the part of the room that was out of the light from the windows. She tried to master the beating of her heart. If she did not secure this position, she would begin to lose confidence in herself. She had already half promised Phil that she would go home without trying further. She would . . . But her thoughts were interrupted by the opening of the door.

He *was* young—no more than thirty at the outside. He was also handsome in a harsh sort of way, she thought to herself. He was of somewhat above-medium height, with a slender, well-proportioned figure, very dark hair and eyes, and a thin, angular, aristocratic face. The sunlight shining through the windows was full on him as he came through the door. In its harsh glare the cold cynicism of his expression made him look somehow satanic. He was expensively and elegantly dressed. Indeed, he looked very much as if he might have been poured into his well-tailored coat and pantaloons—a sure sign that he was a gentleman of high fashion.

He did not look like a kind man. He looked like the sort of man who would devour chambermaids more than he would seduce them. But she must not judge the man before he had uttered even a single word. She felt demeaned again, alone in a gentleman's house without servant or chaperon, because she herself was now a servant—an unemployed one. Her eyes dipped to focus on the carpet before his own found her in the shadows. She concentrated hard on cultivating the manner of a typical governess.

"Miss Duncan?" he said. His voice was as haughty and as bored as she had expected it to be, though it was a pleasant tenor voice. There was no pretense of charm in it. But why should there be? He was conducting an interview for a governess for his children.

"Yes, sir," she said, trying to look dignified but not overproud. She kept her back straight. She was, after all, a lady.

"Please be seated." He indicated a chair that was close by and out of the glare of the sunlight, for which fact she was grateful. Interviews did not get easier with experience.

"Yes, sir," she said, seating herself, keeping her eyes lowered. She would answer the questions concisely and honestly. She would hope there would be no awkward questions.

Mr. Earheart seated himself on a chair opposite hers. He crossed one booted leg over the other. His hessian boots were of shining, expensive leather. His valet must have labored hard to produce such a shine. There was an air of wealth and confidence and power about the man. Charity felt distinctly uncomfortable in the pause before he spoke again.

Chapter 2

How did one conduct an interview for a future wife? the Marquess of Staunton wondered.

"The letter of recommendation from the rector of your former parish is impressive, Miss Duncan," he said.

"Thank you, sir," she said.

"However," he said, "it was written all of one year ago. Have you had employment since then?"

She stared at her knees and appeared to consider her reply. "Yes, sir," she said.

"And what was it, Miss Duncan?"

"I was governess for eight months to three children, sir," she said.

"For eight months." He paused, but she did not pick up the cue. "And why was the position terminated?"

"I was dismissed," she said after hesitating for a few moments.

"Indeed?" he said. "Why, Miss Duncan?" Had she been unable to control the children? He could well imagine it. She seemed totally without character.

"My—my employer accused me of lying," she said.

Well. She was frank at least. He was surprised by her reply and by the fact that she did not immediately proceed to justify herself. A meek mouse indeed.

"And did you?" he asked. "Lie, I mean."

"No, sir," she said.

He knew how it felt to be accused falsely. He well knew the feeling.

"Is this your first attempt to find employment since then?" he asked.

"No, sir," she said. "It is the seventh. The seventh interview, that is."

He was not surprised that she had failed to get past any of those interviews. Who would wish to employ such a drab, spiritless creature to educate his children?

"Why have you been unsuccessful?" he asked.

"I believe, sir," she said, "because everyone else has asked what you just asked."

Ah yes. Her confession doubtless brought any normal interview to an abrupt halt. "And you have never thought to lie?" he asked her. "To pretend that you left your employment of your own free will?"

"Yes," she admitted, "I have thought about it, sir. But I have not done so."

She was also a very moral little mouse. Someone once upon a time had told her that it is wicked to lie, and so she never lied even in the service of her own interests. Even if it meant she would never again be employed. She clung to a puritanical morality. His father would be appalled.

"For which proof of your honesty you are to be commended, Miss Duncan," he said. "I may be able to offer you something."

She looked up into his face for the first time then, very briefly. Long dark lashes swept upward to reveal large, clear eyes that were as blue as the proverbial summer sky. Not the sort of gray that sometimes passes for blue, but pure, unmistakable blue itself. And then the eyes disappeared beneath the lashes and lowered eyelids again. For one disturbing moment he felt that he was about to make a ghastly mistake.

"Thank you, sir," she said. She sounded a little breathless. "How many children are there? Do they live here with you?"

"There are no children," he said.

He waited while she studied her knees, transferred her gaze to his knees, and raised her eyes to his chest—perhaps even to his chin.

"No children?" She frowned. "My pupils, then, sir, are—are . . ."

"There are no pupils," he said. "I am not in search of a governess, Miss Duncan. It is another position entirely that I have to offer."

The little mouse obviously sensed that a big bad cat was about to pounce. She jumped to her feet and turned in the direction of the door.

"I am not about to suggest anything improper, Miss Duncan," he said, remaining seated. "Actually I am in search of a wife. I am willing to offer you the position."

She half turned back to him but did not look directly at him. "A wife?" she said.

"A wife," he repeated. "I am looking for a Mrs. Earheart, Miss Duncan. Temporarily, that is. At least, the marriage would be forever, I suppose, since such things are next to impossible to dissolve by anything less drastic than the death of one of the partners. If you have any romantic notion of marrying for love and living happily ever after, then I must bid you a good morning and proceed with the next interview. But I daresay you have not, of if you have, then you must realize that such a dream is unrealistic for someone in your situation."

She raised her eyebrows but did not contradict him. Her body was still turned toward the door. Her head was still half turned toward him.

"The marriage would be permanent," he said. "But our being together as a married couple would be temporary—for no longer than a few weeks at a guess. After that you would be free again apart from the small encumbrance of being Mrs. Earheart instead of Miss Duncan. And you would be very comfortably well-off for the rest of your life."

She was frowning down at the carpet. But she was not hastening from the room. She was clearly tempted. It would be strange if she were not.

"Will you not be seated again, Miss Duncan?" he asked.

She sat, arranged her hands neatly in her lap again, and studied her knees once more. "I do not understand," she said.

"It is really quite simple," he said. Her face was perhaps heart-shaped, he thought. But that description glamorized her too much. "I need a wife for a short period of time. It has crossed my mind that I might employ someone to act the part, but it would be far more—effective to have a real wife, one who will be bound to me for life."

She licked her lips. "And after the short period of time is over?" she asked.

"I would settle five thousand a year on you," he said, "in addition to providing you with a home and carriage and servants and covering your year-by-year household expenses."

She sat very still and said nothing for a long while. She was thinking about it, he thought. About five thousand a year, about a home and a carriage of her own. About never again having to apply for a position as a governess.

"How do I know that you speak the truth?" she asked at last.

Good Lord! He raised his eyebrows and favored her with his frostiest stare while his right hand curled about the handle of his quizzing glass. But his indignation was wasted on her lowered eyelids. Her hands, he could see, were clasping one another rather tightly in her lap. He supposed that to someone like her there must seem to be the very real possibility that this was all a cruel joke.

"There will, of course, be a written contract," he said. "I will have it here together with my man of business this afternoon, Miss Duncan—shall we say at three o'clock? You may, if you wish, spend some time alone with him and question him about my ability to fulfill my part of the agreement. Are you willing to accept my offer?"

For a long time she did not answer him. Several times her mouth opened as if she would speak but she closed it again. Once she bit into her lower lip, once into the upper. She pulled carefully at each finger of her right glove as if preparing to take it off and then pulled it firmly on again with a tug at the wrist. She spoke at last.

"Seven thousand," she said.

"I beg your pardon?" He was not sure he had heard aright, though she had spoken plainly enough.

"Seven thousand a year," she said more firmly. "In addition to the other things you mentioned."

A quiet little mouse who nevertheless had her eye to the main chance. Well, he could hardly blame her.

"We will of course settle upon six," he said, his eyes narrowing. "You accept my offer, then, Miss Duncan? I may cancel the other interviews I have scheduled to follow yours?"

"Y-yes," she said. And then, more firmly, "Yes, sir."

"Splendid." He got to his feet and reached out a hand for hers. "I will expect your return here promptly at three o'clock. We will marry tomorrow morning."

She set her hand in his and got to her feet. Her eyelashes swept up again, and he found himself being regarded keenly by those steady blue eyes. He resisted the urge to take a step back. She must be looking at the bridge of his nose, he thought. She appeared to be gazing right into the center of both his eyes at once.

"What happens," she asked, "when you meet the lady you really wish to marry and spend your life with?"

He smiled at her rather frostily. "The woman does not exist," he said, "with whom I would consider sharing even one year of my life."

She drew breath to speak again but closed her mouth without saying anything. Her eyes dropped from his.

It had all gone remarkably well, he thought a few minutes later after she had left. He had expected to be peppered with questions, most notably about what she would be expected to do during the weeks before she was set free to live out her life on what must appear to her to be a vast fortune indeed. Miss Charity Duncan had asked nothing. He had expected to be burdened with all sorts of confidences. She had offered none. He knew nothing about her except what had been in her letter of application. She was three-and-twenty years old, was the daughter of a gentleman, could read and write and figure, could speak French and draw and play the pianoforte, and had

had experience in the care and education of children, whom she liked.

He also knew that she was quiet, demure, neither pretty nor ugly, and shrewd. The only thing about her that had surprised him had been her demand for more money than he had offered. No, there had been something else too—her eyes. They were quite at variance with the rest of her. But then even the plainest, dullest woman was entitled to some claim to beauty, he supposed.

And so she was to be his wife tomorrow. He raised his eyebrows and pursed his lips, considering the thought. Yes, she would do, he decided. Very nicely indeed.

She sat by the window, trying to garner the last of the daylight for her task. She was darning the heel of one of Philip's stockings. It was only six o'clock, but the light was fading. The narrowness of the street on which they had lodgings and the height of the buildings on the opposite side did nothing to help. How she longed sometimes for the countryside again. No, it happened more often than sometimes. She sighed.

What was she going to tell Phil when he came home from work? She still could not quite believe even herself in the reality of the day's events. She had gone to Upper Grosvenor Street this morning, hoping with all the power of her will that she would be offered the governess's position. Yet even as she had approached the house her inward concentration on the interview ahead had been distracted by the foolish dream of finding a priceless jeweled necklace in the gutter or of finding some other unexpected road to a fortune.

Instead of offering her a position as governess, Mr. Earheart—handsome, elegant, cold in manner—had offered her marriage. It was like some bizarre fairy tale—except that in a fairy tale he would have offered because he had fallen instantly and desperately in love with her. Mr. Earheart merely wanted a temporary wife, but he was willing to keep her very handsomely indeed for the rest of her life. She had made sure that the written agreement stated that. She would not be cut off in the event that he predeceased her. She would have six thousand a year for the rest of her life, besides the other things he had mentioned during the morning.

She and Penny and the children could live very comfortably on six thousand a year. They could have Papa's debts paid off in no time at all. Philip would not be too happy about not being the one to save them from their impoverishment, of course, but he would come around to reality. And he would be able to marry Agnes.

She knew, of course, what she was going to tell Philip when he came home. She had had many solitary hours in which to rehearse her story. But it went much against the grain to lie. She was not sure she was going to be able to do it. But she must—she had no choice. She could not possibly tell him the truth. For one thing, he might have her carried off to Bedlam. It was difficult even for her to believe that what had happened really had happened.

Oh dear, she thought. She was darning over a patch that had already been darned once. Poor Phil, he spent nothing on himself and everything on his brothers and sisters. She brushed impatiently at her cheek after a tear had plopped unexpectedly onto the back of her hand, startling her.

And then she felt the welling of panic that had been assaulting her at regular intervals ever since she had arrived home after signing those papers. Tomorrow she was going to marry a stranger—and a rather daunting stranger at that. She was doing it entirely for money. But after it was done there would be no going back. There would not—never ever—be a real husband or a real marriage for her. Not that there would have been anyway. But there was something rather frightening about the certain knowledge that . . .

But Philip was home, looking weary after his day's work, and she smiled warmly at him, set aside her darning, and got to her feet to ladle out his soup and cut a slice of bread.

"You look tired," she said, tilting up her cheek for his kiss.

"One is supposed to be tired in the evening," he said. "Mm, that smells good, Charity." He plopped wearily onto his chair.

She sat at the table with him while he ate, her elbow resting on it, her chin in her hand. She did not know how to begin, and so she waited for him to start the conversation. He asked her if there had been any letter from home and then, when she shook her head, assured them both that it was too soon to expect another when they had heard as recently as the end of last week.

"Ah," he said at last, obviously just remembering, "you had an interview this morning. Forgive me for not asking about it sooner. How was it?"

She smiled at him. "I was offered the position," she said.

His spoon paused halfway to his mouth. "Ah," he said again. "Well, that is good news. Are they pleasant people, Charity? Where do they live? How many children are there?"

"Very pleasant," she said. "Wiltshire. Three." She held carefully to her smile. "And yes, it is good news."

He was trying to look pleased for her, she could tell. "It was *Mr.* Earheart who interviewed you?" he asked. "Did you meet Mrs. Earheart, Charity?"

"Oh, yes indeed," she said, "and the children too. They are all exceedingly pleasant, Phil. You would like them. They are leaving for the country tomorrow. I will be going with them."

"Tomorrow," he said, frowning. "So soon?"

"Yes." She smiled gently. "I have made enough soup to last you for three days, and I have made some of the currant cakes you so like—a dreadful extravagance, I know, but I wanted you to have them."

"Perhaps I should ask for an hour off tomorrow," he said, "so that I can see you on your way and assure myself that your new employers are worthy of you. What time will you be leaving?"

"No, Phil." She stretched out her hand to touch the back of his. "There is no need to do that. I would hate saying good-bye to you and then having to be cheerful for the children immediately after. I would much rather you did not come."

Her brother covered her hand with his own and patted it. "As you will, then," he said. "But Wiltshire is not so very far away, Charity. And nothing is irrevocable. If you do not like the position, then you may leave it at any time and return home. Penny will be very happy and the children will be ecstatic."

"Nevertheless it is a position to which I shall commit myself," she said. "Why should you be the one to support us all?"

"Because I am the man of the family," he said.

"Phooey!" She got to her feet, picked up his empty bowl, and refilled it without even asking if he wanted more. Philip, she thought, was going to be very angry with her. And that might be an understatement. But after tomorrow morning he would be able to do nothing about it. The loneliness of facing her own wedding quite alone washed over her for a moment, but she pushed self-pity firmly aside. What did she have to pity herself for? She was going to be a wealthy woman—a pitiable fate indeed!

They did not stay up late. Philip was tired and his days began early. The light had gone and they always used candles sparingly. Besides, partings were always difficult. There never seemed to be anything to say during the last few hours together—perhaps because there was altogether too much to say. And this time was worse than ever because in the little they did say so many lies were necessary. He asked about the children who were to be her pupils and she was forced to invent genders and ages for them.

She hated lying. But how could she tell the truth? There would be a time for the truth, when she was finally able to care for her family herself, when it would be far too late for any of them to exclaim in horror at the madness of what she was doing. Yes, there would be a time. But it was not now.

She got up early in the morning, as she had done every day since joining her brother at his lodgings in town, to get his breakfast and to pack a couple of slices of bread and some lamentably dry cheese for his midday meal—and a currant cake as a special treat. She hugged him tightly and wordlessly when he was ready to leave.

"Take care," he said, his arms like iron bands about her. "I hate the way you feel forced into doing this, Charity, when I am the man of the family. One day you will be free again to live the life of a lady, I promise you."

"I love you," she said. *In a few hours' time, Phil, I am going to be the wife of a very wealthy man. I am going to be a very wealthy woman. Oh, Phil, Phil.* "Tears! How silly I am." She laughed and dashed at them with her hands.

And he was gone. Just like that. The room was empty and cold and still half dark. It was her wedding day. She and Penny had played weddings sometimes as children—they were always joyful, lavish affairs. But this was the reality. This was her real wedding day. She blinked impatiently at more tears.

"Are you quite mad, Tony?" Lord Rowling asked during the weekly evening ball at Almack's while the Marquess of Staunton languidly surveyed the female dancers through his quizzing glass. "Are you really going to go through with this insanity?"

"Oh, absolutely," the marquess said with a sigh. He gestured about him with one jewel-bedecked hand. "Behold the great marriage mart, Perry—Almack's in London during the Season. All the most marketable merchandise is here on display in this very room and all the prospective buyers are looking it over. I am a buyer. Why would I not be? I am the heir to a dukedom—and the duke is reputedly ailing. I am eight-and-twenty years old and growing no younger. I have merely chosen to shop in a slightly different market."

"You *advertised* for a governess and chose a wife," Lord Rowling said, shaking his head. "You chose a total stranger after a short interview. You know nothing about her."

"On the contrary," the marquess said, his glass pausing on one particular young lady and moving slowly down her body from face to feet. "She comes highly recommended by the rector in whose parish she grew up. She was dismissed from her last post after eight months for lying, a charge which she denies. She is a plain, quiet, moral little mouse. And she *bargained* with me, Perry, and squeezed more money out of me than I had offered. She will do admirably. March's chit has put on weight since the start of the Season. Whoever takes her will find himself with a decidedly plump wife within five years. But then some men like plump wives."

"Tony!" his friend said, exasperated. "Your cynicism outdoes anyone else's I know. But this marriage scheme goes beyond the bounds of reason."

"Why?" the marquess asked. "If I were to address myself to the papa of any young lady here present, Perry, he would snap me up in an instant, my reputation as an incurable rake not withstanding. And so would she. I am a matrimonial prize. She would know nothing of me apart from superficial details, and I would know nothing of her. We would be strangers. Is there any real difference between marrying one of these females and marrying a little mouse of a governess who almost salivated at the prospect of coming within sniffing distance of my fortune? There is only one significant difference. The mouse will be easier to shed when she has served her purpose."

Lord Rowling took his snuffbox from a pocket, but he held it unopened in one hand while he stared at his companion. "You are making a mistake, Tony," he said. "A ghastly and an irrevocable one. What if the woman refuses to be shed?"

The Marquess of Staunton merely raised one haughty and eloquent eyebrow. "Like all brides, Perry," he said, "she will promise obedience tomorrow morning. I believe I will dance with Miss Henshaw. She has been warned of my reputation and blushes most prettily and looks away in sweet confusion every time she accidentally catches my eye—which she is at pains to do quite frequently."

He strolled off to pursue his mission, but the main task of the evening had been accomplished. Rowling had agreed to attend his wedding as a witness. Staunton did not often frequent Almack's or any other fashionable ballroom for that matter. He set about amusing himself for the evening. His last evening as a single man. He examined the thought as he danced with the blushing Miss Henshaw and concentrated upon deepening her blushes. But he did not find the thought in any way alarming.

Tomorrow was his wedding day. Merely another day in his life.

Chapter 3

True to his promise, Lord Rowling arrived in Upper Grosvenor Street in good time the following morning to accompany the groom to the church, where the marquess's man of business as the other witness awaited them. The Marquess of Staunton, to his friend's fascination, appeared as coolly composed—and as immaculately tailored—as if he were planning a morning stroll along Bond Street.

"You are quite sure about this?" Lord Rowling asked as they prepared to leave the house. "There is nothing I can say to persuade you to change your mind, Tony?"

"Good Lord, no," the marquess said, placing his hat just so on his head and raising his eyebrows to his servant to indicate that he was ready to proceed out-of-doors.

The church was not one of London's most fashionable. It looked gloomy enough to Lord Rowling as did the street on which it was situated and as did the heavy gray sky overhead. The groom appeared quite unaffected by gloom—or by elation either. He nodded to his man of business and strode without further ado toward the church door. His two companions exchanged glances and followed him.

Inside the church, seated quietly in a shadowed pew at the back, the bride waited. She was dressed as she had been the day before, her bridegroom noticed immediately. She had made no attempt to get herself up in a bride's frippery. He had not thought to give her money to buy herself new clothes, the marquess thought belatedly—a new dress for today, bride clothes to take with her into her more affluent future. And they were to leave for the country soon after the wedding. There would be no time for shopping. Well, no matter. It would be better to take her exactly as she was.

"Miss Duncan?" He half bowed to her and held out his arm for hers.

"Yes, sir." She stood up, looked at him briefly, and then lowered her gaze to his arm. She appeared not to know whether she should lay her own along the top of it or link her own through it. He took her hand in his free one and set it on his wrist. He did not pause to present her to Lord Rowling. He was impatient.

"The rector is waiting," he said.

"Yes, sir." She glanced to the front of the church.

His mouth felt surprisingly dry and his heartbeat surprisingly unsteady. She was a total stranger. She was about to become his wife. For the rest of a lifetime. For a moment his mind touched upon the notion that he might live to regret this day. But he suppressed the thought, as he had done when he had awoken soon after dawn and again while he had breakfasted. He despised last-minute nerves. He led his bride forward.

Without all the pomp and ceremony that had accompanied every society wedding he had ever attended, the nuptial service was really quite short and unremarkable, he found. The rector spoke, he spoke, she spoke, Rowling handed him a ring, which he placed on her finger, and he found that it was too late to wonder if he would regret the day. Miss Charity Duncan no longer existed by that name. She was his wife. His first feeling was one of relief. He bent his head and briefly placed his closed lips close to the corner of her mouth. Her skin was cool.

The rector was congratulating them then with hearty good humor, his man of business was doing his best to look festive, and Rowling was smiling and being charming. There was the register still to sign.

"My very best wishes to you, Lady Staunton," Rowling said, taking one of her hands in both of his and smiling warmly at her.

"Wh-what?" she asked.

"You are unaccustomed to the sound of your own new name," he said, raising her hand to his lips. "My best wishes for your felicity, ma'am."

"You are Charity Earheart," the marquess explained to her, "Marchioness of Staunton."

"Oh," she said, looking full at him with wide and startled eyes—and this time he really did take a step back. "Are you a *marquess*?"

"Staunton, at your service, my lady," he said. He really should have given greater consideration to those eyes yesterday. But it was too late now. "May I present Lord Rowling?"

It was raining when they came out of the church—a chilling drizzle oozed downward out of a gray and dreary sky.

"A good omen," Rowling said with a laugh. "The best marriages always proceed from wet wedding days, my grandmother is fond of saying. I believe she married my grandfather during a thunderstorm and they enjoyed forty happy years together."

But no one seemed prepared to share his hearty optimism. The Marquess of Staunton hurried his silent bride toward his carriage. There was breakfast to take with their two wedding guests, his wife's trunks to collect from her lodgings, and a journey to begin. He had written to his father to expect him tomorrow. He had not mentioned that he would be bringing a wife.

He seated himself beside her in the carriage, lifted her hand to his wrist again, and held it there with his free hand while the other two men seated themselves opposite. He felt almost sorry for her—a strange fact when he had just ensured her a future infinitely preferable to what she could have expected as a governess. Besides, he was unaccustomed to entertaining sympathetic feelings for anyone. For the first time it struck him as strange that no one had accompanied her to her wedding. Was she so totally without friends?

The leather of her glove was paper thin on the inside of the thumb, he noticed. There was going to be a hole there very soon.

He was a married man. The stranger whose gloved hand rested lightly on his wrist was his wife, his marchioness. There was a strange unreality to the moment. And a stark reality too.

She was a married lady. She had walked to that quiet, rather gloomy church this morning, gone inside as herself, as Charity Duncan, and come out again a mere half hour later as someone different, as someone with another name. Everything had changed. Nothing would ever be the same again. She was Charity Earheart, the . . .

She turned her head to look at the taciturn man beside her on the carriage seat. He had not spoken a word since his footman had carried out her small trunk from Philip's lodgings—the carriage had appeared to fill the whole street and had attracted considerable attention—and he had asked her in seeming surprise if there was nothing else.

"No, sir," she had said and had thought that probably she should have called him *my lord*.

She was . . . She felt very foolish. And he must have felt her eyes upon him. He turned his head to look at her. His eyes were very dark, she thought. They were almost black. And quite opaque. She had the peculiar feeling that a heavy curtain or perhaps even a steel door had been dropped just behind his eyes so that no one would ever be able to peep into his soul.

"I am—*who*?" she asked him. She could not for the life of her remember. "You are the Marquess of *What*?"

"Staunton," he said. He had an aquiline nose, rather thin lips. One lock of very dark hair had fallen across his brow above his right eye and curled there like an upside-down question mark. "Eldest son of the Duke of Withingsby. His heir, my lady. We travel to Enfield Park, his seat in Wiltshire so that you may be properly presented to him."

He really was a marquess. Lord Rowling had not been teasing her. He was not after all plain Mr. Earheart. But of course his servants had called him *my lord* and had called her *my lady.* And he was the son *and heir* of a duke. The Duke of Withingsby. He would be a duke himself one day. She would be . . . No, she would not. Not really.

"Why would you marry without your father's knowledge?" she asked. "And why me? I am a gentleman's daughter, but one would expect a future duke to look for somewhat higher qualifications than that in a wife."

His smile was rather unpleasant, she thought, despite the fact that it revealed very white teeth. But the smile in no way touched his eyes. "Perhaps, my lady," he said, "that is just the point."

He had married her to spite someone? His father?

"Do you and your father have a quarrel with each other?" she asked.

He continued to smile—with his lips. "Shall we say," he said, "that the more displeased his grace proves to be, the more gratified I shall be?"

She understood immediately. She would have had to be stupid not to. "So I am a mere pawn in a game," she said.

His smile disappeared and his eyes narrowed. "A very well-paid pawn, my lady," he said. "And one who will be titled for the rest of her life."

It was as well, she thought, that they were to remain together for only a few weeks—just until she had given the Duke of Withingsby a thorough disgust of herself, she supposed. She did not believe she could possibly like this man. What sort of man married a stranger merely to displease his father?

Not that she had any cause for moral outrage, of course. She had accepted the offer he had made yesterday—gracious, was it really only *yesterday*?—without demanding to know anything about the man beyond the fact that he had the means to keep the promises he made her. She had married him for those promises. She was the sort of woman who would marry a stranger for money. It was an uncomfortable admission to make even—or perhaps especially—to oneself.

It would be very difficult for this man to become anything

but a stranger, she thought, even though she was apparently to spend a few weeks in his company. Those eyes! They had no depth whatsoever. They proclaimed him to be a man who chose not to be known, a man who cared nothing for the good opinion of others. They almost frightened her.

"Was it not rather drastic," she asked him, "to marry beneath you merely to score a point in a game? Would not the quarrel have blown over in a short while as quarrels usually do?" She should know. She had grown up in a household with five brothers and sisters.

"Perhaps my father and I should have kissed and made up instead?" he said. "You may spare such shallow observations on life for your pupils, my lady. Though of course there will be no more of them, will there?"

Charity was hurt. Shallow? As the eldest she had learned early to understand others, to identify with them, to be a mediator, a peacemaker. What a thoroughly unpleasant man he was, she thought, to speak with such contempt to a lady—and again she was jolted by the realization that he was her husband. She had promised him obedience. For the rest of her life, even after these few weeks were over and she was back home with the children, she would not really be free. Any time he chose he could demand anything he wished of her. But no, that was a foolish worry. He would be as glad as she to sever all but the unseverable tie that bound them.

"I would have thought," she said after a couple of minutes of silence, "that a man who expects to be a duke one day would have wished to produce some heirs of his own." Even as she spoke she wished she could simply stop and bite down hard on her tongue. She felt as if her cheeks had burst into flames. She had been trying to understand clearly his motives for marrying her—and had unfortunately thought aloud.

"Indeed, my lady?" The tenor lightness of his voice did not at all match his dark, satanic looks, she thought. At the moment it was quite soft—but deadly cold. "Are you volunteering your services?"

She found herself desperately and deliberately wondering if

he had tied the intricate knot of his neckcloth himself or if his valet had done it for him. She lowered her eyes to it. She had lain awake last night wondering, among other things, if . . . His words now seemed to indicate that he had not intended *that* to be one of her duties during the coming weeks.

"You *are* my wife." His voice was still soft and pleasant—and seemingly chiseled out of the ice of the North Pole.

"Yes, sir." She knew very well that his valet must have helped him into his coat. He could never have shrugged into it himself. It fit him like a second skin and displayed admirably the breadth of his shoulders. She wondered if the famous and very expensive Weston was his tailor.

"We are going to have to stop early," he said, looking past her to the window and narrowing his eyes again. "Confound it, it is raining again and heavily too."

She found the rain a welcome relief from the direction the conversation had taken. It was something—one of about a hundred questions—she ought to have asked yesterday before agreeing to anything, certainly before signing any papers. But she had not thought of it until much later, until she was sitting at home darning Philip's stockings, in fact. But then she could hardly have asked the question anyway—"Do you intend to bed me, sir?" The very thought of asking such a thing aloud could turn her alternately hot and cold.

He was very handsome and even rather alarmingly attractive. He was also quite unpleasant. Quite undesirable as either a husband or a l—or a lover.

If it did not happen, of course—and fortunately it seemed very unlikely that it would—then she would go through life without ever knowing what it felt like to be fully a wife. She would never have children of her own. It was something she had fully expected for a long time—certainly since Papa's death and her understanding of the family's poverty. It was also something that seemed even more depressing now that there was no doubt at all, now that there was no hope . . . She would have liked to know . . . She thought she knew what happened, but knowing such a thing and experiencing it were vastly different things, she supposed. But the trend of her thoughts distressed her. They were not the thoughts of a proper lady.

The rain became first heavy and then heavier and finally torrential. The road became a light brown sea of mud, and it was impossible to see more than a few yards from the windows of the carriage. After fifteen minutes of very slow progress and some alarming slithering, the carriage turned into the cobbled yard of a wayside inn that was not at all the sort of establishment one might expect the Marquess of Staunton, heir to a dukedom, to patronize. At least, that was what his disdainful expression told Charity as they waited for the door to be opened and the steps to be set down.

She thought of what Lord Rowling had said of rainy wedding days. If he was correct, theirs should be the most blissful marriage in the history of the world. She smiled rather ruefully to herself.

She was hurried inside the dark, low-ceilinged taproom of the inn beneath a large black umbrella that the marquess held over her head. She stood shaking the water from the hem of her dress and cloak while he talked with the innkeeper, an enormous man who looked more irritated than delighted at the unexpected business the rain was bringing to his inn.

"Come," her husband said finally, turning back to her and gesturing her toward the steep wooden staircase up which the innkeeper was disappearing. "It seems that the inclement weather has made this a popular hostel. We are fortunate to have arrived in time to take the last empty room."

It was not a large room. The ceiling sloped steeply down fully half of it. One small window looked down upon the innyard. There was a washstand and a small table and chair. There was really no room for any other furniture, for the rest of the room was dominated by the large bed.

"You may leave us." The marquess nodded curtly to the innkeeper, who withdrew without a word. "Well, my lady, this will have to substitute for the suite of rooms I have reserved at a posting inn fully twenty miles farther along the road. We must dine in the public dining room and trust that the fare will be tolerably edible."

The bed was like an extra person in the room, unavoidably visible, embarrassingly silent.

"I am sure it will be, sir," she said, tossing her bonnet and her gloves onto the bed with what she hoped was convincing nonchalance.

"You will wish to freshen up and perhaps even to lie down for a short while before dinner," he said. "I shall leave you, my lady, and do myself the honor of returning to escort you to the dining room."

She had no idea where he would go in such a shabby little inn. To the taproom probably to imbibe inferior ale. Doubtless his jaded palate would object quite violently. But she did not really care. She was too busy feeling relieved that at least for the moment she was to be alone in this horribly embarrassing chamber. She had never before thought of a bed as an almost animate thing. She had always thought of beds as merely pieces of furniture upon which one slept. But then she had never before stood in a bedchamber with any gentleman other than her father or her brothers. She had never had to contemplate spending a night in a bedchamber—and in the same bed—with a gentleman.

But she was *married* to this particular gentleman, she reminded herself, lying down on the bed—it was decidedly hard and rather lumpy, though it appeared to be reasonably clean— after removing her shoes and her hairpins. Philip would be thinking about her all through the day, imagining her getting to know Mr. and Mrs. Earheart, her new employers, and their three children. He would be hoping that they continued pleasant and that the children were not taxing her energies too much during the journey. He would be looking uneasily out at the rain, worried for her safety. He would be waiting for her first letter.

What would he be thinking, she wondered, if he knew that she had been wed during the morning, that she was now Charity Earheart, Marchioness of Staunton, one day to be the Duchess of Withingsby? That during the coming weeks she was to be used as a pawn in a foolish quarrel between the marquess and the duke, his father. That after that she would be a lady of substance with six thousand a year in addition to a home and servants and a carriage. Papa had never kept his own carriage. They had only ever had Polly as a servant and she had stayed for the last ten years or so only because she considered herself one of the family and had nowhere else to go.

Oh, Phil, she thought, closing her eyes. He would be able to have their own home to himself. He would be able to take Agnes there, and they could begin their own family. Without the burden of Papa's debts and the necessity of supporting and providing for all the children, he would be able to manage very well as a country gentleman.

Oh, Penny. How was she managing at home alone, without either Phil's help or her own? Penny was just twenty. And pretty and sweet-natured. She should be thinking of beaux and of marriage. Were the children all well? Did they have enough to eat? Did they all have sufficient clothes? Were they missing her as dreadfully as she was missing them?

Soon, she told both them and herself silently. Soon she would be back with them. All would be as it used to be or as they had imagined it to be until Papa had died and they had realized the impoverishment of their situation. They would never be poor again or unsafe—or separated.

Yes, she had done the right thing. How could she have refused such a totally unexpected and irresistible offer? It had been like a gift from heaven. How else could she possibly think of it? She closed her mind to the possibility that it might be just the opposite, especially when one considered the satanic appearance and the flat eyes of the Marquess of Staunton.

Of course she had done the right thing. It was too late now anyway to give in to doubts.

Of course she had done the right thing.

By midnight the rain appeared to have stopped. The Marquess of Staunton stood in the open doorway of the inn taproom, one shoulder propped against the doorpost, gazing out across the cobbled yard and shivering slightly in the chilly air. But it was, of course, far too muddy and far too late to move on tonight.

He was the last of both the taproom's patrons and the inn's guests to linger downstairs. Behind him the innkeeper tidied up for the night with deliberately audible movements. He was clearly hinting that his last remaining customer should consider taking himself off to bed.

"The sun will be shining in the morning, m'lord," he said.

"Mm, yes," the marquess agreed. They would have sunshine for their arrival at Enfield Park. How delightful! His lips tightened into a thin line. He should, he thought altogether too belatedly, have merely ignored his father's summons. He should have made no answer at all to it. Better yet, he should have answered curtly and courteously to the effect that he was too busy with his own affairs to avail himself of his grace's kind hospitality. What concern of his was it that the duke was ailing? Had his father taken any notice of him when he had broken his leg and very nearly his neck too during that curricle race to Brighton six years ago? None whatsoever.

All ties between him and his father had been severed for eight years. He was not bound to Withingsby even by financial ties. He was independently wealthy. He had been under no obligation to pay any attention to that letter when it had come. He wondered why he had felt somehow obligated, somehow caught up in the past again as if it had never been laid properly to rest. As if the bonds had not been fully severed.

He should have ignored the letter. He should have found some way of renouncing his birthright. Let William be duke after their father. Let Claudia be duchess. His lip curled at the thought. What an irony there would be in that. Claudia as the Duchess of Withingsby.

Claudia . . .

The innkeeper was clearing his throat. "Can I get you anything else tonight, m'lord?" he asked.

"No." The marquess straightened up, stepped back inside

the room, and closed the door. "I am for bed. Good night." He
turned toward the stairs.

Consummating his marriage had been no part of his plan.
What possible pleasure could be derived, after all, from bedding an innocent brown mouse? From dealing with skittish-
ness and pain and tears? And blood. Besides, he had not
married for pleasure.

He still had no intention of consummating the marriage. But
the sleeping arrangements the rain had forced upon him in this
sad apology of an inn were a considerable annoyance to him.
For one thing, he was a restless sleeper and did not like sharing a bed. He only ever shared one for sexual activity, never
for sleep. For another thing the very idea of conducting that
most private of all activities—sleeping—in anyone else's company offended his notions of privacy.

Tonight more than ever he felt the need for privacy. Instead
of which, he was doomed to spending what remained of the
night, not only in the same room as his bride, but in the same
bed.

There was enough light from a lantern hung over the stable
door in the yard below to allow him to undress in their room
without the aid of a candle and to slide beneath the covers of
the bed on the side closest to the door. She was lying quietly
asleep on the far side of the bed.

His wife! He found himself wondering if she had any family. Not only had no one come to the church with her, but no
one had come rushing out of her lodgings when his carriage
had stopped for her trunk. Did she have no one at all of her
own? No family? No friends? Well, soon enough she would
have any number of the latter, he thought cynically. It was
very easy to find friends when one was in possession of six
thousand pounds a year. And was it possible that that small
trunk held all she possessed in the world? Where were the rest
of her belongings? Was it really possible to live on so few?

But he was not curious about her. He did not want to know
anything about her other than what he knew already. Most certainly he did not wish to pity her. She was not in any way

pitiable—he had ensured that yesterday in the contract they had both signed and this morning in the marriage service. He would quell all curiosity. She would serve a purpose in his life and then she would be well rewarded. He always rewarded well the women who were of service to him. This one was not performing the usual service, of course, but she would be adequately compensated for her time nevertheless. He need feel no other sense of responsibility toward her.

He addressed himself determinedly to sleep.

Chapter 4

The Marquess of Staunton found that sleep was eluding him. Totally. And he became aware of something gradually—two things actually. He could feel the warmth of her along his right side although they did not touch. He could also feel the stillness and quietness of her—she was far too still and far too quiet to be sleeping. But then it seemed reasonable to suppose that sleeping would be quite as difficult for her as it was for him.

"You should be asleep," he told her. "Tomorrow will be a busy day." He felt an unreasonable annoyance with her for being awake, for intruding even further into his privacy than her mere physical presence already made inevitable.

"I have counted all the sheep in England," she said.

He pursed his lips.

"I had just started on those of Wales when you spoke," she said. "Now I shall have to begin all over again."

He had expected a meek little "Yes, sir." He was reminded somehow of her eyes, which he had found himself unaccountably avoiding during dinner, when she had sat directly opposite him at their table. He found her eyes threatening, though he would have been hard-pressed to explain exactly what he meant by that if he had been called upon to do so or to explain why his mind had chosen that particular word to describe their effect on him. Now her words suggested a certain sense of humor. He did not want her to have a sense of humor—or those eyes. He wanted her to be nondescript, devoid of character or personality.

"And this is the lumpiest bed it has ever been my discomfort to lie upon," she said.

"My apologies," he said curtly. "This was not my choice of accommodation for the night."

She was silent. But not to be ignored. He was aware of her as a wakeful human presence in his room, in his bed. He turned restlessly onto his side, facing her. She did not have her hair decently confined beneath a cap, he could see, his eyes having accustomed themselves to the dimness of the room. It was spread all over her pillow. It looked long and slightly wavy. It looked rather attractive. Again he felt annoyed. He had conceded the fact that she had fine eyes. That was entirely enough beauty for his bride to possess. He had chosen her partly for her plain appearance.

What *did* innocence feel like? he wondered irritably. It was one thing—perhaps the only thing—that was outside his sexual experience. She was lying on her back with her eyes closed. But she turned her head on the pillow even as he watched her and opened her eyes. He could smell her hair. It smelled of soap. He had never thought of the smell of soap as being erotic. And neither was it. He frowned.

"One thousand three hundred and sixty-four," she said after the silence had stretched rather uncomfortably. Her voice sounded strained. Humor, he thought with a flash of insight, was her manner of self-defense. She was in bed with a man for the first time ever, after all. It must be a somewhat alarming feeling for her.

"There is another way," he said and listened in some alarm to the echo of words he had uttered without any forethought. "Of inducing slumber, I mean."

"Pretending that one may sleep all day tomorrow if one wishes?" she said altogether too quickly. "It does work sometimes. I shall try it."

He raised himself on one elbow and propped the side of his head on his hand. "You are my wife," he said, realizing that he was getting into deep waters when he had intended not even to get his feet wet.

"Yes." Her conversation had finally been reduced to mono-syllables. Her eyes were wide, he could see, but in the dark-ness they did less damage than when their color was clearly visible.

"I have no intention of asserting my conjugal rights by force," he said. "However, if sheep have not achieved their purpose and the bed has failed to lull you, I am willing to offer my services." He had bent his head closer to hers. Was he mad? But there was no way of retreating now unless she said no. He willed her to say no.

"Oh," was all she said. But the breathlessness of the word assured him that she understood very well.

"If you wish to try it," he said. He was surprised and not a little alarmed to find that his body had already rebelled against his will and hardened into arousal. Yet he did not even con-sider her desirable. "If you do not, we will address ourselves to sleep again and perhaps try the greater tedium of counting sheep's legs."

She stared back into his eyes only inches from her own. He could see that he had not left her with any monosyllabic an-swer to give. She was silent. But there was no withdrawing from the question now. And now his body was willing her to say yes.

"Do you wish to try it?" he asked her.

"Yes," she said in a whisper.

He would not have been surprised by a refusal. She had been an impoverished gentlewoman just yesterday, forced to earn her living as a governess, forced to suffer any insult or in-dignity her employers cared to subject her to—the last ones had accused her of lying over something. Today she had achieved the respectability of marriage with the prospect of a more than comfortable settlement for life after a mere few weeks spent in company with him. She might very easily have avoided the one aspect of marriage that he understood was generally distasteful to respectable women. He did not imagine that his bride was either a sensual or a passionate woman. Quite the opposite. But he had given her a clear choice—he wondered how many men gave such a choice to their brides on their wedding night—and she had whispered yes.

Well then. So be it.

She expected him to kiss her. His mouth was only inches from her own. She could smell the brandy he had been drinking. If he had kissed her, she could have closed her eyes and concentrated on the sensation created by his mouth against her own—she had found his kiss at church quite shockingly intimate even though his lips had not quite touched her own. If he had kissed her, she might have hidden behind her closed eyes and her feelings while the other thing happened.

She did not understand why she had said yes, except that she was weary of trying to sleep and failing to do so, and she had been strangely disturbed by the warmth of him on the bed beside her, and she knew that this was probably her one and only chance in life to experience the deepest intimacy of all. And because the mere smell of brandy was intoxicating her.

He did not kiss her. Or move his head away. He continued to half lean over her and look into her eyes. His own appeared quite black. His hair was tousled. The hand that was not propping up his head touched her. She felt immediately as if she had been touched by a flaming torch even though it was only her shoulder he touched at first. His hand moved firmly downward to her breast, circled beneath it, lifted it. She thought she might well find it impossible to draw the next breath of air into her lungs. She felt horribly embarrassed. Her breasts were rather large—too large, she always thought.

And then her nipple was imprisoned between his thumb and the base of his forefinger and he squeezed them together almost as if he was unaware that it was there, causing her excruciating pain, though it was not like any other pain she had ever experienced. This was undoubtedly pain, but it shot off upward into her throat and across to her other breast and downward into her belly and along her inner thighs so that she ached and yearned all over. Her breath shuddered and jerked out of her, quite audibly.

She was alarmed. She wished she had said no. Was it too late now? But she was curious too. She wished he would kiss her. Was this not supposed to be romantic? Was it not supposed to be—love? She realized the absurdity of that youthful assumption even as she thought it. This was not love. But it was certainly—exciting. It was not supposed to be exciting. It was supposed to be love—a sweet and gentle thing. Somehow the buttons of her nightgown had come undone and he was repeating his actions on her other breast—her naked breast.

This time pain had her gasping for air.

But his hand had moved on downward beneath the low opening of her nightgown—and on down to the source of the ache the pain had created. She had parted her legs slightly and tilted her hips to allow his hand easier access before her brain understood just where his hand was and exactly what it was doing there. She felt engulfed by embarrassment and by unfamiliar and uncontrollable achings and yearnings. His fingers were parting, probing, stroking. She could hear sounds of wetness. She would have died of embarrassment, she was sure, if such an act had been within the power of her will.

She opened her eyes suddenly. He was still propped on one elbow. He was still looking down at her. He took his hand away and lifted her nightgown—all the way to her waist. Well, this part she knew about, she thought. She knew what to expect. She drew a deep breath and held it. She was not sorry she had said yes. He was a stranger and she did not believe she could ever like him—partly because she did not believe she could ever know him—but he *was* her husband, and he was undeniably attractive. On the whole she was glad there was to be this experience in her life—just this one time.

"Let it out," he told her. "You cannot possibly hold it long enough. Breathe normally."

It was easy enough for him to say that, she thought as he moved over her and a considerable portion of his weight settled on top of her. She could feel his hands pushing beneath her, spreading over her buttocks, holding them firm. Her inner thighs were against the outside of his legs, pushed wide. He seemed to be all hard, unyielding muscle. She felt horribly defenseless. But he had given her the choice, and she had said yes. She would say it again if the choice were given her again. Curiosity and fear and excitement were a heady blend, she found.

At first it was enormously frightening. Apart from the conviction that there could not possibly be room, either in breadth or in depth, there was all the fear of being impaled, destroyed while she was pressed wide and was helpless to defend herself. Then there was the terrified certainty that indeed there was not enough room and that she was about to tear into unbearable pain. Then he was deep, deep inside and holding hard and still there, and she knew with startled surprise that there was after all room and that she would survive—and that it felt unfamiliar and exciting and really rather good.

But she had been right to guess that knowing and experiencing were two quite different things. She could never have imagined the utter carnality of the sensation.

And then she discovered—during several minutes of shocked amazement—that in fact she had not known at all. Only about penetration. She had had no inkling of the fact that penetration was only the beginning. He pumped in and out of her with hard, smooth strokes until the ache his hands on her breasts had already created became raw pain—pain that was not really pain but for which there was no other more suitable word in her vocabulary. And certainly it was beyond bearing and growing more so with every inward stroke.

"Oh," she said suddenly, alarmed and amazed as she pressed her hands to his buttocks in an attempt to hold him still and deep and as inner muscles she had still not consciously discovered clenched convulsively. "Oh."

He answered her mute appeal instantly. He pressed hard into her tightness and held there. "My God," he murmured against the side of her head. "My God!"

Something that she thought might well be death beckoned and she followed without a struggle. Whatever it was closed darkly about her and felt wonderful beyond belief. Nothingness. Total, blissful nothingness.

She was half aware of his moving again, faster and harder than before. She was half aware of a flood of heat deep inside as he sighed and held still again and relaxed his full weight down onto her. Death was not after all to be feared, she thought foolishly and very fuzzily. Death was the fulfillment of all that was most desirable.

She slept. She grumbled only very halfheartedly when the wonderful heat and weight that bore her down into the mattress was lifted away from her and far lighter blankets covered her instead. Yes, she thought with the last thread of consciousness, there was a method vastly superior to counting sheep.

And love was not always sweet and gentle. And love was not always love.

The road had dried sufficiently by the following morning to make travel possible. And the landlord at the inn where they had stayed the night had proved quite correct in his prediction. The sun shone from a sky that was dotted prettily but sparsely with fluffy white clouds. Fields and hedgerows looked washed clean in the morning air.

It was the perfect day for a homecoming.

The Marquess of Staunton gazed moodily and sightlessly out through the window on his side of the carriage. Damn and blast, he was thinking, verbalizing the words in his head with silent venom.

She had actually been blushing when she had joined him in the inn dining room for breakfast. She had looked like the stereotypical bride the morning after her wedding night. She had even been looking almost pretty—not that he had spent a great deal of time looking into her face. He had addressed himself to his breakfast without being in any way aware of what he ate beyond the fact that it was inordinately greasy.

What the devil had possessed him last night? He had felt not one glimmering of sexual interest in her from the moment of spying her in the shadows of the salon where she had waited to be interviewed to the moment during which she had started to talk about sheep and Wales and lumpy mattresses. Not one iota of a glimmering.

And yet he had consummated their union during the very first night of their marriage—and had done so with great enthusiasm and more than usual satisfaction. He had fallen asleep almost immediately after lifting himself off her and had slept like the proverbial baby until dawn.

What if he had got her with child? It had been almost his first thought on waking up—*after* he had rejected the notion of waking her up and doing it again with her. A pregnancy would complicate matters considerably. Besides, children of his own body were the very last things he wanted. The very idea of impregnating a woman made him shudder. He had always been meticulous about choosing bedfellows who knew how to look after themselves—until last night.

He had the uneasy feeling this morning that he might have been at least partly deceived in his wife. True, she had been innocent and ignorant and awkward and virgin. She had also been a powder keg of passion just waiting to be ignited. And he had provided the spark. And had heedlessly spilled his seed in her.

She had proved him wrong in his conviction that he had nothing new to learn sexually except what it felt like to mount a virgin. Very wrong. He had known women come to sexual climax. It happened routinely with all his mistresses. But he had understood last night with humiliating clarity that women faked climax just as they faked delight in the whole process, knowing that for a conceited man it was important not only to receive pleasure in bed but also to believe that he gave it. Thus many women earned their daily bread—making their employers feel like devilishly virile and dashing and manly fellows.

Charity Earheart, Marchioness of Staunton, had taught him a lesson last night—quite unwittingly, of course. The shattering reality of her own untutored, totally spontaneous response to being bedded had exposed all the artificiality of all the other women he had ever known. His wife had made him feel stupidly proud of his performance. She had made him want more—he had wanted it as soon as he awoke.

He was furious, the more so perhaps since he did not quite know on whom to concentrate his fury. On her? She had merely reacted to what he did to her. On himself? His lips thinned. Was he incapable of being alone with a woman—even such a woman as the one he had married—without making an idiot of himself?

"It is pretty countryside," she said, breaking a lengthy silence.

"Yes, it is." She had tried several times to initiate conversation. He had quelled each attempt with a curtness bordering on the morose. He had no wish to converse, especially on such intellectually stimulating topics as the prettiness of the countryside.

It would not happen again, he decided. They would have separate bedchambers at Enfield, of course, and would be expected to keep to them except for brief, discreet, and dutiful couplings. But the doors between their room would remain firmly and permanently closed. He would not touch her again with a ten-foot pole.

"What is Enfield Park like?" she asked him.

He shrugged. "Large," he said. But such a brief answer crossed the borderline between moroseness and downright rudeness. She had done nothing wrong, after all, except to say yes last night. But he was the one who had asked the question. "The house is Palladian in style, massive, with wide lawns and flower beds and ancient trees all about it, sloping down at one side to a lake and up on the other side to woods and planned walks and artful prospects. There is a village, there are farms, some old ruins—" He shrugged again. "There are all the usual trappings of a large estate. It is extremely prosperous. Your husband is like to be a very wealthy man, my lady—far more wealthy than he already is—and quite well able to keep you in comfort for the rest of your life."

"Is your mother alive?" she asked. "Do you have brothers and sisters?"

"My mother died," he said curtly, "soon after giving birth to her thirteenth child. There are five of us still living." He did not want to talk about his mother or about her frequent pregnancies and almost as frequent stillbirths. The number thirteen did not even include the four miscarriages. Devil take it, but he hoped he had not impregnated his wife. "I have two brothers and two sisters."

"Oh," she said. He could see that her head was turned in his direction. He kept his eyes directed beyond the window. "Are they all still at home?"

"Not all," he said. "But most, I believe." Marianne wrote to him occasionally—she was the only one. She had married the Earl of Twynham six years ago. They had three children. Charles must be twenty now. Augusta would be eight—twenty years younger than he. There had been seventeen pregnancies in twenty years for his mother. He did not want to think of his mother.

"How happy you must be, then," his wife said—he had almost forgotten that she shared the carriage with him, "to be coming home. How you must have been missing them."

She set one hand on his arm and he turned his head sharply to look pointedly down at it and up into her eyes. "It is the first time in eight years, my lady," he said, and he could hear the chill in his voice. "And my absence has been entirely voluntary. I come now only because the Duke of Withingsby is in failing health and has summoned me, doubtless so that he can assail my ears with a recounting of my shortcomings and a listing of my responsibilities. There are certain burdens attached to being the eldest of five living children and to being the heir to a dukedom and vast and prosperous estates."

Her very blue eyes had widened. They were a truly remarkable feature, lending considerable beauty to the rest of her features. He felt annoyance that she had kept them hidden through most of their initial interview. They detracted severely from the overall image she projected of a quiet brown mouse. Had she trained them on him from the start of that interview, he would not even have asked her to sit down. He would have

dismissed her almost immediately. And her face was definitely
heart-shaped.

"You have been without your family for eight years?" she
said, her voice warm with sympathy. "Oh, it must have been a
dreadful quarrel indeed."

"It was a matter with which you need not concern yourself,
my lady," he said chillily, attempting to stare her down. It was
something he was adept at doing. Very few people in his experience had been able to hold his gaze when he had no wish for
them to do so.

She gazed right back at him. "I believe you must have been
very deeply hurt," she said.

He clucked his tongue, made an impatient gesture with one
hand, and turned back to the window. "Spare me your shallow
analysis of what you know nothing about," he said, "and of a
person you know nothing of."

"And I believe," she said, "you have protected yourself by
shutting yourself up inside yourself—like a fortress. I believe
you must be an unhappy man."

He sucked in his breath. He felt furious almost to the point
of violence. Except that he had never been one to work out his
anger or his frustrations in violence. He felt the icy coldness
that the effort of control always caused in him. He turned his
head once more to look at her.

"My lady," he said, his voice very quiet, "you would be
very well advised to be silent."

Something flickered for a moment in her eyes—he thought
it was probably fear—and was gone again. She tipped her head
to one side, frowned fleetingly—and held his gaze. But she
obeyed him.

He set his head back against the comfortable cushions of the
carriage and closed his eyes. He kept them closed for a long
time, letting the anger flow out of him, admitting that it was
ill-founded. The woman was his wife and was being taken to
his childhood home to meet his family. It was to be expected
that she would feel some curiosity even if the arrangement
they had was more in the nature of employment than marriage.

He could not expect her to behave as if she were totally inanimate, after all.

He spoke again at last, without opening his eyes.

"You do not have to concern yourself with what will happen when we arrive at Enfield Park," he said. "You need not worry about creating a good impression or any impression at all for that matter. I will speak for you. You may think of yourself as my shadow if you will. You may behave as you did when we met two days ago."

"Why?" It was not a defiant question. It sounded merely curious.

"The Duke of Withingsby is extremely high in the instep," he said. "He has an enormous sense of his own consequence and of that of his whole family. Although his heir has been busily sowing his wild oats for eight years and acquiring an unsavory reputation as a rake—did you know that about your husband, my lady?—his grace will now expect great things of him. A glittering and politic marriage, for example."

"Your marriage to me will of course be seen as a disaster," she said.

"Undoubtedly," he agreed. "I have married a governess, an impoverished gentlewoman. At least I have spared him someone from the *demimonde*."

"And you wish for a wife who is not only of inferior birth and fortune," she said, "but also lacking in charm and manners and conversation. A mere shadow."

"You need not worry," he said. "No one will openly insult you. Anyone who dares do so will have me to deal with."

"But who," she asked in her low, pleasant voice, "will protect me from your insults, sir?"

His eyes snapped open. "You, my lady," he said, "are being paid very well indeed to serve my purpose."

"Yes," she said, looking steadily back at him, "I am."

The words, even her expression, were quiet and meek. Why, then, did he have the distinct impression that war had been declared?

He closed his eyes again.

Chapter 5

Enfield Park in Wiltshire was dauntingly grand. Yet even as the thought flashed into Charity's mind she realized that it was a gross understatement. She had lived most of her life in a cottage that boasted eight bedchambers abovestairs and was set amidst a few acres of pleasing parkland. She had been a frequent visitor at nearby Willowbourne, the home of Sir Humphrey Loring and his family—Cassandra Loring, a mere eight months younger than she, was her particular friend—and had always thought it imposing. Both properties would fit into one corner of Enfield Park and never be noticed.

At first, after the carriage had passed between massive stone gateposts and by a small stone lodge, she mistook the dower house off to the right of the driveway for the main house itself and then felt foolish when she realized her mistake, though she had not spoken it aloud, for she had been almost awed by its size and the classical perfection of its design. And that was just the dower house? It must be—the marquess had murmured the information and the carriage had continued on past.

The driveway wound between flowering hedgerows, beyond which stretched dense and ancient woodlands. They seemed to have passed into a quieter, more shadowed world despite the clopping of the horses' hooves and the creaking of the carriage wheels. Charity stared about her in wonder. But the woods fell away behind them as they approached a river and crossed it over a covered Palladian bridge—it was a magnificent structure, she saw, leaning closer to the window. The driveway climbed slightly on the other side of the bridge, passing be-

tween well-kept lawns and flower beds and the occasional old
tree with massive and gnarled trunk. There were wooded hills
over to the right, Charity could see. But almost before she
could notice them, her attention was taken wholly by the house
itself, which had just come into view.

It was an almost laughable misnomer to call it a house. It
was a vast mansion of classical design. It was grand enough to
do a king justice. It could easily be a palace. But it was the
home of the Duke of Withingsby, her father-in-law. One day
her husband would be duke and owner of it all. And she had
thought yesterday morning that she was marrying a plain Mr.
Earheart.

Charity swallowed. He was very silent—as he had been for
most of the day and yesterday too. She had tried to make conversation, though admittedly she had chosen topics that did not
lend themselves to a great deal of intelligent discussion. She
had expected this morning—naively as it had turned out—that
it would be easier to communicate with him today. Though she
had not for a moment mistaken what had happened the night
before for love and had not expected it to make any difference
at all to his plans for the future, she had nevertheless expected
that there would be greater ease and warmth between them.

How wrong she had been. The opposite was true. The fact
that they had had conjugal relations—though it was very hard
to believe that it had happened with this elegant, almost morose man beside her—appeared to have meant nothing at all to
him and merely made her annoyingly self-conscious. She kept
remembering where and how he had touched her and tried not
to stare at his hands—they were long-fingered, very masculine
hands. She kept remembering that he had been deep inside her
body, and moving vigorously there for what must have been
several minutes. She kept remembering the amazingly intense
pleasure his movements had given her.

It had happened with this immaculately tailored, stern-
faced, very handsome stranger. It should have brought them
closer together, even without the dimension of love. How
could they continue strangers when they had shared bodies?

But she had a great deal to learn, it seemed. He had told her earlier that he had earned a reputation as a rake. That meant that last night's activity was very familiar to him. She was merely one of a long string of women—and without a doubt the least expert of them all. It was a strange thought. To her the experience had been earth-shattering. She was not yet sure whether she was glad to have experienced it or whether in light of the future it might have been better if she had never known.

But the carriage was fast approaching the house—the mansion—and the discomfort she had lived with all day increased tenfold. Even if she were coming here as a governess she would be quaking with apprehension. But she was not coming as a governess. She was coming as the wife of the heir—the temporary wife. The unexpected wife. She smoothed her hands over the folds of her brown cloak and was thankful that her gloves had not worn into holes—yet.

"Ah," her husband said from beside her, "my arrival has been noted." He chuckled softly—a rather chilling sound.

The great doors at the top of the marble steps had opened and two people—a man and a woman—had stepped outside. For one foolish moment Charity forgot that the duchess was deceased. Two such grand personages, both dressed elegantly in black, could only be the duke and duchess, she thought. But of course they were not. They were merely servants—the housekeeper and the butler at a guess.

"His grace observes every occasion of any significance with the utmost formality and correctness," the marquess said. "The return of the prodigal heir is an occasion of significance." His second chuckle sounded just as mirthless as the first.

There was no time for Charity to become even more nervous than she already felt. Liveried footmen had appeared on the terrace, and they opened the door of the carriage and set down the steps almost before it had rolled to a complete halt. And then she was standing on the cobbles, feeling dwarfed by the massive pillars that flanked the steps and overwhelmed by the occasion, watching her husband receive the homage of the black-clad servants with icy courtesy. They turned to precede him up the steps while he offered her his arm.

His face was hard and cold, his eyes opaque. His face was also devoid of all color. He wore so heavy a mask, Charity realized with a sudden flash of sympathy, that there was no penetrating it to the real man behind. Not even through the eyes, usually a mask's weak point. He was coming home to his father and his family after eight years. How different from the homecoming she imagined for herself in a few weeks' time.

He dropped her arm when they reached the wide doorway and stepped inside ahead of her. This was the point at which she was to become his shadow, she thought, but rather than being offended that he did not lead her forward, she was glad of the chance to be insignificant. Her first impression of the hall was of vastness—of marble and pillars and classical busts and a towering dome. It would have been an intimidating room under any circumstances. But these were clearly not any circumstances. Two rows of silent servants, women on the left, men on the right, flanked the central path across the hall to a short flight of wide steps that led up to what might be a grand salon.

At the foot of the steps, arranged as if for a theatrical tableau, was a group of people, clearly *not* servants or even ordinary mortals. In the center, and slightly in front of all the others, a man stood alone. A man who so closely resembled the Marquess of Staunton as he might appear in twenty-five or thirty years that for a moment Charity felt somewhat disoriented.

She was, she realized then, in the presence of the Duke of Withingsby.

The marquess paused for a moment to look left and right, an ironic half smile on his lips. Then he fixed his eyes on his father and moved forward across the hall, his boots clicking hollowly on the marble floor. Charity took one step forward to follow him. But a hand closing firmly about her upper arm stopped her progress. She turned her head to look into the disdainful face of the housekeeper.

"You will move to your left, girl," the woman said quietly, "and stand behind the line of servants until someone can attend to you."

Charity felt a welcome wave of amusement. She had been mistaken for a servant! "Oh, I think not," she said, smiling. But she stood where she was.

"Impertinent baggage," the housekeeper said coldly, her voice still low enough that it did not carry. "I will deal with you myself later. Stand where you are."

The marquess was bowing to his father, who was inclining his head in return. Everyone else in the group—the brothers and sisters?—stood watching. None broke ranks to greet the brother they had not seen for eight years. Charity felt chilled. How different her own homecoming would be, she thought again. She would have brothers and sisters hanging off every available part of her person and all would simultaneously be talking shrilly in order to be heard above everyone else. Nothing but a polite murmuring reached her ears across the expanse of this chilly hall.

And then her husband turned, looked back until his eyes found her, raised haughty eyebrows, and extended one hand. Charity could not resist one cool glance at the housekeeper, whose own eyebrows had disappeared almost beneath the frill of her cap, before moving forward. The hall seemed a mile long. But finally she was close enough to raise her hand and place it in the still-outstretched one of her husband. She kept her eyes on their hands. This was the moment during which she was to become a pawn, the moment of triumph for her husband. Well, she certainly looked the part, she was forced to admit—*that* had just been proved beyond a doubt. She would act it too. He was paying her well enough after all. And it was not a difficult part to play given the circumstances. Heaven knew she felt tongue-tied enough. And her legs were feeling anything but rock-steady.

"Your grace," the marquess said, "allow me the honor of presenting to you the Marchioness of Staunton."

He did not call his father "Papa," Charity noticed, or even

"Father." He called him "your grace." How very peculiar. It must have been a real world-stopper of a quarrel. And he had used his North Pole voice. She curtsied. And disconcerted by the utter silence that succeeded her husband's words, she raised her eyes to look at the Duke of Withingsby.

He looked even more like his son from close up. The only significant difference was the silver hair at his temples and the almost gray tinge to his complexion. He was looking back at her with a stern, set face and hard eyes—even in facial expression and manner he resembled his son. He presented, she was forced to admit, a somewhat formidable aspect.

"My lady." He broke the silence and half inclined his head to her. Even his voice—even the *tone* of it—was like his son's. Except that he had found ice even chillier than that at the Pole. "You are welcome to Enfield Park." Not by the flicker of an eyelash did his grace display shock or even surprise. He looked back at his son. "You will wish to greet the rest of your family, Staunton, and to present them to Lady Staunton."

Her husband had certainly won this round of the game, Charity thought ruefully, even if his father had not given him the satisfaction of collapsing in horror or erupting into a towering rage. He had just learned of his son's marriage and had just met his new daughter-in-law and had greeted her with about as much enthusiasm as he might be expected to show to his lordship's valet. Except that his eyes, with one cold sweep, would probably not have noted and dated and priced every garment the valet wore. She had the peculiar feeling that his grace had even detected the hole that had not yet quite been worn in her glove at the pad of her thumb.

His grace stood to one side.

"William?" Her husband's voice sounded strained and Charity realized anew that his return home was not as lacking in emotion as he would have her believe—and as perhaps he believed himself. He was bowing to a young man on the right of the silent group of relatives, a young man who was clearly his brother, though he was not as tall or as dark in coloring. They must be very close in age. "Claudia?"

The young lady who curtsied to him was extremely beautiful. She was blond and tall and dressed fashionably in a shade
of green that matched her eyes.

"Anthony," they both said.

"May I present my wife?" he asked, and Charity became involved in another round of formal bows and curtsies. "My
brother, Lord William Earheart, my lady. And Lady William."

Was this how an aristocratic bride could expect to be
greeted by her husband's family? Charity wondered as he
turned to the next couple. No hugs? No tears? No smiles or
kisses? Just this stiff formality, as if they were all strangers?
She felt rather as if she were suffocating. But of course most
aristocratic brides would meet their husbands' families before
the ceremony. And would be properly approved by that family. Oh yes, her husband had won this round of the game all
right. This was a disaster.

Lady Twynham—also fashionably and tastefully dressed—
was the marquess's sister. She called him Tony and accused
him of never answering any of her letters and presented him to
the Earl of Twynham, a portly man of middle years, who
looked bored with the whole proceeding. She inclined her
head to Charity and said nothing at all. Her eyes, like her father's, assessed the brown bonnet and cloak that her sister-in-
law was wearing.

Lieutenant Lord Charles Earheart was a slim, fair-haired
handsome young man, who bowed with equal stiffness to both
his brother and his sister-in-law. One could hardly blame him,
perhaps, when the marquess had not even been quite sure of
his identity.

"Charles?" he had said. "You *are* Charles? Lieutenant, is
it?"

He must be younger than Philip, Charity estimated. Nineteen? Twenty? He would have been just a boy when his
brother had left home, and they had not seen each other during
the eight years since. How very sad it was. Perhaps, she
thought suddenly, without this marriage she would not have
been able to see her own brothers and sisters for eight years or

longer—all the younger ones would have grown up without her. It was already a year since she had seen them last.

And then there was the youngest one, a girl. She was expensively dressed and elaborately coiffed and unnaturally quiet and still and dignified for such a young child. She was very dark in coloring, and she had the narrow, aristocratic face of her eldest brother—and of her father. She would be handsome rather than pretty when she grew up.

"Augusta?" the marquess said. For the first time there was some softening in his tone. "I am your brother Anthony. This is my wife."

"How pretty you look in blue, Augusta," Charity said kindly. "And how pleased I am to make your acquaintance."

The child executed two perfect curtsies. "My lord," she murmured. "My lady."

Well. And that was that, Charity thought. The scene had been played out and she would have to say that the Marquess of Staunton had won his point resoundingly. But perhaps the welcome home would have been just as chilly even if she had not been with him. There was no way of knowing. She knew nothing of the quarrel that had sent him from home and kept him away. And she had no way of knowing either what was to come next. She had not thought beyond this moment and she did not know if her husband had either. With a hand at the small of her back he was turning her in his father's direction again. The housekeeper stood just a few feet off. She had doubtless been summoned by some silent communication—a lifting of the ducal eyebrow, perhaps.

"Mrs. Aylward," the duke said, "you will conduct the Marchioness of Staunton to the marquess's apartments, if you please, and see to her comfort there. Tea will be served in the drawing room in precisely half an hour. You will attend me in the library, Staunton."

Did anyone ever *smile* here? Or do anything with any enthusiasm or spontaneity? Charity was supposed to be quiet, dull, and demure, and she had been all three ever since setting foot over the threshold. But she was oppressed by the atmosphere, offended by it. These people were *family.* Family members were supposed to love and support one another. And she was, however temporarily, a member of this family. This silver-haired, stern gentleman was her *father*-in-law. Some gesture was necessary—even imperative—if she was to maintain any of her own identity. She smiled warmly at him and curtsied again.

"Thank you," she said, and she hesitated for only the merest moment, *"Father."*

Nobody said anything—or rather everybody continued to say nothing. But Charity did not believe she imagined a collective stiffening in everyone around her just as if she had opened her mouth and uttered some obscenity. She turned her smile on her husband, who bowed to her.

"I shall see you shortly, *my love,"* he said, throwing just a little emphasis onto the final two words.

They jolted her. He had never mentioned that part of his plan was to pretend that they had a fondness for each other. But then he had not said a great deal at all about his plans. She turned and followed the housekeeper toward a marble arch and the grand staircase beyond it.

"My lady," the housekeeper said stiffly as they began the ascent, "we were not informed of the fact that his lordship was bringing a wife to Enfield Park. I do beg your pardon."

"For calling me an impertinent baggage?" Charity said, laughing. She could just imagine the woman's embarrassment. "I was amused, Mrs. Aylward. Please forget it."

But Mrs. Aylward herself looked far from amused, especially at the open reminder of her own words. It must be a rule of the house, Charity decided, that no one was allowed to smile beneath its roof. Her laughter had echoed hollowly and disappeared without a trace. She felt that sense of oppression again. This was not going to be easy. She must hope that the first stage of her marriage would last for very few weeks. She longed for home and for the familiar, cheerful, *smiling* faces of her family.

The marquess's apartments, on the second floor, consisted

of two large bedchambers, connected by adjoining dressing rooms, and of a study, and a sitting room of equal size. It was clearly an apartment designed for a married couple.

"I shall have the bed aired and made up immediately, my lady," the housekeeper said, leading her into one of the bedchambers, a square, high-ceilinged room, whose predominant colors of green and gold gave it a springlike appearance. It was by far the least oppressive room Charity had seen in the house so far. It was also a chamber into which her room at home would fit four times over, she was convinced.

"What a lovely room," she said, crossing the soft carpet to look out of one long window. It faced across a lawn to a horseshoe-shaped lake and trees beyond. "And what a glorious view."

"I shall see that your luggage is brought up and your maid shown to your dressing room without further delay, my lady," Mrs. Aylward said. "You will wish to change and freshen up for tea."

Oh dear.

"I have no maid," Charity said, turning to smile at her, "and only one small trunk. But a pitcher of hot water and soap and towels would be very welcome. Thank you, Mrs. Aylward."

The housekeeper was too well trained to look appalled, though like many of her breed she had perfected the look of well-bred disdain. She used the look on Charity now. But during eight months as a governess and during six interviews for another position, Charity had grown accustomed to ignoring such looks and reminding herself of her own inherent dignity.

She was, however, made aware of her somewhat embarrassing predicament—one that had not been apparent to her when she had first agreed to marry or even after she knew her husband's true identity. Only now, in this house, among these people, did she become uncomfortably aware that apart from her rather aged gray silk and her well-worn sprigged muslin, she had nothing suitable for wearing in genteel company. And this company was going to be somewhat higher on the social scale than genteel. She had a few other good clothes at home, of course, but she had not thought it appropriate to take them with her when she took employment.

She wondered if her husband realized the poverty of her wardrobe and concluded that he must—he had advertised for a governess, after all, and he had seen her trunk and had even asked if that was all she had. She wondered if he would be embarrassed by her shabby appearance, and concluded immediately that he would not. It was all part of his plan. He wanted her to be just as she was—or as she had appeared to him during that interview in Upper Grosvenor Street. He wanted her to be a drab little mouse, and probably a shabby one too. She could begin to see why. Even the housekeeper had mistaken her for a servant. The Duke of Withingsby must be totally incensed at the knowledge that she was his heir's *wife*. She looked down at her brown cloak and tried to see it through his eyes. Yet there was nothing he could do to alter the situation. Oh yes, her husband must indeed feel that he had won this round of the game.

Charity had no right to feel bitter. She had no reason to feel anything except an eagerness that this charade be over and done with as soon as possible.

Mrs. Aylward left her alone after promising to send up her trunk and assign a maid to her care—until her own should arrive from London, she added with the certain and disdainful knowledge that there was no such person.

Charity looked about at the magnificence of her room and hugged her arms about herself. On the whole she would have preferred to be in a small attic room, about to begin a new job as a governess. Except that then she would have little hope of ever returning to her family or of ever expecting the happy settlement in life of her brothers and sisters.

She had done the right thing. Of course she had.

Chapter 6

As a boy, the Marquess of Staunton had often had the fanciful feeling that the dome above the great hall settled its weight upon his shoulders as soon as he stepped inside the doors, rather like Atlas's world. Eight years after leaving home and setting himself free, he experienced exactly the same feeling as soon as he crossed the threshold again.

It was a feeling of heaviness and darkness. And the people who still haunted his dreams and his nightmares even though he had freed himself from them in all his waking moments were there, waiting to pull him in again, to drag him under until he gasped for air and sucked in water instead and knew himself doomed. He was glad indeed that he had brought a wife with him, that he had the undeniable means with which to defy their subtle influence. And they were *all* there, he saw at a glance.

None of them had ever been to London during the eight years he had spent there. That was a strange fact when one considered their social rank and the adult ages of all of them except the youngest. It was a chilling reminder of the power the Duke of Withingsby wielded over his family. His eldest son and heir had left without his permission. None of his other children would be allowed to meet him and perhaps be contaminated by his influence. Even Twynham must be under the ducal thumb. He had never brought Marianne to town or even come there alone, to the marquess's knowledge. He had never met his sister's husband.

And so in leaving his father he had been severed from his

whole family—even from the baby. It was the choice he had been forced to make—the choice that had almost killed him. He had left behind the baby and twelve-year-old Charles. He noticed the young girl among the silent group behind the duke. She must be that baby. And the very young man must be Charles. He tried not to remember how many times he had tortured himself, especially during the early years, with wondering if it had been cowardly to leave them. And how many times he had felt cruelly punished with the fierceness of his longing for them.

His father looked not a day older than he had looked then, though the grayish tinge to his complexion proclaimed the fact that he had not lied about his failing health.

All these things the marquess noticed and felt during the first seconds after he had stepped through the doorway into the great hall. During those moments he was almost overwhelmed by unaccustomed emotion. He had trained himself not to feel at all. And by God, he would put that training to use now when he most needed it. He looked mockingly at the silent lines of immaculately clad servants before crossing the hall and beginning this charade of a family reunion.

Nothing surprised him. His father welcomed his son home with chill pomp just as if he had not left in bitterness and been gone and living independently for eight years. And—as he might have expected—his father greeted the news of his marriage without a flicker of public dismay—or enthusiasm. He met this daughter-in-law with chill courtesy. So did all the others. But the marquess was glad of the formality. Without it, he did not know quite how he would have looked William in the eye, or Claudia, or how he would have been able to speak to them. He had seen, almost before he was properly through the door, almost before he saw his father, that they were there, side by side, husband and wife. And that Claudia was more beautiful than she had ever been.

It was enormously satisfying to him—even more so than he had expected—to present his wife. To sense the blank shock in his father's whole being. To display to *them* that he had married from personal inclination after all, that he cared not one fig for dynastic considerations. He had not realized until this very moment that he had had more than one reason for choosing a bride as he had and for marrying her before coming home.

And then came the crowning moment. Just as she was about to be led away by the housekeeper, his wife smiled. No, she did not just smile—she lit up the hall with the warmth of her expression and despite the terrible drabness of her clothes she looked suddenly quite startlingly lovely. And she called his grace *Father*. It was a priceless moment. No one had ever been so familiar with the Duke of Withingsby. There was nothing even remotely vulgar in either her smile or her words. They were just shockingly out of place in this household.

And so an idea was born in him and he had called her his love—a definite vulgarity in the ducal vocabulary. He knew a moment of quite exquisite triumph, far in excess even of what he had dreamed.

He followed his father into the library but did not stand just inside the door, as he had always used to do when summoned there, facing the seated duke across the wide expanse of the oak desk in a position of distinct subordination. No, he would never stand there again. He crossed the room to the window and looked out across the lake.

"How are you, sir?" he asked. His father was not languishing on his deathbed, but he was undoubtedly in poor health. And his health was the reason for this homecoming.

His grace ignored the question. "Your marriage is of recent date," he said. It was not a question. The marquess did not doubt that his father was familiar with every move he had made during the past eight years, though not a single letter had been exchanged between them—until the one that had summoned him home.

"Yesterday," he said. "A union that was consummated last night," he added, glad suddenly that it could be said in all honesty. Though he would have been just as married even without the consummation.

"Who is she?" the duke asked.

"She was Miss Charity Duncan, a gentlewoman from Hampshire," the marquess said. "She earned her living as a governess before marrying me."

"I suppose," his father said, "you were seduced by blue eyes and a seductive smile and bold impertinence."

Seductive? Bold impertinence? His quiet little mouse? His lips twitched but he said nothing. His father would soon realize how far wide of the mark his initial judgment of his daughter-in-law was, though it would not hurt at all if she smiled more often. He turned from the window and looked at the duke, who was seated, as expected, behind his desk—from which vantage point he had dispensed chill justice on servants and children alike for as far back as his son could remember. And no love at all.

"I married her," he said quietly, "because I chose to, sir. I passed the age of majority seven years ago."

"You married her," his grace said, "in defiance of me and in defiance of your upbringing. You have married a woman of shabby gentility and questionable manners. She was very carefully chosen, I daresay."

"Yes, sir," his son said, the sense of triumph building in him. "For love."

It was something he had not intended to claim, something he had never even considered claiming since love—in any of its manifestations—was an emotion that gave him the shudders. But the idea had occurred to him when she had so shocked his family with a single word and a dazzling smile. It was a good idea. The Dukes of Withingsby and their heirs did not marry for love—especially shabby gentlewomen. The idea that his heir had been indiscreet enough to form a love match would strike his father as the ultimate vulgarity.

"Tillden will be arriving here tomorrow with his countess and his daughter," the duke said. "They are coming to celebrate the formalizing of a betrothal between Lady Marie Lucas and my eldest son. There is to be a betrothal ball the night after tomorrow. How will you explain yourself to them, Staunton?"

"I believe, sir," the marquess said, "I have no explaining to do."

"You were fully aware of the match agreed upon seventeen years ago," his grace said. "And if you had forgotten, my letter of a couple of weeks ago would have reminded you—the letter you received even before you were acquainted with the present marchioness, I daresay. Tillden may well consider you in breach of contract."

"If there is a contract in existence," his son replied coolly, "it does not bear my signature, sir. If the agreement was verbal, it was not ratified by my voice. The contract is not my concern."

"A young lady who has grown up expecting to be the Duchess of Withingsby one day," his grace said, "is about to be severely humiliated."

"I had no part in raising her hopes," the marquess said. "And I believe you must agree, sir, that this conversation is pointless. I am married. The ceremony has been performed, the register signed and witnessed, and the union consummated."

His father stared at him coldly and quite expressionlessly. It was a moment of acute triumph for his son, who held his gaze.

"It is to be hoped," his grace said at last, "that you know how to dress your wife, Staunton. The garments she wore for travel will disappear without trace after today, I trust? It was my distinct impression that my housekeeper mistook her for a maid."

So that was why she had still been standing just inside the door when he had turned to present her to his father? The marquess smiled inwardly.

"My wife pleases me as she is," he said. "I care nothing for the clothes she wears."

"A nonsensical attitude when the appearance of your wife reflects your own position in society," his grace said. "As she appeared on her arrival, she is hardly fit to occupy a place in the kitchen."

"As my father and our host," the marquess said, the stiffness and chilliness of his voice quite at variance with his secret satisfaction, "you have the right to say so, sir. I will, however, be pleased to debate the issue with anyone else who feels obliged to utter similar sentiments."

What *did* she have in that small trunk of hers? he wondered.

"You will wish to go upstairs before coming to the drawing room for tea," the duke said. "You will wish to escort Lady Staunton down. You will not wish to be late. And you will instruct her ladyship on how I am to be addressed, Staunton."

His son stood looking at him for several moments before moving to the door without another word. He could remember how as a boy he had adored his father, whom he rarely saw, how he had fed off every comment about his own likeness to the duke, how the whole of his boyhood had seemed to be shaped about the desire to please his father, to emulate him, to be a worthy heir to him. All his efforts had gone unnoticed. And yet every failure at a lesson, every episode of boyish mischief, every reported bickering with a younger sibling had brought him to this very room for an interrogation and a lecture, while he had stood before that desk, knowing that at the end of it all there would be the command to bend over the desk for the painful and never brief caning.

He could not count the number of times he had been caned by his father. Neither could he count the number of times his father had shown him affection since there were no such numbers to count.

He might have forgiven his father's harshness toward himself—perhaps. But the duke had shown no love to anyone—not even to his wife, who had borne him thirteen children and had miscarried four others. And his grace had expressed only impatience and irritability when his eldest son had tried to persuade him to see his youngest daughter after her birth—and after the duchess's death.

It had been one of his reasons for leaving home.

He had come to hate his resemblance to his father—the outer resemblance and, more important, the inner resemblance. He had come to hate himself. Until he had freed himself. He was free now. He had come back when summoned, but he had come on his own terms. The Duke of Withingsby no longer had any power over him.

But devil take it, he thought as he took the stairs up to his apartment two at a time, that dome was pressing down on his shoulders again.

The apartments he had occupied from the time he left the nursery until the time he left home had been prepared for him again. They must have been kept for him all this time, he thought. His declaration that he was leaving, never to return, had been disregarded—and indeed, here he was, back again. He had rather expected that the apartments would have been given to William and Claudia. But apparently not. They must be in some lesser apartment.

He found his wife in the private sitting room. She was standing at the window, looking out, though she turned her head as soon as he opened the door. The room, which he had never used, looked strangely cozy and lived-in and feminine, he thought, though nothing had changed in it except for the fact that she was standing there. It was a woman's room, he realized, or a room that needed a woman's presence.

It seemed suddenly strange to have a woman—a wife—in these long-familiar rooms.

For the first time since he had known her she was not wearing brown. She had changed into a high-waisted dress of sprigged muslin. It looked somewhat faded from many washings. Her hair was simply styled and knotted behind. It was lighter in color than he had thought at first. She looked, he thought, like someone's poor relation—a very poor relation. She also looked surprisingly young and pretty. She had a trim figure—a rather enticing figure, as he remembered clearly from his exploration of it the night before.

"The view is magnificent," she said.

"Yes." He crossed the room to stand beside her. He had always been somewhat oppressed by the house. In the outdoors he had known freedom—or the illusion of freedom. The late-afternoon sun slanted across the lake, turning it to dull gold. The woods beyond—his boyhood playground and enchanted land—were dark and inviting.

"You are very like your father." She was looking at his profile rather than out the window.

"Yes." His jaw tightened.

"And you hate being like him," she said quietly. "I am sorry I stated the obvious."

He did not like her insights, her attempts to read his character and his mind. He shared himself with no one, ever—not even his closest male friends. She must understand that she was not to be allowed a wife's privilege of probing into every corner of his life—the very idea was nauseating. She must be reminded that theirs was purely a business arrangement.

"I married you and I brought you here, as you very well know," he said, turning to look at her—she looked very directly back with those splendid blue eyes of hers, "to prove to his grace that I live my own life my own way. No one is allowed to direct my life for me and no one is invited to intrude on my privacy. I am the Duke of Withingsby's heir—nothing but my death can change that. But beyond that basic fact, I am my own person. You are the proof I have brought with me that I will not do anything merely because it is expected of the heir to the dukedom."

"You did not have the courage merely to tell him that?" she asked.

"You, my lady," he said, "are impertinent."

She opened her mouth to speak but closed it again without saying anything. She did not look away from him, though. She stared at him with wide eyes. He had the strange feeling that if he looked deeply enough into them he would see her soul. If she kept herself that wide open, he thought in some annoyance, sooner or later life was going to hurt her very badly indeed.

"You played your part well on your arrival," he said. "You may confidently continue as you began. You need not be embarrassed by your lack of a fashionable wardrobe. And you need not be embarrassed by any lack of conversation—my family is not easy to converse with. We are expected in the drawing room immediately. You may stay close to me and leave the conversation to me. There is no necessity for you to impress anyone."

She half smiled at him. "Augusta must have been very young when you went away," she said.

"She was one week old," he told her. "I stayed for my mother's funeral." He had shed no tears for his mother. He had sobbed painfully, the child in his arms, just before he left. The last tears he had shed—the last he would ever shed.

"Ah," his wife said softly, and he could have sworn that she had slipped inside his head again and knew that he had wept over his last ever contact with love. Over his last foolishness.

He would not have her inside his head—or anywhere inside himself.

"Ours was a brief courtship," he told her briskly. "You were governess at the home of an acquaintance of mine. I met you there, we fell in love, and we threw all caution to the winds. We married yesterday, mated last night, and are embarking upon a deeply passionate relationship today."

She blushed and her eyes slipped from his for a few moments. But she looked back at him steadily enough. "Then, my lord," she said, "you must learn to smile."

He raised his eyebrows.

"You look," she said, her eyes roaming over his face, "like a man who has married a stranger with the sole purpose of angering and perhaps disgusting someone else. You look like a man who is wallowing in bitter and unhappy triumph."

His eyes narrowed. He found himself wondering if one short interview two days before had been sufficient time in which to learn about her character—or what he had thought to be lack of character. But perhaps she had a point, he had to confess.

"You will have your smiles, my lady," he said. "But below-stairs, where they will be seen by others. We have no need of them when we are alone."

"No," she said.

"Take my arm." He offered it. "We are late. His grace does not tolerate unpunctuality."

"That is why we have stood here talking instead of going down immediately?" she asked him. There was a look very like merriment in her eyes.

But he merely waited for her to take his arm.

The Duke of Withingsby's family had moved directly to the drawing room from the hall. Although the fine weather might have tempted some of them out-of-doors to stroll until it was time for tea, they all felt an unexpressed need to remain together and to be out of the earshot of servants.

"One might have guessed," Lord William Earheart said, the first to speak after the door had been closed, "that when he so meekly agreed to return to Enfield scarcely more than a week after his grace wrote to him, Staunton would have a trick or two up his sleeve. I would have advised his grace to leave the letter unwritten if my opinion had been sought."

"Oh, William," his wife said reproachfully, releasing his arm and setting hers about Augusta's shoulders, "you would not have. You know you have longed for Anthony's return as much as anyone."

"What in thunder are you talking about?" He frowned moodily. "Have *you* been longing for his return?"

"I cannot believe it," the Countess of Twynham said, sinking gracefully onto a sofa. "I cannot believe it. How *could* he? It is one thing to run away to town for a few years—I would imagine it is many a young man's dream to do so. It is one thing to live wildly there and to gain a reputation as a—" She glanced at Augusta. "Well, it is one thing. It is another thing entirely to *marry* without his grace's permission and to bring his bride home here without a word to anyone. Did you *see* her, Claudia? I would die of humiliation if my *maid* were seen in such garments."

Claudia, Lady William, had led Augusta to the window and had sat with her in the window seat. "Perhaps, Marianne," she said, "they had a trying journey. There was all that rain yesterday, you will remember. Who would wish to wear good clothes in that weather?"

"But who the devil *is* she?" the Earl of Twynham muttered while busying himself at the sideboard, pouring a glass of brandy while there was still time. No hard liquor was permitted during tea at Enfield. "Did Staunton say? He would have if she had been anyone, you may be sure. It will be a trifle embarrassing when Lady Marie arrives tomorrow, eh?"

"Oh!" Marianne waved a handkerchief in the air as if she were about to succumb to a fit of the vapors, and then pressed it to her nose. "I shall *die*. And it is too late for his grace to stop her from coming. And Tony knew about her coming. He must have known. How could he do this to us? I cannot believe it. He has married a nobody and brought her here to humiliate us all. And she is a dreadfully vulgar creature as was plain for all to see."

Lord William combed his fingers through his hair. "She called his grace *Father*," he said and winced. "She had not been in the house five minutes. Can you imagine Lady Marie calling him *Father*? She would know better. I would not be in his grace's shoes tomorrow for all the tea in China."

"But Lady Staunton does have a lovely smile," Claudia said. "Perhaps we should wait and make her acquaintance before making any hasty judgments. What do you think, Charles?"

Lieutenant Lord Charles Earheart was standing beside her and Augusta, looking out of the window.

"I would not have come home on leave if his grace had not summoned me," he said. "Not when I knew that Staunton had been invited too. I have no thoughts on his arrival or on the fact that he has brought a wife with him. It is nothing to me."

If he had intended to speak with cold dignity, he failed miserably. His voice shook with youthful passion. Claudia reached out and touched his hand. He did not pull away, but neither did he turn his head to acknowledge her smile of sympathy.

"And what do you think of your eldest brother, Augusta?" Claudia asked.

"I think his lordship looks very like his grace," Augusta said. "I think he looks disagreeable. And I think her ladyship is very ugly."

The Earl of Twynham sniggered while his wife waved her handkerchief before her face again. " 'Out of the mouths of babes . . .' " she said. "You are quite right, Augusta. He looked very disagreeable indeed as if he were enjoying the whole dreadful scene. And *she* has no pretense to beauty or anything else either, I daresay. It would not surprise me to learn that Tony had found her in someone's kitchen—or in someone's schoolroom more like. One wonders if she is even a gentlewoman. I will find it extremely difficult to be civil to her."

"His grace will be civil, you may be sure, Marianne," Lord William said. "And he will expect no less of us. She *is* Lady Staunton, after all, whoever or whatever she was before Staunton decided to marry her."

"And she will be the duchess in time," his sister said in deepest disgust. "She will be the head of this family and will take precedence over Claudia, over me—over all of us. It will be quite insupportable. Twynham and I will come to Enfield very rarely in the future, I daresay. Well, there are ways and ways of being civil, Will. I shall be civil."

Lord Twynham sniggered again. "One wonders how Withingsby will manage things tomorrow," he said. "Tillden will not be amused, mark my words. And she already takes precedence over you, Marianne. She is Staunton's marchioness."

"We must all be civil today and let tomorrow look after itself," Claudia said. "Anthony has come home again and he has brought a bride of whom he is fond. He called her *my love.* Did anyone else hear him? I was touched, I must say."

Her husband snorted. "The Dukes of Withingsby and their

heirs do not marry for any such vulgar reason as love," he said, "as you know very well, Claudia."

She flushed and lowered her face to kiss the top of Augusta's head. Lord William had the grace to flush too, but there was no chance for any more conversation. The doors opened to admit the duke. He crossed the room in the silence that greeted his arrival and took up his stand with his back to the unlit fireplace, his hands at his back.

"Staunton is not here yet?" he asked rather unnecessarily. "He is late. We will await his pleasure." The coldness of his words did not invite any response.

His family proceeded to wait in uneasy silence. The Earl of Twynham clearly considered gulping down the last mouthful from his glass, but he regretfully and unobtrusively set the glass down on the sideboard instead. Claudia hugged Augusta, for whom the chance to take tea in the drawing room with the adults was a rare and questionable treat, and smiled reassuringly at her.

Chapter 7

Charity was coming to expect magnificence at Enfield Park. Even so, she found the drawing room quite daunting when she first stepped inside it. The drawing room at home was more in the way of a cozy sitting room, a place where the family gathered when they were all together in the evenings or when they were entertaining friends and neighbors. This room was like—an audience chamber was the only description that came to mind. The high-coved ceiling was painted with a scene from mythology, though she was not at leisure to identify which. The walls were hung with huge paintings in gilded frames—landscapes mostly. The furniture, heavily gilded and ornate, spoke of wealth and taste and privilege. The doorcase was elaborately carved. The marble fireplace was a work of art.

But she had little chance to do much more than catch her breath and focus her attention on the people who occupied the room—the duke standing formally before the fireplace, everyone else arranged about the room, either standing or seated. No one moved or said a thing, though every head turned toward the door as she came through it, her hand on her husband's arm.

Her sprigged muslin felt about as appropriate to the occasion as her shift would have been.

A moment later, after the first shock of the ordeal was over, she could have shaken every one of them. Their *brother* had come home, yet no one spoke a word to him. What, in heaven's name, was the *matter* with them? The answer was not long in coming. Most eyes turned after a few moments toward the duke, and it was clear that everyone waited for him to speak first. He took his time about doing so, though no words were necessary to convey the message that he was displeased.

A man ought not to be allowed to get away with being such a despot, Charity thought—but it was a thought she must certainly learn to keep to herself.

"Now that it has pleased Staunton to favor us with his company," his grace said at last, "we may have the tea tray brought in. Marianne? You will ring for it, if you please. Lady Staunton may be excused from her duties for this occasion."

It took Charity a fraction of a second to realize that she was the one being excused. From pouring the tea? *Her?* But of course, she realized in some shock. As the wife of the marquess she was the most senior lady present. She became even more aware of her sprigged muslin.

"Tony, do come and sit beside me and tell me why you never answer my letters," Marianne said, having got to her feet to pull the bell rope. And since she did not even look at Charity and since the sofa on which she sat could seat only two in comfort, it was clear that her invitation was not meant to include her brother's wife.

But Charity had glanced toward the window and the small group gathered there. Claudia was seated on a window seat with Augusta, one of her arms about the child's shoulders, and Charles stood beside them. Claudia caught her eye and looked on her kindly—or so Charity chose to believe as she crossed the room toward them. She would not be a shadow no matter what her husband wished. She was a lady and ladies were never merely other people's shadows, even their husbands'.

She smiled warmly. "You have been allowed to come to the drawing room for tea, Augusta?" she said. "I am so glad."

"Just for today," Claudia said. "For a special occasion. For Anthony's homecoming. The other children are not so fortunate despite long faces and even some pleading."

"The other children?" Charity asked.

"Anthony has not told you?" Claudia asked. "But then he

has not even met any of them himself yet. There are Marianne and Richard's three—two girls and a boy—and William and my two boys. Perhaps after tea you would care to come up to the nursery to meet them. They would be overjoyed, I can promise you."

Charity could have hugged her as she accepted the invitation. There was at least *someone* human at Enfield Park. How had Claudia been able to find a dress fabric that so exactly matched her eyes in color? she wondered.

"Charles." Charity smiled at him. "You are on leave from your regiment?"

"My lady." He made her a stiff bow. "I was summoned by his grace."

"*My lady*," Charity said softly. "I wonder if you would be so good as to call me by my name since I am your sister? It is Charity. My name, I mean."

"My lady." He inclined his head to her.

Well. Charity turned to look back into the room and found herself being surveyed from head to toe by a very disdainful Marianne. The marquess was seated beside her, looking as cynical and satanic as he had looked during that morning on Upper Grosvenor Street. Lord Twynham—Claudia had called him Richard—was standing by the sideboard, looking morose. William, also standing, was in the middle of the room, staring moodily at nothing in particular. The duke had not moved from his position of command at the fireplace.

Charity wondered what everyone would do or say if she suddenly screamed as loudly as she could and flapped her arms in the air. She was alarmed when she realized that she was quite tempted to put the matter to the test. But she was saved by the opening of the door and the advent of the tea tray and a better idea.

She crossed the room with all the grace she could muster— her mother had often accused her of striding along in unlady-like manner, and even Penny had sometimes hinted the same thing when they walked out together.

"Do set it down," she said to the servants, indicating the

table that was obviously intended for the tray. She walked around the table to the single chair that had been set behind it. She smiled at her sister-in-law. "I shall pour, Marianne, and save you the bother." She turned the same smile on the duke. "Thank you, Father, for the kind thought, but you do not need to excuse me from any of my duties as Anthony's wife." Finally she turned the smile on him and made it ten times more dazzling. She considered blowing him a kiss, but no—she would not be vulgar.

She was convinced for one ghastly moment that the proverbial pin might have been heard to drop on the drawing-room floor if someone only thought of dropping it there—despite the fact that the floor was sumptuously carpeted. But her husband got to his feet just in time.

"You may certainly pour a cup for me, my love," he said. And then he did it, what she had told him he must do. He *smiled* at her—with his mouth and his very white teeth and with his eyes and with his whole face. He smiled and in the process transformed himself into a dazzlingly vital and handsome man, not to mention a knee-weakeningly attractive one. Charity wondered if her hands would be steady enough to lift the teapot and direct the tea into the cup without also filling the saucer. She had to remind herself very sternly that he was merely acting a part and that in a sense so was she.

She had *never*, she thought, had to work so hard to earn her daily bread. It was true that this time she was earning vastly more than just daily bread, more than she could ever have dreamed of earning, in fact. But even so . . .

But even so, she was not sure she would have agreed to all this if she had only known what was facing her.

She had changed into a gown of gray silk for dinner. It had a modest neckline, modest sleeves, modest everything else. It was not shabby. Neither was it in the first stare of fashion—or even in the second stare for that matter, her husband thought. It looked like the sort of decent, unremarkable garment a governess might wear when taking the children down to the drawing room so that their parents might display them before family guests. It was the sort of garment designed to make her invisible. She wore no jewelry with it.

He stood in the doorway of her dressing room, which her new maid had opened to his knock, surveying her with slightly narrowed eyes.

"You may leave," he told the girl, who curtsied and scurried away without even glancing at her mistress for confirmation of the command.

She had done admirable things with his wife's hair. It curled softly about her face and was coiled prettily at the back. He would have preferred the usual plain style, but he would say nothing.

"Why did you choose to preside over the tea tray this afternoon?" he asked her. She had taken him totally by surprise. He had been almost enjoying himself, feeling everyone's discomfort almost like a palpable thing, watching their fascination with his wife, who had been dressed so very simply in her shabby sprigged muslin—and in such marked contrast to the elegant, costly, fashionable attire of everyone else. He had puzzled them all, he had been thinking, thrown them all off balance—even his father, he would wager. They did not know what to make of him or of his sudden marriage. They were all perhaps a little afraid of him. And they were all doubtless fully aware of why they had been summoned to Enfield Park. Part of it assuredly was their father's health—but that was only what had instigated his decision to bring on the moment of his heir's betrothal to the lady chosen for him at birth. There was even a ball planned to celebrate the event very publicly.

"Because, as your father reminded me," his wife said in answer to his question, "it was my duty to do so as the wife of his eldest son."

"There is no necessity for you to—do your duty as you put it," he said. "You know that was not my intention in bringing you here."

"But by choice you married a lady, my lord," she reminded him. "A lady knows what is expected of her after she marries even if she cannot quite dress or act the part of a future duchess. You may rest assured that your family thoroughly despises my appearance and my recent background and my lack of connections and fortune. They are welcome to do so as there is nothing I can—or would—do to alter any of those things. But I will not have them believe also that my upbringing was defective. That would be a lie and a slur on my mother's memory."

So much for his quiet mouse. She did not really exist, he suspected. Miss Charity Duncan had, of course, acted a part during that interview. She had badly wanted the position of governess—she had already failed at six previous attempts—and had behaved as governesses were expected to behave. He had taken the act for reality and had not perceived that there was a great deal of character behind the meekness—he should, of course, have taken more note of those shrewd blue eyes. He had been deceived. But there was truth in what she said now. Everyone this afternoon had treated her with subtle, well-bred condescension. She was not of their world. It must be an appalling thought to all of them that one day she would be wife of the head of the family. His father must feel that everything he had lived for was crashing about his ears.

"No one will openly insult you," he assured her, not for the first time. But now he felt more personal commitment to seeing that it was so. "No one would dare."

She smiled and came toward him. "Insults are only really effective," she said, "when the person insulted cares for the good opinion of the insulter. I will not be insulted here, my lord." She took the arm he offered.

And that, he thought, had been a quiet, charming, very firm setdown. She cared nothing for anyone in this house, her words told him. Well, neither did he. He had not come home because he cared. He had come in order to assert himself and his independence once and for all. And perhaps to lay a few ghosts to rest—though the thought had popped into his mind only now and surprised him. There were no ghosts to lay to rest. Everything that was past was long dead and done with.

"I would know more about your family," she said as he led
her from the dressing room toward the grand staircase, seeming to contradict what she had just implied. "Perhaps you will
enlighten me more tomorrow."

"I have seen none of them myself for eight years," he said.
"There is nothing to tell, my lady."

"But you must have boyhood memories," she said. "William
must be close to you in age, and Marianne too."

"William is one year my junior and Marianne two," he said.
Then the almost annual stillbirths and miscarriages had started.

"It must have been wonderful to have a brother and sister so
close to you in age," she said.

Yes, he had always adored and protected and envied the
smaller, weaker, but sunnier-natured Will. He would have
changed places with him at any time if it had been possible except that he could never have protected Will from all the harsh
burdens of being their father's heir.

"I suppose so," he said. "I do not often think of my boyhood."

"You had not met Lord Twynham before this afternoon,"
she said, looking at him. "But you had met Claudia. Were she
and William married before you left?"

"A month before," he said curtly. He did not want to talk
about Claudia. Or about Will. He did not want to talk.

"She is very beautiful," she said.

"Yes." She was still looking at him. "Yes, my sister-in-law
is a lovely woman."

Fortunately there was no time for further conversation. The
family was assembled in the drawing room, and dinner was
ready. Marianne and Claudia, he saw at a glance—Augusta
doubtless was not allowed to join the family for dinner—were
both splendidly gowned and decked out in jewels. The men
were all immaculately tailored, as was he. Formal dress for
dinner had always been a rule at Enfield, even when they
dined merely *en famille*, as they did tonight.

"My lady?" The duke was bowing and offering Charity his
arm to lead her in to dinner. It was something he would do, of

course, because it was the correct thing to do. He would also seat her opposite himself, at the foot of the table. But how it must gall him to be compelled to show such deference to a woman who looked—and had very recently been—the quint-essential governess.

She smiled warmly at him and laid her arm along his. "Thank you, Father," she said.

The marquess pursed his lips. He had not for a moment ex-pected such warm charm as his wife was displaying, but he was not sorry for it. It was, in fact, preferable to the timid, de-mure behavior he had anticipated and hoped for. Life at En-field had never been conducive to smiles—or to warmth. And none of the Duke of Withingsby's own children had ever ad-dressed him by any more familiar name than *sir*. He wondered if his wife had noticed that, and concluded that she probably had. He almost wished that she would call his grace *Papa*. He suppressed a grin.

But he sobered instantly. Was he expected to lead in Clau-dia as the lady next in rank to his wife? But William, he was relieved to see, was already offering her his arm. William, who had not exchanged a word with him and scarcely a glance dur-ing tea. Once his closest friend and at the last his deadliest enemy. Well, it was all in the past. Twynham and Marianne were going in to dinner together. The marquess brought up the rear with Charles.

Charles also had had nothing to say to him during tea. He had been a twelve-year-old boy eight years ago—an active, in-telligent lad who had looked on his eldest brother with open hero worship. There was no such look now. It had been impos-sible to explain to the boy just why he was leaving. He had not even attempted an explanation. He had left without saying good-bye. He had shed tears over the baby. He had been un-willing to risk them over his young brother.

"So you are the tallest of us all after all," he said now.

"So it would seem," his brother said.

His grace, at the head of the table, bowed his head and they all followed suit. There was, of course, the solemn and lengthy

prayer to be intoned before the food was served. It felt strange
to be back, the marquess thought, to be among people who
were strangers to him at the same time as they were almost as
familiar to him as his own body. And he felt, after an interval
of eight years, as if in some strange way he had carried them
with him for all that time, as close as his own body. He felt all
tangled up with them again, as if he were not free of them after
all. It was a suffocating feeling.

He looked up as the prayer ended to see his wife at the foot
of the table, smiling, and turning to make conversation with
William beside her. He felt such a relief that he had married
her and brought her with him that for the moment it felt almost
like affection.

Charity had lied during dinner. When Marianne had asked
about her family, in the supercilious way that appeared to
come naturally to her, Charity had told the truth about her father—except that she had made no mention of his debts—but
had claimed to be an only child. She had even been forced
then to a second lie in explaining that her father's property had
been entailed on a distant male relative and that as a consequence she had taken employment as a governess.

Despite what she had said to her husband earlier about her
immunity to insult in this house, she had found herself unable
to bear the thought of having her brothers and sisters subjected
to the veiled contempt these people clearly felt for a family so
low on the social scale when viewed from their superior
height. She could not bear to watch the effect of poor Phil's
story on them.

Her family was her own very private property. She would
not even try to share them with these cold people. Part of her
regretted what she had done in accepting the Marquess of
Staunton's strange offer—for a number of reasons, not least of
which was the lie it forced her to live. Part of her hugged to
herself the knowledge that it would all ultimately be worth-
while—she would be reunited with her family and no one
would ever again be able to force them apart.

The duke looked along the length of the table at her when they had finished eating and raised his eyebrows. She smiled at him—how difficult it was to continue smiling and not give in to the oppressive atmosphere of the house!—and rose to her feet to lead the other two ladies from the room.

Claudia was the only one who talked to her. She told Charity more about her two boys, whom Charity had met briefly in the nursery after tea, and said that she must come to the dower house tomorrow to see them again.

"Though of course," she added, "the houseguests are expected tomorrow afternoon. You must come in the morning, then, unless you are a late riser. I daresay you are not, though, if you are accustomed to presiding over a schoolroom." Her words were spoken without any apparent contempt.

The houseguests—yes. The duke had spoken of them at dinner. The Earl and Countess of Tillden and their daughter were coming. It surprised Charity that guests were expected when the duke was clearly ill and it had been his failing health that had caused him to summon her husband home. But perhaps the earl and his family were close friends. Somehow it was difficult to think of the Duke of Withingsby as having close friends.

Certainly the advent of guests would add to her own awkward position. She had no experience with anyone more illustrious than Sir Humphrey Loring. And she had so few clothes, and nothing at all suitable for such company. But she would not allow herself to panic. That was the whole point, after all, was it not? She had been brought here in order to be an embarrassment.

"Lady Staunton," Marianne said loudly when the gentlemen had joined them in the drawing room, "do please favor us with a rendering on the pianoforte. I will not insult you by asking if you play. Teaching the instrument must have been one of your duties as a governess."

"Yes indeed," Charity said, getting to her feet. "And I had the best of teachers too, Marianne. My mother taught me."

The pianoforte was a magnificent instrument. Charity had

been itching to play it ever since teatime. She sat and played, aware as she did so that the duke stood before the fireplace, Marianne began to converse and laugh with her brothers and sister-in-law, Lord Twynham settled low on a sofa for an after-dinner nap, and the marquess stood behind the pianoforte bench.

"Wonderful, my love," he said when she was finished, smiling into her eyes and taking her hand to raise to his lips. "Will you not play again—for me?"

"Not tonight, Anthony," she said, leaning slightly toward him and looking into his eyes with warm affection before he released her hand—she had not really expected when she had agreed to all this that she would be called upon to playact. It felt disturbingly dishonest. But something else had been bothering her. She got to her feet and crossed the room to the fireplace. She hesitated for a moment—the Duke of Withingsby was a very formidable gentleman. It would be so easy to fall into the habit of cowering before him. And it was not part of her agreement to do anything more than be her husband's shadow. But she would not cower. She slipped her arm through his and smiled as his eyes came to hers in open amazement.

"Father," she said, "will you not have a seat? You look very tired. Shall I ring for the tea tray and pour you a cup of tea?" He looked downright ill. He looked as if he held himself upright by sheer effort of will.

A strange hush fell on the room. Even breathing seemed to have been suspended.

"Thank you for your concern, my lady," his grace said after what seemed to be an interminable silence, "but I stand by choice. And I do not drink tea in the evening."

"Oh." She seemed to be stranded now, holding on to his arm with nothing further to do or say and with nowhere to go. "Then I shall stand here with you for a short while. The paintings in this room are all landscapes. Are there any portraits elsewhere? Family portraits?"

"There is a gallery," his grace said while everyone else continued to listen with apparently bated breath. "With family portraits, yes. It will be my pleasure to escort you there tomorrow morning, ma'am."

"Thank you," she said, "I should like that. Is there one of you? And of—of Anthony?"

He pursed his lips and reminded her even more of her husband. And then he told her of the family portrait that had been painted only two years before her grace's passing. He spoke of some older family portraits, including two by Van Dyck, one by Sir Joshua Reynolds.

His hand, Charity noticed, was long-fingered and well manicured, like his son's hands. It was also parchment white, the skin thinly stretched over the blue veins. He had not lied in order to lure his son home, she thought. He was ailing. She felt sad for him. She wondered if he was capable of love. She wondered if he had loved his wife. She wondered if he loved his children, if he loved her husband.

And she reminded herself that she was not interested in this family, that she was here merely to act out a charade, merely to earn her future with her own family. She wanted as little as possible to do with this strange, cold, lonely man and with his silent, morose, troubled family. And with his son, whom she had married just the day before and with whom she had lain last night. Her husband. Her temporary husband.

It had been an odd, disturbing day. She was glad it was almost at an end.

Chapter 8

The Marquess of Staunton had woken at dawn and found himself unable to sleep again even though it had taken him a long time to get to sleep the night before. He had lain down and stared upward in the near-darkness at the familiar pattern of the canopy above his bed. He had stood at the window gazing out at moonlit darkness, his fingernails drumming on the windowsill. There had been a sheen of moonlight across the lake.

He had felt restless. His brain had teemed with jumbled memories of the day—his father's gray complexion, Charles's transformation from an awkward boy to a tall, self-assured young man, Claudia's mature beauty, William's reticence, Augusta's formality, Marianne's affectionate treatment of himself, his wife seated behind the tea tray at teatime, his wife making conversation with Twynham and Will at dinner, his wife playing the pianoforte very precisely and skillfully, his wife with her arm linked through the duke's, smiling at him and forcing him into conversation.

He had smiled himself at that last memory. His grace hated to be touched. He never smiled or was smiled at. No one ever initiated conversation with him. And of course no one ever called him Father.

She was quite perfect. She was far better than the quiet mouse he had thought would do the trick. As a mouse she would merely have been despised. She would not have disturbed the atmosphere of the house. As she was, she was causing alarm and outrage. Doubtless the very, *very* correct Duke of Withingsby and his offspring thought her vulgar. She was not, but in their world spontaneity was synonymous with vulgarity. And she was his *wife,* the future duchess. The knowledge would gall them beyond bearing.

And he had understood, standing there at the window, one definite reason for his insomnia. She was in the next room, only their two dressing rooms separating them. She was his wife. The night before he had consummated their marriage and she had responded with flattering passion. He would not at all mind repeating the experience, he had realized in some surprise—he really did not think of her as desirable.

He had gone back to bed and lain awake for some time longer, remembering the smell of her hair. It was strange how a smell—or the absence of a smell—could keep one awake. And soap! He had never found even the most expensive of perfumes particularly alluring. He could remember breathing in the smell of her hair very deliberately as his body had pumped into hers, and enhancing his own sexual pleasure with the sense of smell.

There had been definite pleasure, not just physical release.

At dawn he was awake again and could not get back to sleep. The sky looked bright beyond the curtains at his windows. There was a chorus of birdsong in progress. It was an aspect of country living he had forgotten. He threw back the bedclothes impatiently. He would go for a ride, blow away some cobwebs, rid himself of the feeling of oppression the house brought to him.

But when he stepped through the front doors some minutes later, on his way to the stables, he stopped short at the top of the marble steps. On the terrace below him stood his little brown mouse, her head turned back over her shoulder to look up at him. She was up and dressed and outside at only a little past dawn?

"Good morning, my lady," he said, amazed that he could have lain awake last night wanting this drab creature—even her eyes were shadowed by the brim of her brown bonnet.

"I could not sleep," she said. "The birds and the sunshine

were in conspiracy against me. I have been standing here undecided whether to walk to the lake or up onto the hill."

"Try the hill," he suggested. "A picturesque walk has been laid out there and will lead you to several panoramic views over the park and estate and surrounding countryside."

"Then I will go that way," she said.

He tapped his riding crop against his boots, undecided himself for a few moments. "Perhaps," he said abruptly, "you will permit me to accompany you?"

"Of course." She half smiled at him.

He walked beside her, his arms at his sides. She clasped hers behind her. She walked with rather long strides, he noticed, as if perhaps she was used to the countryside. But she walked gracefully too. What had life with her father been like? How long ago had her mother died? Was she dreadfully lonely? Had the father been quite unable to make provision for her, even knowing that his estate had been entailed on a male relative? Had the relative been unwilling to provide for her? Did she miss her home and the countryside and the life of a lady? Had there been love in her home? Had there been love *outside* it—had there been a man she had had to leave behind in order to work as a governess? He was glad when she spoke and made him aware of the direction of his thoughts. He had no wish to feel curiosity about her or to know anything about her beyond what was necessary for his purposes.

"Your father really is ill," she said. "Have you discovered what is wrong with him and how serious it is?"

He had spoken briefly with Marianne in the drawing room last evening. "It is his heart," he said. "He has had a few mild attacks during the past few months. The physician has warned him that another could be fatal. He has advised almost constant bed rest."

"I believe," she said, "that your father finds it difficult to accept advice."

"That," he said, "would probably be the understatement of the decade."

"Perhaps," she said, "he would listen to you if you spoke

with him. Perhaps he invited you home with the hope that you would speak, that you would lift the burdens of his position from his shoulders."

He laughed, entirely without humor, and her head turned in his direction.

"Do you love him?" she asked quietly.

He laughed again. "That is a foolish question, my lady," he said. "I broke off all communication with him for eight years. During those years I deliberately made myself into everything he would abhor. I lived recklessly, I involved myself in business and investments, I made a fortune independently of the land, and I became—"

"A rake." She completed the sentence for him when he hesitated.

"I freed myself," he said, "from him and from all this. When I returned, I came as myself, on my own terms. No, I do not love him. There is nothing to love. And I am incapable of love even if there were. You were perfectly correct yesterday when you commented on my likeness to my father."

"Why *did* he ask you to come back here?" she asked.

"With the intention of asserting his dominance over me once more," he said. "With the intention of making me into the person he had planned for me to be since birth so that I might be worthy of carrying on the traditions he has so meticulously upheld."

"And perhaps," she said, "so that he might see his son again before he dies."

"Tell me, my lady," he said, his voice testy, "do you read romantical novels? Sentimental drivel? Do you picture to yourself an affecting deathbed scene in which father and son, drenched in tears, the rest of the family sobbing quietly in the background, are finally reconciled? Finally declare their love for each other? Promise to meet in heaven? *Pardon and Peace*—the book might be called that. Or *The Prodigal Son,* though that title has already been spoken for, I believe?"

"But not in a sentimental novel," she said. "In the Bible, my lord."

"Ah. *Touché,*" he said.

She smiled softly at him and said no more. He was agitated. Her silence had deprived him of the opportunity to work off his irritation on her. They had reached the rhododendron grove and the graveled path began to climb. Soon it would turn and they would reach the little Greek folly, from which there was an uninterrupted view down over the house and the lake beyond it.

Perhaps it was time she knew the full truth behind their marriage. "His grace summoned me home in order to marry me to the bride he chose for me seventeen years ago," he said and felt a sense of almost vicious satisfaction when her head jerked around so that she could gaze at him. "A dynastic marriage, you will understand, ma'am. The lady is the daughter of the Earl of Tillden, a nobleman of ancient lineage and vast properties, a man as high in the instep as Withingsby himself."

Her eyes widened—he could see them clearly now even beneath the brim of her bonnet. "They are the visitors expected here this afternoon," she said.

He smiled. "I was expected to come home and to conduct a very brief courtship of Lady Marie Lucas, to celebrate my betrothal to her at a ball planned for tomorrow evening, and to marry her before summer is out," he said. "I was expected then to do my duty by getting my heirs and my daughters on her annually for the next twenty years or so. The Duchesses of Withingsby are chosen young, you see, so that there are sufficient fertile years ahead of them. It is a pity, after all, to waste such impeccable lineage on a mere couple or so children, is it not?"

She had stopped walking. They stood facing each other. "And so you advertised for a governess and offered your chosen candidate marriage," she said. "What a splendid joke." She did not sound amused.

"I thought so," he said, his eyes narrowing. "I still think so. The guests will arrive this afternoon, my lady, unaware that they come in vain."

Her eyes searched his and he felt the familiar urge to take a step back. He did not do so. There was something unfamiliar in her eyes—anger? Contempt? He raised one eyebrow.

"I believe, my lord," she said, "you were less than honest with me. I did not know I was to be used as an instrument of cruelty. I believe I might have rejected your offer had I known."

"Cruelty?" he said.

"How old is she?" she asked.

"Seventeen," he said.

"And she is coming here today for her betrothal," she said. "But she will find you already married—to me. To a woman who is older than herself and by far her social inferior. Oh yes, my lord, you are to be congratulated. It was a diabolical plot and is working very nicely indeed."

Her quiet contempt goaded him. How dared she!

"It seems to me, my lady," he said, "that you were ready enough to take my money and enrich yourself for a lifetime. You asked precious few questions about what would be required of you as my wife. The only question that seemed to concern you was my ability to fulfill my financial commitment to you. You forced up my price. You insisted upon an extra clause that ensured a continuation of your annual allowance in the event that I predecease you. And are you now to preach morality to me?"

Her chin jerked upward and she continued to look at him, but she flushed deeply.

"I have never made any promise to Lady Marie Lucas," he said. "I have never had the smallest intention of marrying her."

"But it did not occur to you to write to your father explaining this," she said, "telling him firmly that it would not do and that he must inform the Earl of Tillden of your decision. Instead you married me and brought me here to embarrass and humiliate them all."

"Yes," he said curtly, thoroughly irritated with the way she was making him feel *guilty*. He had no reason for guilt. His life was his own. He had made that clear eight years ago, and if the message had not been taken, then he was making it crystal clear now.

She opened her mouth as if to speak, but she closed it again and turned to walk on. He fell into step beside her. "Perhaps," she said at last, "she has had a fortunate escape, poor girl. One would not wish an innocent child of seventeen on you."

"You, of course," he said, "are far better able to handle me."

"I do not have to," she said. "When may I leave? After today's humiliation is complete?"

"No," he said. "I will need you for a while yet." He must stay here for a while yet. There would be no real need to do so after today. He could return to his life in town and feel assured that his family would never trouble him again. But having come back, he knew he could not go again so soon or so easily. His father was ill, probably dying. William and Charles were his brothers. Marianne and Augusta were his sisters. Having seen them again, he felt the burden of the relationships again. And one day—perhaps soon—he would be head of the family. No, something had to be settled before he left Enfield—and before he could set his wife free. He was not sure what he meant by a settlement—not at all sure.

They walked onward in silence until she noticed the folly and stopped again.

"Walk around to the front," he told her. "There is a splendid view. There is even a seat inside the pavilion if you wish to sit for a while."

She did as he suggested though she did not sit. She stood for a long while in front of the folly, looking down at the house and beyond it. The scene was at its best, bathed in early-morning sunshine. If they had heard a chorus of birdsong from the house, there were whole vast choirs of them at work here.

"It will all be yours," she said after a lengthy silence. She seemed to be speaking more to herself than to him. "Yet you do not feel the need to pass it on to a son of your own."

He turned his head sharply to look at her. She stood with a very straight back and lifted chin. Such a proud, erect posture was characteristic of her, he realized. Dressed differently, she would look like a duchess. And dressed differently, she would look beautiful. It was a jolting thought. Not that dress created beauty, of course—it merely enhanced it. But he was already familiar enough with her face to admit—reluctantly—that it possessed far more beauty than he had thought at first. She had been wearing a careful disguise of nonentity when she came to her interview on Upper Grosvenor Street. Only the eyes had almost given her away and she had been clever enough to keep them hidden most of the time.

"You would do well to hope," he said, his eyes sweeping over her, "that I do not change my mind."

She looked back at him—and blushed.

"I will not change my mind," he said despite the alarming surge of desire her words and the look of her had aroused. "What happened between us two nights ago, though pleasant enough, was a mistake. It might yet have consequences. We will have to hope not. But you may rest assured that I will never again put you in danger of conceiving."

She did not look away from him despite the blush, which did not recede. She tipped her head to one side and prolonged the gaze. "I believe," she said at last, "that you must have loved your mother very deeply."

For a moment he was almost blinded by fury. He clasped his hands very tightly at his back, drew a few slow breaths, and was very thankful for the iron control he had always been able to impose upon his temper.

"My mother," he said very quietly, "is not a topic for discussion between us, my lady. Not now, not ever. I trust you understand?"

It was a question that could be answered in only one way and with only one word, but nevertheless she appeared to be considering the question.

"Yes," she said. "Yes, I believe that perhaps I do."

"Shall we climb higher?" He indicated the continuing path with one hand. "There are some different and equally magnificent views from higher up." He should have gone riding, he thought. He should have kept to himself.

"I think not this morning," she said. "Your father is to show me the portrait gallery after breakfast, though I shall try not to keep him there too long. I shall try to persuade him to rest afterward."

"You do that," he said, pursing his lips.

"And then I am to call upon Claudia at the dower house," she said.

He nodded curtly. Let her do that too. Let her make friends with Claudia and with Will and with the whole lot of them if she could. She might find it harder than she imagined. Let her make friends with Tillden and with Lady Marie this afternoon. He should be feeling more than ever triumphant this morning. But she had succeeded in making him feel thoroughly out of sorts.

"Allow me to escort you back to the house for breakfast, then," he said. Though he doubted anyone else would be up even yet.

"Perhaps," she said, "you would care to accompany me? To the dower house, I mean. You did not have much opportunity to talk with your brother yesterday. And I suppose you have not yet met your nephews."

"My heirs after William?" he said. "No, I have not. Unfortunately I have other plans for this morning."

She circled around the folly ahead of him and they set off down the slope. They walked in silence, not touching.

But he spoke again as they approached the house—reluctantly, not at all sure he wanted to do what he was about to say he would do.

"Perhaps my other business of this morning can be postponed," he said. "Perhaps I will accompany you to the dower house." That was where they lived, he had discovered last evening, William and Claudia and their two sons. "After all we have been married for only two days and are deep in love and will not wish to be separated unnecessarily." His tone sounded grudging even to his own ears.

"And William is your brother," she said, smiling at him.

Yes. And William was his brother. And there were some ghosts to lay to rest, as he had realized yesterday.

Perhaps the Duke of Withingsby lacked the ability to love, Charity thought, though she was by no means convinced of it—she did not really believe that it was possible to be human and incapable of love. But certainly he was capable of a pride bordering on love.

He had been at breakfast when she and her husband had returned from their early-morning walk and had entered the breakfast parlor together. He had stood and made her a courtly bow, at the same time sweeping her brown walking dress and her simple chignon—she had not summoned her maid when she had risen early—with haughty eyes.

Immediately after breakfast he had brought her to the portrait gallery, which stretched along the whole width of the house, and had proceeded to show her the family portraits and to describe their subjects and, in certain cases, the artists who had painted them. He displayed a pride and a degree of warmth she had not seen in him before.

"The people Van Dyck painted," she said, stepping closer to one canvas displaying a family grouping, "all look alike. It is not just the pointed beards and curled mustaches and the ringlets that were fashionable at the time. It has something to do with the shape of the face and the eyes—and the sloping shoulders. His paintings are easily distinguishable anywhere."

"And yet," he said, "I believe you will agree, ma'am, that the Duke of Withingsby depicted here bears a remarkable resemblance to your husband."

He did. She smiled at the likeness. "And to you too, Father," she said. "But then I think I have never seen a father and son who so resemble each other." And who so love and so hate each other, she thought. She did not believe she was wrong.

"That terrier," he said, pointing with his cane to a little dog held in the arms of a satin-clad, ringleted boy, "is reputed to have saved his young master's life when the boy fell into a stream and struck his head. The dog barked ceaselessly until help arrived."

"The boy who is holding him?" she asked, stepping closer still to examine both the child and the dog.

"The duke's heir," he said. "My ancestor."

"Oh." She turned and smiled full at him. "So you owe your life too to that little dog."

"And you owe your husband to it, ma'am," he said, raising haughty eyebrows.

"Yes." She felt herself blushing for some unknown reason. But she knew the reason even as she realized that her father-in-law was noting and misinterpreting her flushed cheeks. She blushed because she was deceiving him, because even though she really was married to his son, she was not truly his wife. She did not want to deceive. It would have been far better if her husband had come alone to Enfield Park to confront his grace, to assert his determination to live his life his way and to choose his own bride in his own time.

He moved along to the next painting and the next until they stood at last before the most recent. She gazed at it mutely, as did his grace.

He looked a good deal younger in the portrait. With his very dark hair and healthy coloring, he looked more than ever like his son. The Marquess of Staunton—proud, youthful, handsome—stood at his shoulder. The other young man must be Lord William, though he looked different in more than just age from the man she had met the day before. He looked—sunny and carefree. Marianne had not changed a great deal. The solemn child must be Charles. No one had smiled for the painter, though William seemed to smile from within.

"She must have been beautiful," Charity said. She referred to the duchess, who sat beside her husband, looking full at the beholder. Though the least striking in looks of any of them, she seemed, strangely enough, to be the focal point of the portrait, drawing the eyes more than the child did, or than the haughty duke himself, more than her proud eldest son. The painter, Charity thought, had been fascinated by her. There was a look of faded beauty about her, though it was probable that the artist had downplayed the faded part. But he had not erased the look of sadness in her eyes.

"She was the most celebrated beauty of her time," the duke said stiffly.

Was that why he had married her? For her beauty? Had he also loved her? She had borne him thirteen children. But that fact proved neither love nor lack of love. She was Anthony's mother, Charity thought. The woman about whom he still felt so deeply that he had turned to ice this morning when she had suggested to him that he must have loved her.

"She was the eldest daughter of a duke," his grace continued. "She was raised from the cradle to be my bride. She did her duty until the day of her death."

Giving birth to Augusta. Charity felt chilled. *Had* he loved her? More to the point, perhaps—had she loved him? She had done her duty . . .

I am the daughter of a gentleman, she wanted to say. *I was raised to be a lady. I too know my duty and will perform it to the day of my death.* But it was not really true, was it? She had married just two days ago and had made all sorts of promises that would never be kept. She had made a mockery of marriage—for the sake of money. Her husband had been very right about that this morning, when she had been outraged to discover just why he had married her in such haste and brought her here. She felt a pang of guilt and was surprised that she should feel so defensive, so eager to justify herself to this stern man who never smiled and who appeared to have inspired no love in his children.

"Father," she said, taking his arm, "you have been on your feet for long enough. I am truly grateful that you have brought me here and shared your family—Anthony's family—with me. But let me take you somewhere where you may rest. Tell me where."

"I suppose," his grace said, "Staunton did not even offer to clothe you in suitable fashion for your change in station."

He had silenced her for a moment. She was horribly aware

of her drab walking dress, from which she should have changed for breakfast and certainly for this visit to the gallery. But she had so little else into which to change. She did not release his arm. "We married in haste, Father," she said. "Anthony wanted to come here without delay. He was anxious about your health. There was no time for shopping. I do not mind. Clothes are unimportant."

"On the contrary," he said, "appearance is of the utmost importance—especially for a woman of your present rank. You are the Marchioness of Staunton, ma'am. And of course he married you in haste. I wonder if you know *why* he married you. Are you naive enough to imagine that you are beloved, ma'am, merely because of melting looks and kisses on the hand and the conjugal activity that doubtless occurred in your bedchamber last night? If you harbor dreams of love and happily-ever-afters, you will without a doubt be severely hurt."

She swallowed. "I believe, Father," she said as gently yet as firmly as she could, "it is for Anthony and me to work out the course of our marriage and the degree of love it will contain."

"Then you are a fool," he said. "There is no *we* in a marriage such as yours. Only Staunton. You are a wife, a possession, ma'am, of sufficiently lowly rank to enable him to demonstrate to me how much he scorns me and all I stand for. He will get children on you so that he may flaunt to me and to the world the inferiority of their mother's connections."

This, Charity thought, still clinging to his arm, almost dizzy with hurt, was how she was earning her money. For Phil. For Penny. For the children. She would not lose sight of the purpose of it all. How *glad* she was now that she had had the foresight to declare herself an only child.

"Do you *feel* scorned, Father?" she asked. "Are you hurt by Anthony's marriage to me?"

He did not answer her for several silent moments. "If I am, ma'am," he said at last, "Staunton will never have the satisfaction of knowing it. You will see that I am not without resources of my own. Most games are intended for more than one player. And most games are truly interesting only when the participants play with equal skill and enthusiasm. Yes, my dear ma'am, I am feeling fatigued. You may help me downstairs to my library and then ring for refreshments for me. You may read the morning papers to me while I rest my head and close my eyes. You are promised to Lady William for later this morning? I will spare you after an hour, then, but not before that. My son came home to me yesterday, bringing me also a daughter-in-law. It behooves me to become acquainted with her. It would not surprise me to discover that I will grow markedly fond of her."

His voice was chilly, his eyes more so. But it did not take a genius, Charity thought, to guess what game it was his grace had decided to play. She had known from the start, of course, that she was to be a pawn. She had just not known the extent of her involvement in that role. But it seemed that every hour brought her a fuller understanding of what she had got herself into.

She supposed she deserved every moment of discomfort that had already happened and that was still to come.

Chapter 9

He was not looking forward to the rest of the day. He was not enjoying himself at all. But then he had not expected enjoyment. Only a satisfying sense of triumph. There was still that, of course, but his wife had dampened it considerably during their early-morning walk by accusing him of cruelty. Cruelty to a young lady he could remember only as a plain and gawky child playing with Charles.

If he had come alone, he thought, he probably would have ended up marrying the girl. Even after the eight years of independence and the conviction that he was free of his father. If he had come home alone, and if Tillden had come with his daughter, he would have found it extremely difficult to avoid the betrothal everyone expected. It would have seemed more cruel then to have said no.

He was not a cruel man, merely one who wished to be left alone to live his own life. But when one was the heir to a dukedom, one did not belong to oneself, not unless one went to unusual lengths to assert one's independence.

He was walking down the driveway with his wife, on the way to the dower house to call upon Claudia. He had had no chance to assess his feelings about the visit. He did not want to assess them. He wondered if William would be at home. He wondered if he would be forced to meet the children.

"You went into the village earlier?" his wife asked.

"Yes," he said. "I went to talk to his grace's physician. The man has been brought from London merely to tend to his health, but according to his own complaints, he is abused and ignored at every turn."

"Your father is sick," she said. "He tires very easily."

"He is dying," he said. "It *is* his heart. It is very weak. It could fail him any day or it could keep him going for another five years. But he refuses to rest and to turn over his responsibilities to a steward's care, as he has been advised to do."

"Then we must persuade him to do so," she said.

They had stepped onto the Palladian bridge and had stopped by unspoken assent to view the river and the lawns and trees through the framework of the pillars.

We? He looked at her sharply and raised his eyebrows. "We must?" he asked.

She was alerted by his tone and turned her head to look back at him. "He called you home," she said. "He must have found it difficult to do so, to make the first move when he is such a proud man. He wants to settle his affairs, my lord. He wanted to see you married to the lady of his choice. He wanted to see you take over from him here so that he could rest and face his end in the knowledge that the future was assured."

"He wanted the feeling of power again," he said curtly.

"Call it what you will," she said. "But you came. Oh, it was on your own terms, as you keep assuring both me and yourself. But you need not have come at all. You had made your own life and your own fortune. You had left intending never to return. But you did return. You even took the extraordinary step of marrying a stranger before you did. You came."

She had the unerring ability to arouse intense irritation in him. It must be the governess in her, he decided. "What are you trying to say, ma'am?" he asked.

"That you never did break free," she said. "That you still love your father."

"Still, my lady?" he said. "*Still?* Your powers of observation are quite defective, I do assure you. Have you not seen that there is no love whatsoever in this family—or in your husband? You see what you wish to see with your woman's sensibilities."

"And he still loves you," she said.

He made an impatient gesture with one arm and signaled her to walk on. The picturesque view was lost on them this morning anyway.

"You can make his last days peaceful," she said, "and in the process you can make some peace with yourself, I believe. There is the embarrassment of this afternoon to be faced, and of course there will never be the eligible alliance your father had hoped for. But all may yet turn out well. You can stay here—there is nothing in London that makes it imperative that you return there, I daresay. And I believe your father may come to accept and even to like me a little."

There was so much to be commented upon in her short speech that for a few moments he was rendered quite speechless.

"His grace may come to *like* you a little?" he said at last. Did this woman suffer from delusions in addition to everything else?

"He showed me the gallery," she said, "and of course thoroughly exhausted himself in the process. He allowed me to help him downstairs to the library and to set a stool for his feet and a cushion for his head. He allowed me to read the papers to him while he closed his eyes. He would spare me at the end of an hour, he said, only because I had promised to call upon Claudia."

The devil! He was speechless again.

"I know you came here for a little revenge," she said, "but you can stay for a more noble reason, my lord. We can make him happy."

"We." He might have shouted with laughter at the notion of the Duke of Withingsby being happy if he had not also been pulsing with fury. "You, I believe, my lady, are forgetting one very important thing. His grace may live for five years, or conceivably even longer. *We* could make him happy for all that time? How, pray? By proving to him that it is a marriage made in heaven? By presenting him with a series of grandchildren?

Are you quite sure you wish to expand our business arrangement to include so much time and so much, ah, activity?"

He had silenced her at last. And of course, as he fully expected, she was blushing rosily when he turned his head to look at her. But an idea struck him suddenly. She had no family. Apparently she had no friends. She had no one. Perhaps . . . Exactly what was she up to?

"Perhaps," he said, his eyes narrowing on her, "it is what you hope for, ma'am. Perhaps you would like to emulate my mother with seventeen pregnancies during the next twenty years. I might be persuaded to comply with your wishes. My own part in such an undertaking would, after all, be slight— and not by any means unpleasurable."

"I would be a fool," she said quietly, "to want a relationship of any extended duration with you, my lord. You are not a pleasant man. The only reason I endure you at all is that I cling to the belief that somewhere behind your very carefully shuttered eyes is a person who perhaps would be likable if he would only allow himself to be seen. And there is nothing so very horrifying about large families. They happen. The agony of losses in childbirth or infancy is often offset by the great happiness of family closeness and love."

"Something you would know a great deal about," he said. He heard the sneer in his voice at the same moment as he saw the tears spring to her eyes. She had no one. Even her parents were dead, and she was only three-and-twenty.

"I beg your pardon," he said stiffly. "Please forgive me. The words were spoken heedlessly and hurt you."

When she looked at him, her eyes were still large with tears. How could he ever have convinced himself that she was plain? he thought. But irritation saved him from feeling more discomfort. Damn it all, but she was becoming a person to him. A person with feelings. He did not want to have to cope with someone else's feelings. When, for God's sake, was the last time he had apologized to anyone? Or felt so wretchedly in the wrong?

"You have a father," she said, "and brothers and sisters and nephews and nieces. They are all here with you now. Perhaps tomorrow or next month or next year they will all be gone. Perhaps you will be separated from them and it will not be easy or even possible to be with them again. Pride and other causes I know nothing of have kept you from them for eight years. You have been given another chance. Life does not offer unlimited chances."

Lord. Good Lord! Deuce and the devil take it! He had married a preacher. One with large, soulful blue eyes that he would fall into headlong and drown in if he did not watch himself.

An avalanche of leaves cascading downward over his hat and into his face broke his train of thought. He was aware of his wife waving them away from her own face and exclaiming in surprise. There was the sound of muffled giggles. Well. He and Will had done the same thing once with gravel and had been soundly spanked for it, the two of them, by the head gardener, who had soothed their pain when he was finished by promising not to report them to his grace.

His wife was looking upward, her head tipped right back. "It must be autumn," she said with loud and exaggerated surprise in her voice and in her expression, "and all the leaves are falling off the trees. I believe if you raise your cane, my lord, and swish it through the lower branches, you will dislodge more of them."

More smothered giggles.

"It is not autumn, my lady," he said, "but elves. If I poke them with my cane, they are like to fall out of the tree and break their heads. Perhaps I should give them a chance to come down on their own."

The giggles became open laughter and one small boy dropped onto the driveway in front of them. He was dirty and untidy and rosy with glee.

"We saw you coming, Aunt Charity," he said, "and lay in ambush."

"And we walked into the trap quite unsuspecting," she said. She looked up again. "Are you stuck, Harry?"

Harry was. It seemed that he was marvelously intrepid about climbing trees but found it quite impossible to descend again—or so his brother claimed. The marquess reached up and lifted him down. He was quite as dirty as the other child. He was also blond and green-eyed and scarcely past babyhood. He was just as his own son might have looked, the marquess thought, if he had married. . . .

"You may make your bows to your Uncle Anthony," his wife was saying. "These two elves are Anthony and Harry, my lord."

"I was named for you, sir," the elder boy said. "Papa told me so."

Ah. He had not known that. So these were the two children they had produced, Will and Claudia.

"I am going to tell Mama that you are coming," Anthony said, taking to his heels.

"And I am going to tell Papa. You are not to tell first, Tony." Harry went tearing along behind. He would not catch up, of course. Younger brothers never did. Until they grew up and could use stealth and deceit.

"We must be close to the dower house." His wife smiled at him.

"We are." And Will must be at home. "Take my arm. We are supposed to be in love, after all."

"You must smile, then," she reminded him.

"I shall smile," he promised grimly.

He not only smiled. He slid an arm about her waist and drew her closer to his side as they approached the house through neatly laid-out parterre gardens. But his arm, she could feel, was not relaxed. Neither were the smiles on the faces of Claudia and William, who had come out of the house to meet them. The little boys came dashing out ahead of them.

But at least they were smiling. They were all smiling.

"Charity," Claudia said, "I am so glad you came. And you brought Anthony. How delightful."

"Anthony?" William inclined his head. "My la—" He looked acutely embarrassed. "Charity. Welcome to our home."

There was something, Charity thought. Something very powerful. It was not just that he had offended them by going off eight years ago. They had married one month before he left. One month before Augusta's birth, before the duchess's death. Claudia was very beautiful. William and his elder brother were very close in age. Had her husband loved Claudia too?

"Thank you," she said. "It is very splendid. In fact yesterday when we were arriving, I mistook it for Enfield Park itself and was marvelously impressed."

They all joined in her laughter—all of them. She had never heard her husband laugh before. He was looking down at her—he should be on the stage, she thought—with warm tenderness in his eyes.

"You neglected to tell me that yesterday, my love," he said.

"You would have laughed at me," she said, "and I cannot abide being laughed at. Besides, I could not speak at all. I had my teeth clamped together so that they would not chatter. You would not believe how nervous I was."

"With me by your side?"

Her stomach performed a strange flip-flop. On the stage he would draw a dozen curtain calls for each performance.

"You were just as nervous," she said. "Confess, Anthony." She turned her face from him and smiled sunnily at the other two adults. "But the ordeal of yesterday is over and we may relax in congenial company—until this afternoon, that is. Your Anthony and Harry mounted a very successful ambush on us out on the driveway. We were showered with leaves. We had no chance at all to take cover."

"I will not ask if they were up in a tree," William said dryly. "There is a strict rule in this family that no tree is to be climbed unless an adult is within sight."

"There was an adult within sight," the marquess said. "Two, in fact. So no rule was broken."

"Uncle Anthony had to lift Harry down," Anthony said.

"Hence the rule," his father added. "Harry would find a whole day spent in the branches of a tree somewhat tedious, I do not doubt."

And so, Charity thought, they had established an atmosphere of near-relaxation through some pleasant and meaningless chitchat. But preliminaries had clearly come to an end.

"Charity." Claudia stepped forward to take her arm. "Do come inside. I plan to tempt you. But perhaps we should consult Anthony first. We never go to town, a fact about which I make no complaint at all. But I do like fashionable clothes and it pleases William to see me well dressed—or so he declares when I twist his arm sufficiently. And so twice a year he brings a modiste from town down here to stay for a week or so with her two seamstresses. They are here now and I am trying my very best not to cost William a fortune. It has occurred to me that since the two of you married in such a hurry that you had no time to shop for bride clothes, you might wish to make use of her services too."

"Oh." Charity flushed and was afraid to turn her head in her husband's direction. The poverty of her wardrobe was very deliberate on his part. But was there any more to be proved by it now?

"I am to be saved after all, then," he said, "from the faux pas of having been so besotted and so much in a hurry to wed that I forgot I was bringing my wife directly from the schoolroom to Enfield? It is no excuse, is it, to protest that to me Charity would look beautiful dressed in a sack. Clearly his grace would disagree. Will you have clothes made, my love? For all possible occasions? However many you wish?"

Poor Anthony. He had been given very little choice. Charity could not resist looking at him and smiling impishly. "You may be sorry for offering me carte blanche," she said.

"Never." He grinned back at her and tipped his head toward hers. For one alarming moment she thought he was going to kiss her. "You must have something very special for tomorrow evening's ball."

The ball that was to have celebrated his betrothal to the Earl of Tillden's daughter? Would it still take place? She supposed it must. All the guests would have been invited. And she was to attend it? A full-scale ball? As the Marchioness of Staunton? She was not sure if the weakness in her knees was caused more by terror or excitement.

"Oh, splendid," Claudia said. "Come along, then. We will leave William and Anthony to become reacquainted—and to look after the boys since their nurse has been given the morning off. Have you ever seen such ragamuffins, Charity? But in *this* house, you see, I insist that children are allowed to be children. And William supports me."

The two men, Charity saw, had been left standing face-to-face in the midst of the parterre gardens, looking distinctly uncomfortable. They were brothers, one year apart in age. What had happened between them? Was it Claudia?

But her mind did not dwell upon them. She would have had to be made of stone, she thought, as Claudia took her into the house, not to be excited at the thought of new clothes. And not just one new dress, but dresses for all occasions. As many as she wanted. It was a dizzying prospect. And a ball gown!

They stood quietly facing each other while their wives walked away toward the house, arm in arm. The two little boys were running about the paths dividing the parterres, their arms outstretched. They were sailing ships, blown along by the wind.

The Marquess of Staunton met his brother's eyes at last. It was an acutely uncomfortable moment, but he would not be the first to look away—or to speak.

"She seems very—amiable," his brother said at last.

"Yes," the marquess said. "She is."

"I have feared that Lady Marie would not suit you," Lord William said. "I am glad you shocked us all to the roots and married for love after all, Tony."

"Are you?" The marquess looked coldly into his brother's eyes. "You have changed your opinions, then."

"I had hoped that in eight years all that business would be behind us," Lord William said with a sigh. "It is not, is it?"

"You argued most eloquently once upon a time against my making a love match," the marquess said, "and against my marrying beneath myself in station."

"An elopement would have been disastrous," his brother said. "And it would have been the only possible way. His grace would never have forgiven you."

The marquess smiled—not pleasantly. "Well," he said, "you showed a brother's care, Will. You saved me from myself and from our father's wrath. You married my bride yourself."

"She was not your bride," Lord William said sharply.

"And when I challenged you to meet me," the marquess said, "you went running to his grace for protection. I am glad you approve of my marrying for love, Will. Your good opinion means a great deal to me."

"Your eyes were clouded, Tony," his brother said. "You were beside yourself with worry over Mother—"

"Leave our mother out of this," the marquess said curtly.

"Mother was at the center of everything," Lord William said.

"Leave her out of it."

Lord William looked away and watched his sons blow out of control in the midst of an Atlantic storm and sail through a forbidden flower bed. He did not bellow at them, as he would normally have done.

"Come and see the stables," he said. "I have some mounts I am rather proud of." He called to the boys, who went racing off ahead of them, sailing ships and Atlantic storms forgotten. "I was less than thrilled when I knew you were coming home, I must confess, Tony. Time had only increased the awkwardness. But we had to meet again sooner or later—his grace cannot survive another attack as severe as the last, I fear. Can we not put the past behind us? There are parts of it I am not proud of, but I would not have the outcome changed. I am comfortable with Claudia—more than comfortable. You do not still have—feelings for her, do you?"

"I love my wife," the marquess said quietly.

"Yes, of course," his brother said. "Everything has turned out rather well, then, has it not?"

"Admirably," the marquess said. "The stables here did not used to be in such good repair."

"No." Lord William paused in the doorway and looked to see that no groom was within earshot. "Friends, Tony? There is no one whose good opinion I crave more than yours."

"Perhaps," his brother said, "you should have thought of that, Will, before taking his grace's part over my chosen bride merely so that you might steal her from under my nose."

"Damn it all to hell!" Lord William cried, his temper snapping. "Is Claudia a mere object? A possession to be wrangled over? She had to consent, did she not? She had to say yes. She had to say *I do* during the marriage service. She said it. No one had a pistol pointed at her head. She married me. Did it ever occur to you that she loved me? I always took second place to you, Tony. You were so damned better this and better that at everything from looks to brains to sports, and of course you were the heir. I never resented any of it. You were my elder brother, my hero. But I do not suppose it even occurred to you that in one significant matter I outdid you. She loved *me*."

The Marquess of Staunton stood very still, his nostrils flared, his hands balled at his sides, reining in his temper. "This is all pointless stuff now, Will," he said. "You and Claudia share an eight-year marriage and two sons. I have recently married the woman of my choice. We will forget the past and be brothers again if it is what you wish. I wish it too." Damn his prim wife and her harping about family affection and second chances. Here he was *forgiving* the brother who had betrayed him?

Their eyes met once more—hostile, wary, unhappy.

Lord William was the first to hold out a hand. The marquess looked at it and then placed his own in it. They clasped hands.

"Brothers," Lord William said, but before the moment could become awkward again his two sons came dashing out from some inner stalls and wanted to show their uncle their ponies.

And then they wanted their uncle to see them ride their ponies. They mounted up and rode about a fenced paddock, displaying the fact that they had been given some careful and superior training despite their youth.

Will loved his boys, the marquess thought, watching his brother's face as much as he watched the two children. There were pride and amusement and affection there—as well as a thunderous frown and a loud bellow of stern command when the older boy began to show off and threw his pony into confusion. Will had not followed in their father's footsteps. But then Will had always been able to withstand the gloom of Enfield better than the rest of them. He had been superior in that way too.

Had he really felt so very inferior?

Had he really won Claudia's love?

She had not married him in bitter resignation after it became obvious that she was not going to be allowed to have the man of her choice—himself—because she was a mere baronet's daughter?

Had she married for love?

It was a thought so new to him that he could not even begin to accept the possibility—the humbling possibility—that it might be true.

Chapter 10

"You are probably furious with me," she said, "and that is why you are striding along looking shuttered and morose."

There were too many people at Enfield Park looking that way, she had decided. She was not going to be drawn into becoming one of them. And she was no longer going to be a meek observer—though from the start she had not been quite that. She had spent a splendid hour and a half with Claudia and Madame Collette—whose elaborate French accent acquired suspicious cockney overtones from time to time. They had pored over patterns and rummaged through fabrics. They had laughed and talked and measured and planned. The modiste, it appeared, was all but finished with Claudia's new clothes and had been planning—reluctantly, she declared—to return to London within a few days. But now she had agreed with great enthusiasm to go back to work, to produce a complete and fashionable wardrobe for her ladyship in very little more time than it took to snap her fingers—thus. The ballgown, of course, would take priority over all else.

Claudia had told all about the session when they had finally rejoined the men, and had forced from the marquess the declaration that he had never been so happy about anything in his life. He had smiled that dazzling smile again—directly into Charity's eyes.

But now he was striding along the driveway, staring straight ahead of him, looking too morose even to be satanic.

"*What?*" He stopped walking and swung around to face

her, causing her to jump in some alarm. "Shuttered and morose, ma'am? Am I to grin inanely at the treetops? Am I to wax poetic about the beauty of the morning and the wonder of life? And why would I be furious with you?"

"You like me in brown," she said. "You approve of my sprigged muslin and my gray silk. You are not sorry for the fact that they are the full extent of my smart wardrobe. Now you are about to spend a fortune clothing me in lavish style for what remains of our few weeks together. You were trapped into it. But so was I, you must confess."

"I like you in brown!" he said, his eyes sweeping her from head to toe. "They are loathsome garments, my lady. The sooner they find their proper place at the bottom of a dustbin, the happier I shall be."

"Oh," she said. "You do not mind too much, then, that I will be replacing them soon—that *you* will be replacing them?"

"It was part of our agreement, was it not," he said, turning abruptly and walking on, "that I keep you in a style appropriate to your rank?"

Except that at the time he had not told her exactly what that rank was to be. And except that the agreement had referred to what she would be given *after* their separation. But she would not argue the point. She had always had sufficient vanity to enjoy acquiring new clothes. But very rarely had she had more than one new garment at a time. Claudia had insisted on a whole array of new clothes. Even the restricted number Charity had finally agreed to was dizzying.

So it was not her new clothes that had set her husband to striding homeward, looking as if he had swallowed sour grapes. He had spent that hour and a half with William and the children. With his own brother and nephews.

She touched his arm and looked into his face as she walked beside him. "Did you *talk* to William?" she asked. "Did you settle your quarrel?"

He stopped walking again, but he continued to look ahead, his lips pursed. "Tell me," he said, "have you always been a pestilential female?"

Philip would say so, though not perhaps in those exact words. Penny would not—Penny was always loyal and had often expressed admiration for her elder sister's unwillingness to sit back and allow life merely to happen around her. The children might agree, especially when she forced them into a room together after they had quarreled instead of separating them as any sane adult would do, and would not allow them out again until they had settled their differences.

"Yes, I have," she said. "What was the quarrel about?"

His nostrils flared.

"It was about Claudia, was it not?" she said and then wished she had not. Some things were best not known for certain. It was true that she was not his wife in any normal sense and would not be spending more than a few weeks of her life with him. But even so she *was* his wife and she was still in the process of living through these few weeks.

He took her upper arm in a firm grasp suddenly and surprised her by marching her off the driveway and among the trees of the woods beyond it. It was dark and secluded and seemed very remote from civilization. He was angry. But she was not afraid.

"In the days of my foolish youth," he said, "when I believed in love and loyalty and fidelity and happily ever afters and all those other youthful fantasies, I set my sights upon Claudia. We practically grew up together—she is the daughter of a baronet who lives a mere six miles from here. I confided in my dearest friend, my brother, who was sympathetic yet sensible at the same time. He was sensible in the sense that he advised against the elopement I planned after his grace refused to countenance the match—Claudia was merely the daughter of a baronet and in no way worthy of the Marquess of Staunton, heir to Withingsby. Besides, a match had already been arranged for me. My brother advised patience. My mother advised boldness—love, she told me, was the only sound reason for marriage. But she was increasing again and very ill and I was loath to elope and leave her. And so my brother released me from all my dilemmas. He married Claudia himself—with his grace's blessing."

They had slowed their pace. He had released his hold on her upper arm. She wondered if he realized that he was holding her hand very tightly, his fingers laced with hers.

"He was afraid to tell you of his own feelings for her," she said. "And so he said nothing, even when it became imperative that something be said. People do that all the time. People can be such cowards especially with those closest to them. He must have tortured himself over it for the last eight years."

"He need not have done so," he said. "I had a fortunate escape. I grew up. I learned the foolishness of all emotions. I learned how self-deluded we are when we believe in love."

"What do you believe in, then?" she asked him. "Everyone must believe in something."

"I believe in myself," he said, looking at her with bleak eyes, "and in the control I have over my own life and my own destiny."

"Why did Claudia marry William," she asked, "if she loved you? If I loved you, I could not possibly marry anyone else, least of all your own brother."

"You *are* married to me," he said, and there was a thread of humor in his voice for a moment. "But you would be well advised never to love me, Charity."

Yes, she thought, she would. It would be a painful thing to love Anthony Earheart, Marquess of Staunton, her husband. But he had not answered her question.

"Did Claudia love you?" she asked.

"I believed so," he said. "She was all smiles with me and charm and friendly warmth—and beauty. Will says that she loved *him,* that theirs was a love match. It is the only explanation that would make sense of that marriage, perhaps. I used to torture myself wondering what power they had exercised over her, the two of them—Will and his grace."

"She never *told* you that she loved you?" Charity asked. "She never told you that she wished to marry you, that she would elope with you?"

"You have to understand this family," he said. "Nothing is done here with any spontaneity. I knew the difficulty with Claudia's lineage. Lady Marie Lucas was already nine years old. She had come here several times with her parents. I could not offer for Claudia before I knew quite certainly what I was able to offer and when I would be free to offer it. I was, after all, only twenty."

"I begin to understand," she said, "why eventually you decided to break free altogether. I can even understand why you gave up everything except your trust in yourself."

She could understand it, but she could not condone it. She wondered if he realized that life had lain dormant in him for eight years and was just beginning to erupt again. She wondered if he would allow it to erupt. But the choice might no longer be his. He had spoken with William earlier—William had told him that Claudia had loved *him*. Perhaps something had already begun, something that could not be stopped.

The trees thinned before them suddenly and she could see that the lake was directly ahead of them—and the lawns and the house beyond. But whereas all was open and cultivated on the opposite bank, here the trees grew almost to the water's edge, and beyond them were tall reeds. There was a wildness and an unspoiled beauty here—and civilization beyond.

They stopped walking. He was still holding her hand, though less tightly, less painfully.

"Without these woods and this lake," he said, his eyes squinting across the sun-speckled water, "I do not know how I would have made my boyhood supportable."

She said nothing to break his train of thought. He looked as if he had become unaware of her and was immersed in memory.

"Will and I played here endlessly," he said. "These woods were tropical jungles and underground caves and Sherwood Forest. Or they were a mere solitary retreat from reality. I taught Charles to climb trees here. I taught him to swim, to ride." He drew a deep breath and let it out slowly.

Yes, she knew all the power of childhood imagination,

childhood companionship. She knew all the joy and sense of worth that nurturing younger brothers and sisters brought.

"Who taught you to be such a good listener?" he asked suddenly. His voice, which had become almost warm with memory, was brisker again. And his hand, she noticed, slid unobtrusively from hers—or in a manner that he must have hoped was unobtrusive. "Was it lonely growing up without brothers and sisters?"

She regretted her lie. She hated not speaking the truth. "I had childhood playmates," she said. "I had a happy childhood."

"Ah." He turned his head to look at her. "But it did not last. Life deals cruel blows quite indiscriminately. Life is nothing but a cruel joke."

"Life is a precious possession," she said. "It is what one makes of it."

"And you have been given the chance of making something quite bearable of yours after all," he said. "You are to be commended for seizing the chance without hesitation."

The mocking tone was back in his voice, the sneer in his face.

"And you have been given the chance," she said sharply, "of putting right what was wrong with your life when you ran from it eight years ago."

"Ah," he said. "You have an incurably impertinent tongue, my lady. But you mistake the matter. I ran away from suffocation. I ran to life."

"Are we late for luncheon?" she asked.

"The devil!" he said and surprised her by grinning until his eyes danced. "I would wager we are. It will be quite like old times except that his grace will probably not refuse to allow us to eat at all this time and probably will not have me wait in the library until he has finished eating and then invite me to bend over the desk to take my punishment. Hunger was never quite punishment enough, you see."

"Sternness, even excessive sternness, does not necessarily denote lack of love," she said.

He laughed and offered his arm. "You are a prim little moralist, ma'am," he said, "and talk with seeming wisdom on matters quite beyond your experience or comprehension. But then I married you for your primness, did I not? And for the hideous garments. You lied about one thing, though."

She raised her eyes to his as he hurried her through the trees in the direction of the bridge.

"You pretended to be a plain little mouse," he said. "You hid yourself very nicely indeed and should be thoroughly ashamed of yourself. I did not even suspect at the time that you are beautiful."

It was ridiculous—despicable—that such a grudging, back-handed compliment should please her so thoroughly that her knees felt weak. He thought her beautiful? Really? Even before he had seen her in her new clothes? Not that it made any difference to anything, of course. He was still a man from whom it would be an enormous relief to free herself in a few weeks' time. She was still merely the shield he had brought home with him so that he might prevent his family from penetrating his defenses. But he thought her beautiful?

"That has silenced you at least," he said.

He sounded, she thought, almost in a good humor.

The Duke of Withingsby had decided against greeting his old friend the Earl of Tillden with all of the pomp he had shown his son the day before. The family was excused from gathering in the hall and were informed instead that they would be prompt in their attendance in the drawing room for tea. He sent a message to that effect to the dower house.

"Staunton and I will meet Tillden and his countess and daughter in the hall," he said.

They were sitting at the luncheon table. The marquess had already been made to feel his grace's silent displeasure for arriving ten minutes late for the meal. But he would not fall mutely into old habits.

"My wife will accompany us," he said.

"Lady Staunton," his grace said, "will await us in the library."

And it was after all pointless to argue further, his son decided. He did not do so.

And so he stood alone with his father a few hours later after word had been brought that the earl's carriage had been seen to cross the bridge. He felt nervous and embarrassed and despised himself heartily. None of this was his concern. He had never expressed an interest in Lady Marie Lucas. He had not been consulted on the decision to invite her, with her parents, to Enfield Park on the very day following his own expected arrival. His grace had taken a great deal for granted after eight silent years. The marquess had nothing for which to blame himself.

And yet he was nervous and embarrassed—and very relieved that his wife was waiting in the library, dressed in her sprigged muslin again and looking pale and calm.

The Earl of Tillden had not changed, the marquess thought as the man stepped into the great hall ahead of his womenfolk—as he himself had done just the day before, of course. Large in both height and girth, bald head gleaming, the earl might have looked genial if it had not been for the permanent frown line of dissatisfaction between his brows and if his mouth and nose had not been so unfortunately positioned in relation to each other that he always looked as if he were sniffing in disdain.

The countess appeared behind him, small and wraithlike, a perpetual smile on her face—and yet it appeared to be a smile of apology rather than of happiness. Sweet and spiritless she had always seemed—and still seemed.

Beside her was—Lady Marie Lucas. At least the marquess assumed it must be she. She was no longer, of course, the thin and gawky child he remembered. She was small, slender, and dainty, with a face of exquisite sweetness beneath hair that had used to be an almost carroty red but was now a vibrant auburn. She was a beauty by anyone's definition. And in the few moments before the duke began the ceremony of welcoming his guests, her hazel eyes found him and widened and she blushed.

She was an innocent child despite her seventeen years and her fashionable clothes and her great beauty, the marquess thought with considerable annoyance and discomfort.

"Tillden," his grace said, inclining his head graciously. "Your coachman has made good time. Ma'am, you are welcome to Enfield Park. I trust you had a pleasant journey. Lady Marie, you are welcome too."

There was a spirited exchange of greetings and bows and curtsies.

"Ah, Staunton," the earl said at last. "You arrived before us, then? Good to see you, my boy."

The Marquess of Staunton bowed. "Sir," he murmured.

"You will be surprised and doubtless gratified to see that our little Marie has grown up while you have been away," the earl said heartily, rubbing his hands together.

"And has grown into a great beauty," his grace said.

His son bowed again.

"You will do me the honor of stepping into the library before my housekeeper shows you to your rooms," his grace said.

"And how are you, Withingsby?" the earl asked as his grace offered his arm to Lady Tillden, and the marquess, for very courtesy's sake, offered his to Lady Marie. She smiled prettily and laid a delicate little hand on his sleeve. "You are looking remarkably well."

In truth his father looked gray even to the lips, his son thought.

Charity was standing quietly by the library window. The marquess, disengaging his arm from Lady Marie's, was about to cross the room to her, but his father forestalled him by reaching out a hand toward her.

"Come here, my dear," he said.

How it must gall his father to have to call her that, the marquess thought, staying where he was beside Lady Marie as

Charity crossed the room and set her hand in the duke's. She smiled at him and—*he smiled back.*

"I would present you to my guests, my dear," he said. "Tillden? Ma'am? Lady Marie? Allow me to present the Marchioness of Staunton. She and Staunton were married in London two days ago."

The marquess was aware of Lady Marie beside him drawing a sharp breath.

"I am so very pleased to make your acquaintance," Charity said, smiling warmly at all three of their guests in turn. "Will you not be seated? And you too, Father? You are overtaxing your strength."

She was behaving as if she had been born a duchess. Except that most duchesses of the marquess's acquaintance did not exude warm charm.

"Married? Two days ago?" The earl's brows almost met across his frown line.

"I am pleased to meet you, I am sure, Lady Staunton," Lady Tillden said kindly, sinking into the chair closest to her. "And I wish you every happiness. As I do you, my lord." She smiled nervously at the marquess.

"Married?" The earl, unlike his wife, was not prepared to turn the moment with empty courtesies. "Is this true, sir?"

"Indeed." The marquess smiled. "His grace informed me of his poor health and naturally it was my wish to hurry home without delay. But I found myself quite unwilling to leave behind my betrothed for an indeterminate length of time. We married by special license."

"Your mama must have been distressed not to have a proper wedding to arrange, Lady Staunton," the countess said. "But under the circumstances . . ."

"My parents are both deceased, ma'am," Charity said. "I had no one's inclination to consult but my own."

"And no guardian to become stuffy about the matter," the marquess said. "Lady Staunton was working as a governess when I met her, ma'am."

"Oh, dear me," her ladyship said faintly, one hand straying to her throat.

"I want a full explanation for this, Withingsby," the Earl of Tillden said. "And I want it *now*."

"My dear." His grace patted Charity's hand. "Mrs. Aylward will be waiting in the hall. Would you be so good as to escort Lady Tillden and Lady Marie to her? You need not return here. Tea will be served in the drawing room, ladies, precisely at four."

The marquess opened the door for them and bowed as they left. His wife smiled at him as she passed. He closed the door and stood facing it for a few moments. Then he turned. This after all, was why he had come. To shake their influence and the illusion of power they held over him once and for all. To prove to them that the Marquess of Staunton was no one's puppet.

"I believe I must demand satisfaction for this," the Earl of Tillden said, his voice tight with bruised dignity.

Good Lord! Was he talking about a duel?

"Sit down, Tillden," his grace said, doing so himself. He looked quite ill, the marquess noticed—and the twinge of alarm he felt took him by surprise. "My son has reminded me since his arrival that he has never been a party to any contract concerning Lady Marie Lucas, either written or verbal. And I must concede that he has a point."

"He does not have to be a party to it, by thunder," the earl said, his voice raised far above the level of courteous discourse. "It was an agreement made between his father and her father. When were the parties to such a match ever consulted for their consent? Do you have no control over your offspring, Withingsby, that your eldest son—your *heir*—has had the impudence to ignore an agreement entered into seventeen years ago by his father in order to marry a woman from the gutter?"

The marquess stood close to the door, his hands at his back. He spoke very quietly. He would be drawn into no shouting match. "You will choose your words with care, sir," he said, "when you speak of my wife."

"What?" The earl's ample fist banged on his grace's desk with force enough to send a fountain of ink spurting upward from the inkwell. "You insolent puppy. Do you dare open your mouth without your father's permission? And to threaten me?"

"I am eight-and-twenty years old, sir," the marquess said. "I have been living independently of my father since I was twenty. I live my life according to my own principles. I have married the lady of my choice, as is my right. I am sorry indeed for any embarrassment my marriage has caused you and Lady Tillden, and more sorry than I can say for any distress I have caused Lady Marie. But I will acknowledge no misbehavior in neglecting to honor a long-standing agreement concerning me in which I had no voice."

"I will demand recompense for this," the earl said, pointing a finger first at the marquess and then at the silent duke. "I will blacken both your names to such a degree that you will be unable to show your faces in society for the rest of your lives." He stood up. "I will have my carriage brought around again and my wife and daughter summoned. I will not remain one hour beneath this roof, where honor is not worth a farthing."

"Sit down, Tillden," his grace said, his voice wearily haughty. "Unless you wish to make yourself a laughingstock and your daughter unmarriageable. No one outside my family knows why you have come here, though doubtless there is speculation. There was never any written contract. There was never a formal betrothal. You are here as my friend, as you have been a number of times over the years. You are here out of concern for my health. No one has ever said that the ball arranged here for tomorrow evening was to be a betrothal ball. It has been arranged to celebrate Staunton's return home and the unexpected joy of his bringing a bride with him. It has been arranged to celebrate my family's being together again for the first time since her grace's funeral. And to celebrate the visit of my oldest friend, the Earl of Tillden. This thing can be carried off with dignity."

The earl had sat again and was clearly considering the wisdom of rethinking his initial impulse.

"I am most insulted, Withingsby," he said. "I hope to hear from you that Staunton and his—his *wife* are to be severely disciplined."

"Staunton has heard my displeasure," his grace said. "Lady Staunton is quite blameless. And in the day since I have made her acquaintance I have grown decidedly fond of her."

The marquess raised his eyebrows.

"Even though she is an upstart nobody?" the earl asked. "Even though she was nothing more than a governess on the lookout for—"

But even as the marquess took a step forward, his father spoke coolly and courteously—and quite firmly.

"I have grown decidedly fond of my daughter-in-law, the Marchioness of Staunton," he said.

The Earl of Tillden, the marquess could see, would stay at Enfield, at least until after tomorrow evening's ball. He had realized that the scandal he would dearly love to visit upon the two of them would also involve his own family in ridicule and humiliation.

"You will ring for the butler, Staunton," his father said. "He will show you to your rooms, Tillden. I trust you will find everything for your comfort there. You will escort the ladies to tea at four?"

Chapter 11

She sat at her dressing-table mirror, brushing her hair long after she had dismissed her new maid for the night. There was little point in going to bed. She would never sleep. Her brain teemed with activity.

It had seemed so easy at first. In return for a lifetime of security for herself and her family, all she had to do was marry a man and spend a few weeks with him, meeting his family. She had very deliberately asked no questions. She had not needed to know.

It had still seemed relatively easy even after she had discovered exactly who her new husband was and who his family was. It had been somewhat nerve-racking, of course, to come to Enfield Park and to be presented to the Duke of Withingsby and everyone else. A great deal more had been expected of her than she had at first anticipated. But even so, it had been fairly easy.

If she had just done as she had been told. If she had just been content to be quiet and demure, to be his shadow. To be a quiet mouse. If she had only not looked about her and seen people—just human people caught up in the drama of life and really not doing very well at it at all. If she had just not come to care.

She sighed and set her brush down on the dressing table. She was not even going to try to sleep yet. She would go into the sitting room and write some letters—one to Philip, one to Penny and the children. It was time she wrote to them. She had been avoiding doing so. What, after all, could she write but lies? Not that there was any point in hiding the truth any longer, she supposed, since it was too late for any of them to stop what she had done. But she could not tell them in a letter. It must be face-to-face.

She seemed to have done nothing but lie for—for how long was it? Yesterday they had arrived at Enfield. The day before that they had married. Was it really less than three days altogether? Four days ago she had not even met the Marquess of Staunton. She had merely been feeling jittery at the prospect of being interviewed by Mr. Earheart.

She took a candle with her into the private sitting room of their apartments and lit two more when she got there. She found paper and pen and ink in the small escritoire and sat down to write.

"Dear Phil . . ."

The Earl of Tillden had acted all evening as if she did not exist, even though his grace had seated him to her right during dinner. The countess had nodded sweetly and nervously in her direction whenever their eyes had met but had avoided coming close enough to make conversation necessary. Lady Marie Lucas had been taken firmly under Marianne's wing. She was a beautiful, elegant young lady, who fit into the drawing room at Enfield and blended in with the family there as if she had been born to it all—as indeed she had.

The marquess had not wished to marry her. Hence his marriage to *her*. But he had not seen Lady Marie for eight years or longer. She would have been a child. It must have been a shock to him to see her today. She wondered if he regretted . . . But she dipped the pen firmly into the inkwell. If he did, it was his problem.

"Dear Phil, You must think I am lost. Two whole days and I am only now writing to you. Everything has been very busy and very new. I am only just settling. There are four children, not three, but the youngest is not ready for my services yet. He is a plump, adorable baby, who crawls into everything he is not supposed to crawl into, who puts everything he finds into his mouth, and who considers everything that happens—especially the exasperation of his nurse—worthy of a chuckle."

It was hard to believe that such a happy child could have come from Marianne and Richard. He had her thinking wistfully of motherhood. But no matter. She would be the world's most attentive and indulgent aunt to Phil and Agnes's children and to Penny's.

"The oldest child, Augusta, is eight years old," she wrote. "She is a grave little girl who has never learned to be a child, and she is hostile to me and to"—Charity brushed the feather of the quill pen across her chin for a moment—"Mr. Earheart. But I did coax first a smile and then a giggle from her after tea today when I told her about the lodgekeeper's two children ambushing me this morning by hiding in the branches of a tree and showering me with leaves as I passed beneath. I believe she must be fond of those children. I will have to see if I can arrange for them to play together occasionally. I do not believe she has been allowed a great deal of time simply for play."

She had told Augusta about some of her own childhood exploits, including the time she had climbed to the topmost branches of a tree close to the house to rescue a kitten who was mewing most piteously while Penny wept and Phil sniveled on the ground below. The kitten had tired of its perch and removed itself to the ground long before Charity had climbed laboriously to the top to find it gone. And then the inevitable had happened—just as it had this morning to a lesser degree with Harry. It had taken a gardener, their father, and a passing peddler—not to mention oceans of tears and much anxious and conflicting advice from the other two children and their mother—to get her down again. Charity had milked the story for all it was worth when telling it to Augusta.

Charity stopped writing. She frowned and brushed the feather absently across her chin again. She had invented ages and genders for the three mythical children she was to teach. What exactly had she told Phil? She must be careful not to completely contradict herself. That was the trouble with lies. A good memory was essential if one was going to start telling them.

But something happened to distract her. The sitting room door opened. She looked over her shoulder in some surprise.

Her husband was standing there. He was wearing a wine-colored brocaded dressing gown with leather slippers. His hair was disheveled but only succeeded somehow in making him look even more handsome than usual. He stepped inside and closed the door behind him.

"Ah," he said, "it *is* you. What are you doing?"

She half covered her letter with one hand, trying not to look too secretive about it.

"I thought I would write a couple of letters before going to bed," she said. "I am sorry. Did the light disturb you?"

"Not at all," he said. "To whom do you write?"

"Oh." She laughed. "To some friends."

"At your old home?" he asked. "I was under the impression that you were alone in London."

She was thankful that his curiosity did not extend to strolling across the room to look over her shoulder.

"At my old home, yes," she said.

He stood just inside the door, his hands at his back, his lips pursed, looking almost awkward. As if he felt he did not quite belong there. As if he were embarrassed. Yet he was in his own apartments in his own boyhood home.

"I never used this room," he said as if in answer to her thoughts. "It seems like a woman's room."

"It is cozy," she said.

"Yes. Well, good night." He turned back toward the door.

"Good night, my lord," she said.

He hesitated, his hand on the doorknob. "Would you mind if I sat here while you write?" he asked. "I will not disturb you."

This was the Marquess of Staunton—that cold, haughty, cynical man? This uncertain, almost humble man?

"I would not mind at all, my lord," she said. "Please do join me."

He sat on a cozy love seat, set his elbow on the arm, and rested his closed fist against his mouth.

"Proceed," he said when she continued to look at him.

His eyes looked darker than usual—it must be a trick of the candlelight. But no, she thought as she turned back to her letter. It was more than that. Something had been lifted behind his eyes. But she would not turn back to see if she had been correct.

It had been a difficult letter to write even when she was alone. It was next to impossible now. In the course of fully twenty minutes she limped her way through another few sentences and brought a very unsatisfactory letter to an end. She waited for the ink to dry before folding the page carefully. She would have to take it into the village tomorrow. She could not set it on the tray downstairs addressed to Mr. Philip Duncan.

"I have finished." She turned and smiled—and was jolted to find that he was sitting exactly as he had been twenty minutes before. He was still watching her.

"It is a very short letter," he said. "And it is only one. I broke your concentration."

"It does not matter," she said. "I can write another letter tomorrow."

"You are gracious, Lady Staunton," he said. "Always gracious. My father appears to have grown remarkably fond of you."

"He is kind," she said.

He laughed softly. "'My dear,'" he said in his father's voice. "'Dear daughter. My dear daughter, come and seat yourself on this stool at my feet.' And then a careless hand resting lightly and affectionately on your shoulder. A soft look in his eyes."

"He is kind," she said again. The duke had made a potentially impossible evening really rather pleasant for her.

"His grace is never kind," he said, "and never affectionate. He plays a game with you, my lady. Or rather he plays a game with me. We play cat and mouse with each other."

By each pretending to an affection for her to infuriate the

other. Neither of them felt the fondness for her that they showed in public.

"Does it hurt you?" he asked.

Yes, it did. It hurt dreadfully to be seen and used as a pawn rather than as a person. But she had freely agreed to be so seen and so used and she had ignored the advice to make herself into a mere shadow. Shadows had no feelings of personal hurt or of pity for those who did the hurting.

She shook her head. "It is just a temporary arrangement," she said. "It will soon be over."

"Yes." He gazed at her and she was sure she had not been wrong about his eyes. Some of the defenses had been allowed to fall. Perhaps he felt safe with her here in his own apartments late at night.

She got to her feet. "It is late," she said. "It is time I went to bed. Good night, my lord."

"Let me come there with you," he said as she reached the door and lifted her hand to the knob.

She realized her naïveté then. She had felt the atmosphere ever since he stepped inside the room, and she had thought it to be mere self-consciousness on her part. She recognized the tension now for what it had been from the start. They both—oh yes, *both*—wanted to lie with each other again. It was open now in his words and the tone in which they had been spoken. And it was open too in her body's response to his words. There was a heavy throbbing in that most secret inner place where he had been two nights ago—and where she wanted him again.

It would not be wise. It was not love or even affection. It was not even marriage. It was need, the need of a twenty-three-year-old woman to mate, to celebrate her womanhood. It was a need that had lain dormant and almost unfelt in her until two nights ago. Now it was a need aroused with almost frightening ease. It was a need, she suspected, that might well grow into a constant craving if she gave in to it and became more familiar with the earth-shattering delights she had discovered two nights ago.

"You may feel free to say no," he said. "I will not force you or even try to persuade you."

And yet if she was honest with herself she would admit that it was already too late to prevent the craving. It had been there last night, it had been one reason for her staying up tonight, and it would be a demon to be fought for years to come. Tonight she had a chance to experience that delight again, to savor it, to commit it to memory for the barren years ahead.

"Allow me to open the door for you, my lady." His voice came from just behind her. "It was no part of our agreement. You must not feel coerced. I will not trouble you by asking again."

"I would like to lie with you," she said.

One of his hands touched her shoulder. The other reached past her to open the door. "I will take you to my bed, then, if you have no objection," he said.

"No," she said. "No, I have none."

His bedchamber was identical in size and shape to her own, but his was a masculine room, decorated in shades of wine and cream and gold. It smelled masculine—of leather and cologne and wine and unidentifiable maleness.

Did it matter that it was not for love? Or even for conjugal duty? Did it matter that it was just for need—for craving? Did the absence of either love or duty make it immoral? He was her husband. She turned to him and looked up into his eyes. Her very temporary husband. She would think about morality when he was no longer her husband, when she was alone again. Alone with her family.

Alone.

It had been the day of his final triumph, the day when he had at last won his undisputed independence and had more-over forced his father publicly to accept it. He had come home and faced his demons and even made some peace with them. It would no longer be a place to be avoided and his family would no longer be people to be avoided. He could be civil to Will again.

He should be rejoicing. He should be planning his return to his own life. He should be turning over to his man of business the matter of his wife's settlement.

He was not rejoicing. He was restless. He tried lying down. He tried willing sleep. It would not come. He was going to have to stay at Enfield, he admitted to himself at last. His father was gravely ill—dying, in fact. The admission brought him momentary panic. They were going to have to talk—really talk. His father was going to have to be persuaded to let go the reins of power so that he could relax and perhaps prolong his days. That meant that he, Staunton, was going to have to take over. He was going to have to stay. Indefinitely. He could not—would not—let his father die alone.

He could not keep his wife here indefinitely. He stood at the window of his room looking out into the darkness. Clouds must have moved over—there was no moonlight. There was no need to keep her here longer than a few days more, in fact. Once Tillden and his family returned home, she might be allowed to leave too. After all, he had not deceived his father about the true nature of his marriage, and he had no real wish or need to deceive him. The point was that the marriage was real and indissoluble. His father, being a realist, had accepted that. She had served her purpose. Now, soon, she might be allowed to go.

The marquess set his hands on the windowsill and leaned on them. He drew in a slow and audible breath and admitted something to himself. He wanted her. Now—in bed. But it was not she specifically he wanted, he told himself. He wanted a woman. Probably because he knew he would not have a woman for a long time. His grace had always been particularly strict about any dalliances his sons showed signs of initiating with local wenches. And his eldest son quite agreed with him. There were places enough where one might slake unruly appetites. The place where one exercised mastery and carried out the responsibilities that came with it was not one of them. He wanted his wife because she was close by—in the next bedchamber—and because she would not be there for long and he was going to be very womanless. He laughed softly in self-derision.

He wondered how she would react if he were to walk into her bedchamber now, demanding his conjugal rights. Perhaps she would give them to him without argument. His nostrils flared. He would go into his study, he decided. He would find something to do there. Some of his favorite books were there. If he thought hard enough, he would surely think of someone to whom he owed a letter. If that failed him, then he would dress again and go tramping about outside in the darkness.

But as he approached his study, he saw the light beneath the sitting-room door. And so he went there instead and invited himself to sit with his wife as she wrote her letter—and what had kept *her* up so late? he wondered. She was wearing a very plain, very serviceable white cotton dressing gown. Her hair was loose and lay in shining waves down her back.

He still wanted her. And he would admit to himself now that it was not just a woman he wanted. He wanted *her*—her innocence, her wholesomeness. He had found them enticing qualities two nights before. She had played her part well, he thought, watching her as she wrote, her posture correct yet graceful. More than well. She had shown a warmth and a charm and a graciousness that had affected them all with the possible exception of Marianne. Even Charles had watched her this evening as she sat on the low stool by their father, a puzzled frown on his face.

She had done well. He had caught himself feeling proud of her, pretty and dignified in the appallingly dull gray silk, before realizing that pride was not an appropriate feeling under the circumstances. Not a *warm* pride, anyway.

He wondered to whom she wrote with such difficulty. Was it someone to whom she merely felt duty-bound to write? Or was it someone of whom she was so fond that she was inhibited by his presence? But he had no right to his curiosity. And no wish to be curious. When she left him, he wanted to be able to forget about her.

But tonight he wanted her. He wanted her beneath him. He

wanted his face in her hair. The sooner she was out of his life the better it would be for him.

He gave in to weakness—and thought that she was going to refuse him. It would be as well if she did, though he did not know what he would do for sleep. But she did not refuse.

"I would like to lie with you," she said after he had got to his feet to open the door for her.

His wife did not mince words. And so he gave in to another weakness. He wanted her in his own bed. He wanted the memory of her there—though the thought, which took him completely by surprise, had him frowning in incomprehension.

There was no timidity in his wife—it seemed laughable to him now that he had mistaken her for a quiet mouse only a few days ago. She turned to him when they were in his bedchamber and looked full into his eyes—her own as wide and defenseless as they had ever been. He hoped they did not denote vulnerability. He hoped no one would ever hurt her deeply.

He undid the sash of her dressing gown and pushed the garment off her shoulders. He undid the buttons of her nightgown, opened back the edges, drew it down her arms, let it fall to the floor. She stood still and unresisting—and looked into his eyes.

She was beautifully proportioned without being in any way voluptuous. He had always thought that he preferred voluptuous women—until tonight.

He removed his dressing gown and pulled his nightshirt off over his head. Her eyes roamed over his body.

"We will lie down," he told her.

"Yes," she said.

He liked a great deal of foreplay and he had many skills. He liked to mount the bodies of his women just for the final vigorous ascent to release. He never kissed his women—not on the face at least. A kiss was too intimate a thing—too emotionally intimate, that was. A bedding was a purely physical thing with no emotional overtones whatsoever.

He did not kiss his wife. His hands went to work on her in the long-familiar ritual. But although he was aroused, he could not seem to get his mind involved in what he did. The pattern had become wearying. It would no longer satisfy. Not with her. He wanted to be lying atop her body. He wanted to be warmed by her heat, soothed by her softness. He wanted to be inside her, enclosed by her femininity. He wanted his face in her hair.

And so he let go of the pattern, the ritual, the familiar skills. He lifted himself over her and lowered his weight onto her. He nudged her legs apart. He had no idea if she was ready. It took women a long time to be ready for mounting. He slid his hands beneath her and pushed carefully inside. She was smooth with wetness.

It was strange, he thought, breathing in the erotic smell of soap, how one could be taut and pulsing with arousal without feeling any of the usual animal urges to squeeze the last ounce of pleasure out of the experience. He wanted merely to be in her, to ride her, to be close to her, to be this close, to be a part of her, of her grace and her warmth and her charm, to breathe in the essence of her. He stopped thinking.

He followed instinct. He had nothing else to guide him. He had abandoned skills and expertise and familiar moves. He followed instinct, mating with her with slow and steady rhythm, prolonging with unthinking instinct the exquisite and regrettable moment when they would become even more nearly one for the merest heartbeat before becoming two and separate once more. He did not know when she twined her legs about his but was only aware of the more comfortable unison of the rhythm they shared.

He sighed into her hair. She made low little sounds of contentment. It amazed him during one lucid moment that there was no great excitement in either of them. Only something far, far more dangerous—but he shut down the thought before it could be articulated.

She lost rhythm first. Her inner muscles began to contract convulsively. Her breathing became more labored. She un-twined her legs from his and braced her feet against the mattress. She pushed upward, straining against him. He thrust hard into her and pressed his hands down on her hips.

There were several moments of rigid tautness in her before she surged about him in utter, reckless abandon. She came to him in silence. She came to him with everything she had. He felt gifted, which was a strange feeling when all that had happened was that she was having a good sexual experience. A purely physical experience.

He let her relax beneath him. He savored the warmth and softness and silence of her. He waited for her breathing to become normal. Then he drove himself to the place where he longed to be, the place where he had always longed to be. Always. All his life. Though it was not a place exactly. It was . . . He heard himself shout out. He felt her arms come about him. He felt her legs twine about his again. He heard her murmur something against his ear—something exquisitely sweet and totally incomprehensible.

He felt as if he were falling and was powerless to stop himself.

Chapter 12

She did not sleep a great deal. At first she was uncomfortable—his weight was heavy on her and made breathing a conscious effort, and her legs stiffened from being pressed wide. Strangely she did nothing to lessen the discomfort. She did not try to wake him or to somehow alter her position. Quite the contrary. She lay very still and relaxed so that he would *not* move. She was very conscious of the fact that they were naked together, that part of his body was still inside part of hers, that they had been man and wife together. Discomfort seemed unimportant.

Even after he had stirred and rolled off her, grumbling incoherently and keeping his arms about her so that she stayed cuddled warmly and now comfortably against him, she did not sleep much. She dozed fitfully.

Nothing had changed. Nothing at all. It had not been love. She would be very, very foolish to imagine that it might have been. She must not even for a moment romanticize what had not contained even one element of romance. They were a man and a woman with physical needs. Conveniently they were married to each other and occupying the same apartments. And so they had fed those needs and been satisfied. She was very glad that she had learned such an invaluable lesson. New knowledge was always worth acquiring. She had learned that love and romance on the one hand and what happened between a man and a woman in bed on the other were so vastly different that one might as easily compare oranges and hackney cabs.

Nothing had changed. Except that foolishly and typically—

oh, so *very* typically—she had become involved. With all of
them—the whole unpleasant, morose, mixed-up lot of them.
Why could she not merely have continued to see them that
way and held herself aloof?

She had always been the same. She might have been married
when she was one-and-twenty, to a gentleman who was person-
able and eligible and of whom she was fond. But her mother
had been dead for only four years and everyone still needed
her, she had insisted—even though Mama's widowed sister had
been quite prepared to take over the care of the family. After
Papa's death, when the whole world came crashing about their
ears, she had insisted on becoming involved in supporting the
family and paying off the debts even though everyone had tried
to persuade her that she was needed more at home. And at her
last employment, of course, she had caused her own dismissal
by becoming involved in the distress of a pretty chambermaid
who was too weak-willed to stand up for herself.

And now she had done it again. She cared. She cared for the
Duke of Withingsby, who loved no one and whom no one
loved—or so they all thought, foolish people. She cared about
Augusta, who had a childhood to retrieve, and about Charles,
who still felt betrayed by the brother who had abandoned him
when he was still only a lad—oh yes, she had worked that one
out for herself. She cared about Claudia, who had caused a bitter rift between two brothers, and who must know it and be
distressed by it despite all her smiling charm. She cared for
William, who must be torn by guilt and by some indignation
too if it was true—it probably was—that Claudia had always
loved him. The only ones she did not particularly care about
were Marianne and Richard, though she loved their children.

Oh yes, she cared all right. Stupid woman. And she cared
for this man, this poor, troubled man who thought he was in
such firm command of his own life. How very foolish men
could be. How very like children they were—blustering and
bullying and glowering and utterly vulnerable. She had been
almost frightened by his vulnerability earlier when he had
shouted out just at the moment when she had been realizing

that the extra heat she felt inside was his seed being released.
He had sounded so lost. She had wrapped herself about him,
feeling an overwhelming tenderness, and murmured comfort
to him just as if he were one of the children who had fallen
down and scraped a knee.

"It will be all right," she had assured him. "Everything will
be all right, dear."

Dear! She hoped fervently he had not heard. The Marquess
of Staunton was not exactly the sort of person one called *dear*.
Or about whom one felt maternal. She felt anything but maternal at this particular moment. He was awake. His hand was
moving in light circles over her back and her buttocks and then
moved over her hip to slide up between them to one of her
breasts. He stroked it and brushed his thumb over her nipple.

"Mm," she said.

It was all either of them said. He lifted one of her legs to fit
snugly over his hip, drew her closer, and came into her. She
was so very naive. She had not known where his caresses were
leading. She had not realized it could be done again so soon—
or while they were lying on their sides. But when she tightened those newly discovered inner muscles, she could feel him
all enticingly hard and long again. And deep. He withdrew and
entered again. She did not believe there was a lovelier feeling
in the world. She wished it could last forever.

She slept deeply after it was over. He had moved her leg to
rest more comfortably on the other one and had drawn the
blankets snugly about her ears. But he kept her close—closer.
He kept their bodies joined. She must leave, she decided before she slid into sleep. There could be no real reason for her
to stay longer. He had made his point and his marriage was indissoluble. He was beyond the power he had imagined they
wielded over him. She must leave, put her life back together
again, proceed to live happily ever after with her family and
her six thousand a year.

But she would think about it tomorrow.

There had been some rain during the night. Drops of mois-
ture glistened now on the grass and there was still some early-

morning fog obscuring the hills and the distant trees. But it was a fine morning for a ride. The Marquess of Staunton stood on the marble steps outside the front doors, breathing in lungfuls of the damp, cool air and tapping his riding crop against his boots.

This morning there was no little brown mouse standing on the terrace below him. He had left her in bed. At his suggestion she had settled for sleep again after he had woken her for a swift, vigorous bout of lovemaking. She had turned her face into his pillow and slid her arm beneath it. She had been sleeping before he had tucked the bedclothes warmly about her.

He strode off toward the stables. Was he insane? Totally out of his mind? Three times last night, once three nights ago. What the devil would he do if he had got her with child? *If?* Four times and he was thinking in terms of *ifs?*

But he had come outside in order to refresh his mind and in order to renew his energies after a night of expending them. He scowled. Why the devil had she been sitting up at such a late hour writing letters? If she had not been, none of that would have happened. He had already resisted the temptation to pay a conjugal visit to her room.

But he was saved after all from such troublesome thoughts. Charles was already mounted up in the stableyard when he arrived there, and was firmly establishing with his frisky mount which of them was in charge.

"You have not forgotten your first lessons in horsemanship, then," he called from the gateway.

His brother clearly had not seen him until that moment. He touched his whip to the brim of his hat and nodded curtly. "Staunton," he said.

"But you have learned considerably more in the years since," the marquess said. "You are a cavalry officer, of course. I suppose riding comes as naturally to you as walking."

"As it does to all gentlemen I believe," Charles said. "Excuse me, Staunton. I will be on my way."

The marquess did not move from the gateway. "For a morning ride?" he said. "It is my purpose too. Shall we do it to-gether?"

His brother shrugged. "As you wish," he said.

It was all the fault of that pest of a wife of his, the marquess thought as he prepared his own horse, having waved away the groom who would have done it for him. That little prude with her character analyses and her moralizing, and her insistence that they were a family merely because his grace had fathered them all. When was the last time he had forced his company on someone who wished him to the devil? On that of a young puppy who had been all but insolent to him? It was all her fault that he felt this need to talk.

"You have seen active service?" he asked as they rode out of the stableyard and headed out to the open fields and hills behind the house.

"Not beyond these shores," Charles said. "I have been in a reserve regiment."

"Have been?" The marquess looked across at him. Dressed in scarlet regimentals his brother must be irresistible to the ladies, he thought, his lips quirking. It was still hard to believe that his younger brother was no longer a twelve-year-old boy.

"We sail for Spain within the month," Charles said. "I intend to be there."

"Does his grace dispute that?" the marquess asked.

His brother did not answer.

"I suppose," the marquess said, "that he did not even approve of your choice of career. He intended you for the church, did he not?" He remembered occasionally broaching the topic with their father. He remembered promising a rebellious Charles that he would take his part and see to it that he was not forced into a way of life that held no attraction whatsoever for him. But he had left before he could keep his promise.

Charles had clearly decided that this was a conversation in which he did not choose to participate. He had taken his mount to a brisk canter.

"But I do not remember your ever saying," the marquess

said, catching up to him, "that you wished to buy a commission. Your interest in a military career is of fairly recent date?"

His brother looked at him with hard, hostile eyes. "You make conversation for the sake of being sociable, Staunton," he said. "Since when have you been interested in my career or my reasons for entering it? And do not say it is because you are my brother. You are no brother of mine except by the accident of birth."

Ah. Charles had been far more deeply hurt by his desertion than he had ever expected. He had thought that the boy would recover quickly and with the resilience of youth attach his affections to someone else—perhaps Will. It had been a naive assumption. But then he had been only twenty himself at that time—Charles's age now.

"You wanted a gentleman's life," he said. "You wanted land and farms and responsibilities—even if you did not own the land, you said. You hoped that Will would enter the church or the army and that his grace would allow you to help run these estates or one of the more distant ones. I thought I might be given one of the other estates. We used to joke about it. I would allow you to live there and run it for me while I went raking off to London."

"Which is exactly what you did," Charles said. For the first time an open bitterness crept into his voice. "With vast success from all accounts."

"Do you know why I left?" the marquess asked him.

"Yes." His brother laughed. "His grace would not allow you to rut with any female within ten miles of Enfield. And with Mother dead there was nothing and no one to keep you here."

The marquess winced. Perhaps he should have forced himself to say good-bye. Perhaps he should have tried to explain. But no—there had been no way to explain the pain, the outrage, the humiliation.

"And Will would have knocked your teeth in if you had gone near Claudia," Charles added.

Ah. Twelve-year-olds sometimes noticed and understood far more than adults realized.

"I loved Claudia," he said. "I thought she loved me. But once she was married to Will, I never would have gone near her."

"You always were insufferably arrogant," his former admirer said scornfully. "Anyone with eyes in his head could see that it was Will she wanted and that Will lived in a sort of hell because he thought you were going to have her and he dared not fight you over the matter. You are not the sort of man to appeal to Claudia, Staunton. Claudia, for all her beauty, likes safety and security and tranquility. She likes Will."

Good God! Had he been so blind? So humiliatingly self-deluded? Apparently so.

"I left for other reasons," he said. "Life had become intolerable and Will's marriage and Mother's death pushed me very close to the edge. Not over it, though. There were still you and the baby." He drew a deep and ragged breath. He had not thought of it specifically for years. He did not know now if he could talk of it. "Something else pushed me over."

If Charles did not prompt him, he would not say it, he decided. It was all in the past. He had got over it, recovered his life and his pride, forged an independence for himself.

"Well?" Charles said impatiently and rather impertinently.

"He accused me of stealing," the marquess said. "His grace, I mean. He had searched my rooms himself and found it. He was waiting there for me with it in his hand. He hit me across the face with it in his open palm. It drew blood."

He did not even look at his brother, who said nothing in the short silence that followed.

"He ordered me downstairs to await him in the library," the marquess said. "I knew what would be at the end of the wait, of course. Any one of us would have known, would we not? I was twenty years old and innocent. I told him that I would do it, that I would wait there, that I would not fight with him or argue with him further. I told him that I would take the whipping just as if I were still a helpless child. But I told him too that I would be gone before the day was out, that I would never set foot on Enfield property again, that he would never set eyes on me again. His grace would never bow to such threats, of course. It was the severest whipping he had ever given me. I had great difficulty riding my horse afterward, but I would not spend another night under the same roof with him."

Charles still said nothing.

"When I made the threat, I did not speak in haste," the marquess said. "I knew exactly what I was saying, and I knew the choices I was making. I knew that I would have to leave the baby, whom he would not even look at, and I knew I would have to leave you. You were the most precious person left in my world. But I will not use such an argument with you in self-defense. You were a child. You needed me. And I did not even have the courage to say good-bye to you. I would not have been able to leave if I had done so and I had to leave. More than my self-respect was at stake. I felt as if my very life, my soul were at stake. When one is twenty, Charles, as perhaps you will admit, one sometimes dramatizes reality in such a way. Perhaps, in retrospect, my self-respect and my life and my soul were of less importance than a child to whom I was something of a hero."

He realized then in some horror why Charles was saying nothing.

"The devil!" he said. "This is not a tale that calls for tears, Charles. It is a foolish and sordid episode from the past. The long-forgotten past. I could not even keep my vow, you see. I am here on Enfield property again after just eight years. I am on almost civil speaking terms with his grace."

Charles spurred on ahead and the marquess let him go. Twenty-year-olds who were also cavalry lieutenants did not enjoy being seen crying.

He drew his own horse to a halt. No, he would not even ride after his brother in a few minutes' time. Charles would be devilishly embarrassed, and he might feel it necessary to comment on what he had been told. Nothing more needed to be said on the matter. Charles now knew at least that he had left not merely to take his rakish pleasure in town after their mother's death had released him from any need to stay at Enfield. It would not make a great deal of difference. Certainly his reason for leaving was no excuse for what he had done. He had broken the bonds of love and trust. And he was not the only one who had suffered as a result.

He turned his horse toward home, changed his mind, and went trotting off in a different direction. He would find some open countryside and take his horse to a gallop until they were both ready to collapse.

Charity slept for only half an hour after her husband had left. Despite the fact that she had slept for only the last few hours of the night and even that sleep had been disturbed when her husband had woken and wanted her again, she found that old habits refused to be ignored. She had always been an early riser.

She breathed in the smell of him on his pillow and mentally examined the mingled feelings of soreness and well-being and languor and energy that all laid claim to her. It must be very pleasant, she thought, to be married permanently, to wake every morning like this. But hers was not a permanent marriage, nor did she wish it to be. This family had more troubles than she could list on her ten fingers. She had a family of her own with whom she was quite contented. And she would be with them soon. There was the ball tonight. Tomorrow or the next day she did not doubt the Earl of Tillden would remove his family from Enfield. Then her function would be quite at an end.

Tomorrow morning she would ask the Marquess of Staunton when she might leave. He would probably want her to stay a few days longer, but by this time next week she could reasonably expect to be home. She threw back the bedclothes and sat on the edge of the bed. How excited they would be to see her. How excited she would be! And what wonderful news she would have to share with them. She would tease them at first. She would pretend to them that she had lost her position and was destitute. And then she would watch their faces as she told them the real story.

Penny would not approve. And Phil would be thunderous. He might even refuse to touch a penny of the money or allow her to pay off any of the debts. But then she had been fighting Phil all her life. And she was the elder, after all. Somehow she would persuade him.

A short while later—she had not summoned her maid, but there had been an embarrassing moment when she had passed through her husband's dressing room, clad only in her nightgown and with her hair all tangled and disheveled, and found his valet there clearing away his shaving things—Charity descended to the breakfast room. It was still very early. She hoped no one else would be there yet. She hoped *he* would not be there. She would not quite know how to look at him or what to say to him. But only Charles was there, looking youthful and handsome in his riding clothes.

"Oh, good morning," she said, smiling warmly. "Are you an early riser too? But I daresay you are if you are a military officer."

"I have been out riding," he said. He had risen from his place and held out a hand for hers. When she gave it to him, he raised it to his lips. It was a wonderfully courtly gesture from so young a man.

"Have you?" she said. "Did you see Anthony? He got up very early too and said he was going riding." She flushed when she realized what her words had revealed.

"I rode a short way with him," he said.

"Did you?" She seated herself and leaned a little toward him as a footman poured her coffee. "And did you two talk? I have never known a family in which the members did less talking on important matters."

His eyes looked suddenly guarded. "We talked," he said.

"Good." She helped herself to a round of toast from the toast rack. "And have you forgiven him for abandoning you when you were just a boy?"

"He has told you, then?" he asked.

"No," she said, smiling. "Even to me he has said very little about the past. I do not know what happened, only that something did and that until everyone is willing to talk about it, nothing will ever be healed. You loved him once."

"Yes," he said. "More than anyone else in the world. He could do no wrong in my eyes even though I was aware of his faults. Arrogance, for example."

"I think arrogance comes naturally from his position and upbringing and his looks," she said, sharing a conspiratorial smile with him.

"Do you love him?" he asked softly.

Her hand paused halfway to her mouth and she set down the piece of toast she had been about to bite into. How could she answer such a question? Only one way, she realized. She had committed herself to a lie when she had accepted the Marquess of Staunton's proposition.

"Yes," she said. "Faults and all. Even though I have wanted to shake him until he rattles from the moment we arrived here. He is so foolishly *reticent*."

He smiled and Charity found herself pitying any very young lady on whom he turned the power of that smile—if he did not intend offering his heart with it.

"I thought you were a fortune hunter," he said. "I hated Tony when he arrived here, but even so I found myself outraged on his behalf. I thought he had been duped. I am sorry. I have seen since that I completely misjudged both you and Tony's ability to choose a bride wisely. I like you."

"Thank you," she said. "Oh, thank you." She felt around in vain for a handkerchief—her face had crumpled quite ignominiously. "How very foolish."

"No," he said gently, and he pressed a large gentleman's handkerchief into her hand. "You have been treated abominably here, though even his grace was thawing by last evening. You have shown great courage in continuing to smile and treat us civilly when we gave you such a cold welcome."

"Well." She blew her nose. "I believe I have had enough

breakfast." She had had two bites of toast and half a cup of coffee. "No, you need not get up."

She wanted nothing more than to rush from the room and find somewhere dark to hide herself. He had thought she cried because he had been kind to her and told her he liked her. That was not the reason at all. It was the other thing he had said—*I thought you were a fortune hunter.* The words had torn at her like a barbed whip.

But she was not to escape so easily. The door of the breakfast room opened and Lady Tillden stepped inside with Lady Marie Lucas. There were curtsies and bows all round and considerable embarrassment. Charity and Lady Tillden settled into a dreary and thoroughly predictable discussion of the weather, which had been rainy last night and was now a little foggy, though there were signs that the fog was lifting, and there was considerable hope that the clouds might move right off later. Perhaps the sun would even shine—as it often did by day when there were no clouds. They were in amicable agreement with each other.

Beyond their own conversation Charity was aware of Lieutenant Lord Charles Earheart bowing over the hand of Lady Marie, as he had bowed over hers a short while ago, and raising it to his lips and exchanging a smile and a few quiet words with her.

"Good morning," he said. "How pleased I am to see you again. It has been all of eighteen months."

"I did not think you would be here," she said. "I thought you would be away with your regiment."

"I am on leave," he explained.

"I hoped you would not be here," she almost whispered.

"Did you?" he said, sounding unsurprised. "But I am, you see."

"Yes," she said.

"And are you still sorry?" he asked her, looking very gravely into her eyes.

But the weather as a topic of conversation had been exhausted, and Lady Tillden, with a sweet and nervous little smile for Charity's benefit, turned her attention to the conversation between her daughter and Lord Charles. They began to discuss the weather.

Charity excused herself and left the room. She ascended the first five stairs to her room at a walk. She took the rest at a run and two at a time.

I thought you were a fortune hunter.

Chapter 13

By the time he dressed for the ball, the Marquess of Staunton was feeling better pleased with the day than might have been expected. He had succeeded in keeping himself at some distance from the houseguests while being perfectly civil when he was in company with them. It helped that both Marianne and Charles had exerted themselves to see to the entertainment of the guests, Marianne taking the carriage into the village with the ladies in the morning, Charles taking the barouche with all three of them during the afternoon on a drive about the park and a picnic at the ruins.

The Earl of Tillden, it seemed, had decided upon the wisdom of behaving as if the idea of a betrothal between his daughter and the Duke of Withingsby's heir had never for one moment disturbed his mind. He was spending an amicable few days with an old friend.

Charles himself had been quiet. He had made no attempt to seek out his brother with any comment on what he had heard during their early-morning ride. On the other hand he had not deliberately avoided him either. And the hostility had gone from his eyes, to be replaced by a blank look that was hard to read. On the only occasion he had been forced to use his brother's name, though, he had not addressed him as *Staunton,* or even as *Anthony,* but as *Tony.* The marquess almost despised himself for the warmth the sound of that name brought him.

Then there was William. He had come to Enfield during the morning to discuss some small matter of estate business with his father. His grace had summoned the marquess to the library, had directed his younger son to spend an hour with him explaining various aspects of the running of the estates, and had left them alone together. They had been awkward and businesslike at first until some trivial detail had amused them both simultaneously and they had laughed together. After that, though they had looked self-consciously at each other and there had still been some awkwardness for a while, something had changed. Something indefinable. They had become brothers again without anything having been said—they had merely continued to discuss the matter at hand.

And the marquess, thinking afterward of Claudia, had realized that all that sordid and rather humiliating business was indeed past history. He felt nothing for her beyond a very natural appreciation of her beauty. The bitterness was gone. Perhaps—probably—after all, she had not been coerced. And after all, perhaps Will had not acted dishonorably except in a very understandable reluctance to admit to his brother that they loved the same woman. Will had been only nineteen years old at the time. One could hardly expect him to act with the firmness and maturity of a man.

Even Augusta had thawed during the day. Not so much to him, perhaps, as to Charity, but she had smiled at him and had looked like a child. He had walked as far as the bridge with Will to enjoy the sunshine that had succeeded the morning mist—and had met Charity and Augusta coming in the opposite direction. Charity had been to the dower house for more fittings, especially for the ball dress that was being prepared in great haste for the evening. She had taken Augusta with her to play with the boys. How had she managed to pry his sister from the schoolroom in the middle of the morning? By the simple expedient of asking his grace and asking Miss Pevensey, the governess.

His grace had released his daughter from the schoolroom merely because his daughter-in-law had asked it of him?

"But of course," his wife had said when he put the question

to her. "He agreed that such a beautiful morning ought not to be wasted."

She had blushed rosily as soon as they met and while they talked, he had noticed. She had clearly been remembering the night before, something he would prefer to forget if he could.

And so he had tried to focus on Augusta, who was, he had noticed, both dirty and disheveled—and for once looking like an eight-year-old child.

"You bring back distinct memories, Augusta," he had said, first fingering the handle of his quizzing glass and then lifting the glass to his eye, "of tree climbing and games of chasing and hide-and-seek. Except that I believe Will and Charles and I—and even Marianne on occasion—usually sported cuts and bruises and torn clothes as well as mere dirt."

She had glanced at him with considerable fright in her eyes.

"You will, of course," he had said, "change your frock and wash your hands and face and comb your hair before his grace sets eyes on you at luncheon. And if he should invite me to the library in the meanwhile and put me to the torture, I shall grit my teeth and swear that when I met you at the bridge there was not even one speck of dirt on your person, even on the soles of your shoes."

That was when she had smiled at him—a huge, sunny child's smile, complete with wrinkled nose.

Yes, the marquess thought now as his valet finally perfected the knot in his neckcloth and picked up his dark evening coat to help him into it, the day had gone rather well. Though of course, with all the preparations for the night's festivities in progress and with the Earl of Tillden and his family still at Enfield as guests, there had been very much a sense of meaningful activity being suspended. There was more to be settled, he realized, than getting on more comfortable terms with his brothers and sisters—and that had been no part of his original plan in coming here. There was something to be arranged and settled with his father. And there was his wife to deal with.

He must send her on her way soon, he had decided during the day. For one thing, she had already fulfilled her function.

He had been accepted as a married man who could not be made to fit into anyone's preconceptions about how the Marquess of Staunton should live his life. For another, it would be easier for her to leave now and cause another commotion within his family before they had quite recovered from the first. It might as well all be settled once and for all. And then too she might as well go before he could increase the already strong chance that she was with child. And before he could become too accustomed to her convenient presence in the room next to his own at night.

He had hired Miss Charity Duncan to do him a service. That service had not included warming his bed at night.

He leaned closer to the looking glass in order to place a diamond pin in the center of the folds of his neckcloth. But his hands paused in the task. He was also wearing a jeweled ring. What jewels did his wife have to deck herself out with? At least she would not have to wear the atrocious gray silk to the ball. Claudia's modiste had finished the ball gown for her. He expected that it would be pretty and fashionable and of suitably costly fabric. But she would have no jewels to wear with it.

It had been the whole point, of course—to bring to Enfield a bride who had clearly been impoverished when he married her, to flaunt before his family the fact that birth and fortune and fashion and beauty—all the usual reasons why a man of his rank chose a bride—meant nothing to him.

And yet now he felt strangely guilty. How must she have felt for the past few days, as different in appearance from his family and their guests as it was possible to be? How would she feel tonight, in her new ballgown, her throat and wrists and ears bare of jewels? And yet she was his wife, the most senior lady in rank at tonight's ball. Word had quickly spread in the neighborhood that the ball, which rumor had had it would be a betrothal ball for the Marquess of Staunton, was in fact being held in celebration of his marriage.

Why had he not thought to buy her a wedding gift—a bracelet, a necklace, a ring? Even Anna, who had served as his

mistress for six weeks earlier in the spring, had been dismissed
with rubies.

He closed his eyes and thought. There was the gold chain
and locket that his mother had given him on his eighteenth
birthday, a miniature of herself inside. He had worn it constantly for a year after her death. He had it with him. He also
had with him—ah yes—a string of pearls he had bought as an
enticement for the young dancer he had intended to employ
after Anna. He had changed his mind about her and about his
need of a mistress from the *demimonde*. He still had the pearls.
He had brought them with the vague notion of presenting them
to Marianne or Augusta.

He dismissed his valet and found them. They were rather
splendid—he had always lavished the best of everything on
mistresses and prospective mistresses on the cynical assumption that a generous protector could usually command the best
services and exclusive services.

He did not know what her gown looked like. He did not
even know the color. She had laughed when he had asked—
and looked remarkably pretty and youthful doing it—and told
him that it was a secret. But it did not matter. Pearls would
match anything. He warmed them in his hand. Perhaps it
might be argued that he owed her nothing since her payment
was very well looked after indeed in the agreement they had
both signed. But she had done her job well, and more than
well—though the pearls would not be payment for sexual fa-
vors. He frowned down at his hand. The thought was distasteful. She was his wife.

He would give her the pearls because she was his wife.
They would be a wedding present even though theirs was not a
normal marriage.

He tapped on the door of her dressing room a minute later
and waited for her maid to open it. But her ladyship was not
there, the girl informed him, bobbing him a curtsy. She had already gone down to the drawing room, summoned there by his
grace.

Well. He slipped the pearls into a pocket and followed his

wife downstairs. His grace had chosen to show an affection for his daughter-in-law that he had never shown his own children. It was deliberate, of course. He was attempting to discompose his son, to convince him that he was not at all rattled to have been presented with a future duchess chosen from the lower ranks of the gentry, a future duchess who had until recently earned her living as a governess.

It did not matter. The marquess was not disconcerted. It amused him that his grace was lavishing attentions on Charity. He looked forward to seeing her in her new ballgown. He would present the pearls to her in a more public setting than he had intended. He would clasp them about her neck himself. Perhaps she would favor him with one of her warm smiles.

Her gown was of white silk covered with a tunic of white lace embroidered all over with gold rosebuds. The embroidery was slightly larger and more densely spaced at the hem and the cuffs of the short sleeves and at the neckline, which was quite fashionably low. Claudia had produced a pair of long gold evening gloves and had insisted that she wear them. Her new maid, who was very clever with her hands, had performed wonders with her hair, so that it was all curls and ringlets without looking in any way too girlish for her age or marital status.

She felt, Charity thought, gazing at her image in the glass, quite beautiful. She found herself totally enchanting, and then grinned at herself and her own self-conceit. But she did not care if she was being conceited. She was not expressing her thoughts to anyone else but herself, after all. She thought she looked quite, quite beautiful. She felt like a princess going to a grand ball—and that at least was not far off the mark. She was the Marchioness of Staunton, daughter-in-law of the Duke of Withingsby, and she was going to her very first ball—in a ballroom whose splendor had quite taken her breath away when she had peeped in at it late in the afternoon—as the guest of honor. She was even to stand in the receiving line with his grace and her husband.

Would he think her beautiful? It did not matter if he did or not, she decided. But oh, of course it mattered. He had found her desirable last night—her cheeks had been turning hot at regular intervals all day long at the memory of last night. But she really did not know whether that had been just because she had been there and available—and willing—or whether he found her personally attractive. It did not matter if he found her attractive or not. Yes it did—she grinned at her image again. She was going to enjoy tonight. She was going to forget that all this was only a very temporary arrangement. She was going to forget that she was only a sort of Cinderella—except that no prince would scour the countryside searching for her, slipper clutched in one hand, after she had gone. She was simply going to enjoy herself.

She waited impatiently for her husband to come to escort her to the drawing room. There was dinner to be sat through first, of course, before any of the outside guests would begin to arrive for the ball. But she would feel that the evening had started once she left this room. She wondered if they would all look on her in some shock now that she was dressed appropriately for the part she played. She wondered how *he* would look on her when he came into her dressing room. She intended to be looking right at him so that she could see his first reaction.

She *hoped* he would approve of her appearance.

She smiled brightly when his knock came at the door and nodded at her maid to open it. She cooled her smile—she must not look like an exuberant schoolgirl. But it collapsed all the way when she saw that it was a servant, not her husband. His grace requested the honor of her company in the drawing room immediately. She hesitated. Surely her husband would not be long. Should she tap on his dressing room door? But somehow, despite her relationship to him and the intimacies they had shared, the Marquess of Staunton did not seem quite the person with whom one felt free to take such liberties.

"When his lordship comes, Winnie," she said to her maid, "please tell him that his grace has summoned me to the drawing room."

Fortunately she felt familiar enough by now with the family not to feel too awed to walk into a room alone. Of course this evening it was more difficult. She felt dreadfully self-conscious of her very different appearance. Even the footman who opened the door into the drawing room for her looked startled, she thought, until she realized the absurdity of the thought. Footmen were trained not to look startled even if a herd of elephants wearing pink skirts galloped by.

Claudia beamed at her and William pursed his lips and looked very like his brother for a moment. Marianne raised her eyebrows and Richard exerted himself enough to bow. Charles took her hand, bowed over it—he was himself looking irresistibly handsome—and told her with a roguish wink that Tony was a lucky devil. The Earl of Tillden and his family had not yet come down. His grace stood with his back to the fireplace and looked her over with keen eyes. She smiled at him and curtsied.

"You wanted me, Father?" she asked. His face looked less gray than usual. He must have been resting, as she had advised him to do and as he had promised to do.

"Yes. Come closer, my dear," he said.

She stepped closer and smiled at him. The attention of the rest of the family was on them, of course. He held something in one of his hands, she saw when he brought it from behind his back.

"I gave her grace a gift on our wedding day," he said. "On her passing it reverted to me. It is my wish to give it as a gift to the bride who will one day hold her grace's title and position. To my eldest son's bride. To you, my dear."

She looked down at his open palm. It was a large and beautiful topaz surrounded by diamonds and set into a necklet of diamonds. It was an ornate and heavy piece of jewelry that must be worth a king's ransom. Not that it was its monetary value that turned Charity's mouth and throat dry. It was the other value of the piece. It had been his gift to his wife—his wedding gift. And now he was giving it to her? It matched her gown, though it was altogether too heavy for the gown's delicacy. But that did not matter. The necklet blurred before her vision and she blinked her eyes rapidly.

"Father." She looked up into his eyes. "You must have loved her very much." Extremely silly words that had no relevance to anything. She did not know why she had said them— or whispered them rather. She had not spoken aloud.

She would not have been able to put into words afterward even if she had been called upon to do so what happened to his eyes then. They turned to steel. They turned to warm liquid. Neither description would have served and yet both were close, opposite as they were.

"Oh yes," was all he said, so quietly that she doubted that even in the quiet room anyone had heard the exchange.

"Turn," he said. "I shall fasten it about your neck."

She turned—and met Marianne's eyes. They were full of disbelief, resentment, envy. Marianne was the elder daughter. She must have expected that her mother's most precious piece of jewelry would be given to her or left to her at her father's death. It felt cold and heavy and alien about Charity's throat. Her father-in-law set his hands on her shoulders and turned her when he had clasped the necklet in place.

"It is where it belongs," he said and then shocked her by lowering his head and kissing her first on one cheek and then on the other.

"Thank you, Father," she said. She was choked with gratitude, with discomfort, with—with love. She cared so very much for him, she thought. She did not know why except that there was a deep sadness in her for him and a deep tenderness. She loved him. He was her father—her husband's father.

A very dangerous thought.

She moved to one side so that she would not monopolize his attention, using the tray of drinks on the sideboard as an excuse. She picked up a glass of ratafia. She had just finished drinking it a few minutes later when the door opened and she saw that her husband had arrived. She stood very still, watching him, waiting for him to notice her. In his dark evening clothes and crisp white linen and lace he looked even more

handsome than ever. And more satanic. But if she had ever
been even a little afraid of him, she was so no longer. She just
wished she did not have certain memories. . . . But for this
evening she would not try to force them from her mind. This
was the evening she had set herself to enjoy.

His eyes found her almost immediately. As his father had
done a short while ago, he stood still and swept her from head
to foot with his eyes. She read admiration there and something
a little warmer than admiration. She smiled at him.

And then his eyes came to rest on her throat.

Something in his look alerted her. She felt cold, breathless.
She felt danger even though his expression did not change and
he did not move for a few moments. Even when he came
slowly toward her his face was expressionless. She felt panic
catch at her breath. She felt the urge to turn and run. Yet she
could not understand the feeling. She continued to smile at
him.

"Where did you get that?" His voice, very quiet, stabbed
into her like a sharp needle. His eyes looked suddenly very
black.

Her hand went to the necklet. "It was your mother's," she
said foolishly.

"Where did you get it?" His nostrils flared.

"Your father gave it to me," she said. "As a bridal gift. It is
very beautiful." *I will give it back before I leave.* But she could
not say those last words aloud. They had an audience—a very
attentive audience.

"Take it off," he said.

"Your father—"

"Take it off." His face was white. And suddenly she was
terrified of him.

She did not move her hands fast enough. He raised one of
his own, curled it about the topaz, his fingers grazing over her
skin none too gently, and jerked at the necklet. The catch held
fast and she grimaced with pain.

"Turn around," he said.

She turned and tilted her head forward. His fingers fumbled

at the catch for what seemed endless moments before she felt the weight of the necklet fall away from her neck into his hand. She did not lift her head or turn around—everyone was behind her and everyone was loudly silent. So silent that she heard the words her husband spoke to the duke after he had crossed the room to the fireplace.

"This is yours, I believe, sir," he said.

"On the contrary, Staunton," the duke said, "it is Lady Staunton's. I have made it a gift to her."

"I decline the gift," his son said. "I will provide any clothes and jewels that my wife will wear."

"It is her ladyship's," his grace said. "I will none of it."

"Then it will lie there until someone chooses to pick it up," the marquess said. And there was the thud of something falling to the floor.

The door opened at the same moment to admit the Earl and Countess of Tillden and Lady Marie Lucas.

William was stooping unobtrusively to pick up the necklet as Charity turned. But it was all she saw. She hurried from the room with her head bowed. She was not even sure she would go up to her room to fetch her things. She was not sure she could bear to stay at Enfield even that long. But a hand closed about her arm before she had taken half a dozen steps away from the drawing-room door.

"Charity?" It was Charles's voice.

"No," she said, pulling her arm loose. "No, please."

But he would not let her go. He stepped in front of her and she ran right against his chest. She did not have the energy to push away again. She rested her face against him and breathed in noisy, shaky gasps.

"Let me take you to another room," he said, "where you may recover yourself. You did nothing wrong. You must believe that. You got caught in the middle. You did nothing wrong."

"No, she did not." The other voice was quieter and came from behind her. "I'll take her, Charles."

"Only if you promise on your honor not to harm her," Charles said, his voice hardening. "Her neck is bleeding."

"I promise," the marquess said. His voice was bleak and dull.

"I suppose it was *that*," Charles said, "to which you referred this morning."

"Yes," the marquess said. "He has come straight from hell, Charles. We have the devil himself as our sire. A noble distinction. Come with me, Charity, please?" His hands touched her shoulders.

She straightened up. "Thank you, Charles," she said. "I hope I have not damaged your neckcloth."

"It is not nearly so elaborate as Tony's anyway," he said, smiling. "I tied it myself." He strode back into the drawing room.

"Come with me," her husband said, and she felt the soft warmth of his handkerchief being pressed against the back of her neck, which she was only just beginning to realize was sore. "Please? I will not hurt you again. I promise I will not."

He took her into the small salon next to the drawing room and closed the door.

"You were, as Charles said, caught in the middle," he told her. He seated her on a chair and dabbed gently at her neck with his handkerchief. "That necklet was my mother's. She always said it was to be mine after her. She gave it to me before she died. She was very positive about her wish that I have it. I was the most precious person in her life, she always told me. My father missed it from her jewel collection right after her funeral while I was out riding, trying to clear my head after the emotions of the day. When I came home, he was in my room, the necklet in his hand. He accused me of stealing it. He would listen to no defense, no explanations. He punished me by whipping me. I could easily have avoided the whipping—I was twenty years old and at least as strong as he. I did not even try to avoid it. But I told him before he administered it what would happen if he did it."

"You left home," she said.

"Yes." He blew cool air against the graze on the back of her neck. "I swore I would never come back. But I came. On my own terms."

"With me," she said.

"Yes. My anger was not directed against you just now," he said. "I was blind with fury. It is no excuse, of course. I beg your pardon."

"He gave it to me deliberately," she said. "He knew it would hurt and infuriate you more than anything else he could possibly do."

"You were quite right," he said, "at the very beginning when you said that you would be a pawn in a game. I am sorry you have been physically hurt too. Does it hurt badly?"

"No," she said, getting to her feet. "Hardly at all. We have a dinner to attend."

"Now?" He laughed. "I am going to take you away from here tonight. We will return to London and then you will tell me where you wish to settle and I will have the arrangements made as swiftly as possible. You have done well. You have earned your future of comfort and security."

"We have a dinner to attend," she said firmly, "and a ball. Perhaps you are lacking in courage, my lord, but I am not. You ran away once and have never been able to outrun the demons or ghosts or whatever you may care to call them. You will not run again, I think, when you have taken a moment to consider."

He gazed at her, his expression unreadable. He drew a deep breath at last. "And so to dinner, then, my little brown mouse," he said. "But will you wear these for me? Will they hurt your neck?"

A string of pearls was lying across his palm. They were delicate and perfect and made her want to cry.

"They are a gift," he said. "A thank you, if you will. A wedding gift perhaps."

"I will wear them," she said, turning and dipping her head again so that he could clasp them about her neck. "They are beautiful."

"But not nearly as lovely," he said, "as their wearer."

Chapter 14

It was not so very difficult after all to get through dinner, the marquess found. His grace behaved as he always did; so did he. That is, they were both reticent, formally correct and courteous. It had become second nature to him to hide all feeling so deep that no one else would suspect that it was there at all.

Except that his wife suspected it. She sat in her place at the foot of the table, quite dizzyingly beautiful, smiling, animated, flushed, bright-eyed—and gazing straight through the defenses that had held everyone at bay for years to understand that he was deeply disturbed by what had just happened. At least it seemed to him that she saw through his defenses. Perhaps it was fanciful thinking. And fanciful too to imagine that she looked with just as penetrating an understanding at his father—only to discover, surely, that there was nothing behind his grace's facade. Only coldness and emptiness and even perhaps evil.

It was not even very difficult to stand in the receiving line just inside the ballroom later in the evening, greeting the guests as they arrived, presenting his marchioness to neighbors and acquaintances. It was not difficult, because although his father stood in the line too, she stood between them and was as animated, as charming, as beautiful as she had been in the dining room.

He found his mind counting back days as he smiled and bowed and made small talk with the arriving guests. But no matter how often he did the calculations he always arrived at the same conclusion. One week ago he had not even met Miss

Charity Duncan. One week ago he had glanced through her letter of application and after some hesitation had set it on the pile of those to be given more serious consideration.

And now, just one week later, he was falling in love with her. The thought verbalized itself in his mind without any prior warning, and he pushed it impatiently away. He was no boy to be gulled by shallow emotion.

"I have never been so nervous in my life," she said, smiling at him during a lull in arrivals.

He raised his eyebrows. He never would have guessed it. She looked as if she had been standing in receiving lines for years. "Not even on your arrival here, my lady?" he asked.

"Oh." She laughed. "I was not nervous then. I was terrified." But she would not exclude his grace from her conversation even though he had used her shamefully earlier in the evening. She turned and set a hand on his arm. "Will you sit, Father? No one will remark upon it if you do. Almost everyone must have arrived by now, and Anthony and I can greet the latecomers." She spoke with a gentle concern that sounded almost affectionate.

As for himself, the marquess thought as, to his amazement, his father allowed himself to be led toward a vacant chair, he did not care what happened to the duke. He would not stay to concern himself with his father's health or with Enfield affairs. Tomorrow he would be on his way back to London with his wife. He would see her settled comfortably in a home of her choice and then he would resume his old life just as if there had not been this disruption of a few days. And really that was all it had been—a few days.

They did not remain in the receiving line much longer. It was their duty to lead off the first set of country dances, and the guests would be impatient to begin. The ballroom at Enfield looked remarkably festive, the marquess was forced to admit, and far more architecturally splendid than most of the London ballrooms he knew. It was a betrothal ball that had been rapidly converted into a wedding ball. The flowers and ribbons and bows that decked the room were predominantly white. But then, of course, his grace was adept at arranging such things.

Did his wife dance? he wondered suddenly. But she surely would have said something to him if she did not. And indeed she danced the steps flawlessly and gracefully. Will, he saw, had led Lady Marie into this opening set. He had not spoken to the girl himself beyond the exchange of a few courtesies. But it did not seem to him that she was nursing a broken heart. He hoped not. He did not doubt that, like him, she was merely a victim of two despotic men who assumed that it was their right to organize the lives of their offspring down to the last detail. Perhaps now she would be given a little more choice of husband, though he doubted it.

His father, he noticed, was observing the proceedings like a king from his throne, his expression proud and unreadable, his complexion tinged with gray. But he would take no notice of that last fact, his son decided. A serious illness did not hinder his grace in the pursuit of evil. He remembered being so blindly furious just a few hours ago that he had tried to yank his mother's necklet from his wife's neck without pausing to undo the catch first. He had drawn blood from the back of her neck.

And he remembered the day of his mother's funeral. He had returned from his vigorous ride, weary from the emotions and grief of the previous days, to find his father waiting in his rooms. For one moment—or perhaps for the mere fraction of a moment—his heart had leapt with something like gladness as he thought his father had come to share his grief. And then he had seen the topaz necklet in his father's hand.

In the pattern of the dance, he and his wife passed each other, back to back. "Smile, my lord," she said. "It is by far the best revenge."

And then they were back in their separate lines, performing other figures of the dance, unable to exchange anything more than looks. She was still smiling, an expression that involved her whole face and appeared to reach back far into her eyes. Perhaps, he thought in some surprise, she wore a mask as impenetrable as his own. Could she really be feeling as happy as she looked? She had been horribly shamed earlier, in front of his whole family. She had been given a precious gift and accepted into the family, so to speak, by the Duke of Withingsby himself. And then her husband had arrived, talked to her coldly in front of them all, torn the gift from about her neck, and abandoned her in her embarrassment and humiliation so that he might have his moment of confrontation with his grace.

It was Charles who had offered her comfort first. And for once—the only time during the days he had known her—she had lost her quiet self-possession. She had sagged against Charles, her breathing labored.

Yet now she had come to face his family again rather than run away as she had had the opportunity to do—it had been his full intent to take her away. She had faced them, not with anger or cold dignity or righteous recriminations, but with smiles and charm and grace. With a dignity worthy of a duchess—or of a marchioness maybe.

For his sake? Was she doing this for him? Because she had made a bargain with him and was determined to earn the generous settlement that would be hers for the rest of her life? Or was she doing it for herself? To show them all that she was not ashamed of who she was, that she could be more the person of true gentility than the best of them?

He really was falling in love with her. This time he allowed the thought to remain in his conscious mind. They crossed in front of each other in the middle of the set and he smiled at her.

"It is certainly something you should do more often," she said before she moved out of earshot again. "It is a deadly weapon."

She was referring to his smile, he thought after a moment of incomprehension. She was *flirting* with him. But even as his pulses quickened involuntarily, he knew that she was not. She was playing a part and she was doing it magnificently well. She was drawing admiring eyes despite the relative simplicity of her appearance—or perhaps because of it. She looked fresh and new and innocent and . . .

And the sooner he got her settled to a comfortable life of her own, the sooner he could retreat to the life that was familiar to him. The safe life. He did not want to be unsafe again. There was too much pain.

He bowed in the line of gentlemen and she curtsied in the line of ladies to signal the end of the set. He took her hand on his and led her toward Claudia.

"I will wish for the honor of your hand for the waltz after supper, my love," he said, relishing the chance to use the endearment. He bowed to her and raised her hand to his lips while Claudia looked on with a smile. "You will reserve it for me?"

"A waltz?" she said. "Oh yes. But I cannot think my hand will be so in demand, my lord, that you need to *reserve* the set with me."

There was no chance for further conversation. Sir John Symonds, Claudia's eldest brother, had arrived to solicit the hand of the Marchioness of Staunton for the quadrille that was to follow.

She looked endearingly startled, her husband saw.

Charity had made a discovery during the ball—two actually. The one was that the Marchioness of Staunton was a very important person indeed and more gentlemen wished to dance with her than there were sets in the evening. She amused herself with wondering how many of the same gentlemen would even notice her existence if she could suddenly appear at the ball as the person she had been just the week before—and clad in her gray silk.

The other discovery was of far greater significance and she longed to discuss it with someone, but Claudia, her obvious choice of confidant, was always in company with other people between sets, and so was she, Charity, for that matter.

Charles had eyes for Lady Marie Lucas. And Lady Marie Lucas had eyes for Charles. They danced the second set together and watched each other covertly during every set that followed it—all of which each of them danced with other partners. At supper they sat close enough to exchange some conversation even though they were not supper partners.

They were just perfect for each other. All of Charity's maternal and matchmaking instincts came to the fore. Penny, she thought, would recognize the gleam in her eye and begin to protest—she tried to hide the gleam in her eye. They were close in age, they were both beautiful people, and they were probably friends. Had not she heard that the Earl of Tillden had brought his family to Enfield a number of times over the years? Charles and Marie had probably been playmates. He was three years older than she. He had probably been her hero. And he had probably been protective of her. She wondered when childhood friendship had blossomed into love. And she wondered too if the Earl of Tillden would countenance a match between his only daughter and the youngest son of a duke—a mere cavalry lieutenant.

She had been woolgathering at the supper table and was not giving her partner the attention that was his due. She was brought back to the present when she met her husband's eyes across the room. He looked his usual cold, arrogant self, staring at her with pursed lips and hooded eyes. But he did not deceive her for a moment. The incident with the topaz necklet had shaken him dreadfully—far more than it had her. It had shaken him to the very roots, exposing wounds that he had covered over and hidden from sight for so long that doubtless he had thought them long healed.

And there was her father-in-law, sitting with the Earl of Tillden and two ladies whose identities she had forgotten, with the identical haughty, shuttered look on his face. How foolish human nature was sometimes. But she was back to woolgathering. She smiled and turned her attention to the conversation at her table.

The waltz she had promised to reserve for her husband came directly after supper. There had never been waltzes at any of the assemblies at home, but Philip had learned the steps elsewhere and had come home and demonstrated them, first with her and then with Penny and finally with Mary. They had all made very merry with the foolish dance. And she had dreamed ever since of waltzing in a real ballroom with a real partner—brothers did not qualify as real partners. Her husband, on the other hand, was as real as any partner could be.

"I know the steps of the waltz," she told him as they took their places on the floor, "but I have never danced it. I hope I will not disgrace you and trip all over your toes or mine."

"You will merely provide me with an excuse for holding you closer," he said.

She wished she had not developed the annoying habit of blushing hotly at the merest suggestion of a compliment. She had done it earlier when he had made that grossly flattering remark about the relative beauty of the pearl necklace and its wearer. She did it again now. There was something in his eyes—a slight drooping of the eyelids. She recognized the look actually. She had learned something last night about sexual tension.

"I shall try not to make it necessary," she said.

His face remained immobile. But his eyes smiled. It was a wicked, knee-weakening expression. She should, she thought very much too late, have allowed him to hurry her back to London as he had wanted to do earlier.

She need not have worried about the dance. After the first few faltering steps she picked up the rhythm of the waltz without any trouble at all. How could she not do so when she had such a superb partner? He twirled her about the perimeter of the ballroom and she could almost imagine that her feet did not touch the floor. She had never in her life felt so exhilarated, she was sure. And not just exhilarated. His eyes held hers, breaking contact only occasionally to roam over her face and her shoulders. And that strange smile lingered there. Those very dark eyes of his had lost their disturbing opaque quality again.

"Has anyone reserved the next set with you?" he asked

when she was beginning to feel regret at the knowledge that the set must be almost at an end.

She shook her head. She had not missed a single set, but apart from this one, none had been reserved ahead of time.

"Then you will remain with me," he said. "And since at Enfield strict rules of etiquette must be observed and I dare not dance a third set even with my wife, we will go outside, my lady. We will stroll down to the lake. Unless you are reluctant to drag yourself from the festivities for half an hour, that is."

Her first foolish thought was that it would be quite improper to be alone with him. For she knew from long experience when a gentleman merely wanted to take a little air with the lady of his choice and when he hoped to take more than just a little air. The Marquess of Staunton intended to take liberties with her person.

Her second foolish thought was that she was afraid to let him kiss her. It was extremely foolish in light of what they had done together in the privacy of his bed the night before—three separate times—and in light of the fact that she was his wife. But somehow, strangely—she would not at all have been able to explain the feeling—there was something vastly different about lying with her husband and walking out into the moonlight with him while a ball was in progress. Walking out was infinitely more dangerous.

And every bit as tempting.

And just as impossible to resist.

"Fresh air and a stroll will be very pleasant, my lord," she said.

That smile in his eyes took on a dimension of true amusement. "You look," he said, "as if you are agreeing to attend your own execution."

"Oh," she said and felt her blush return with full heat. He knew that she knew he was taking her outside to kiss her. She glanced at his mouth. She had felt it once—at their wedding—coming to rest lightly beside her own mouth. It had shocked her to her toenails. What would it feel like directly against her own? It was very silly to feel breathless when she had received his body right inside her own four times in all.

But a kiss was different. She felt breathless. And the music was coming to an end. Yes, there was no doubt about it. The dance had finished.

They would stay for dinner and for the ball, she had said. They would not run away. They would stay and show his family a thing or two about courage. Well, they had stayed, and even his grace would have to agree that all had gone smoothly enough. The ball was a grand success. It could almost compare to a London squeeze. He doubted that anyone had refused the invitation.

The point had been made. Tomorrow he would return to London and set his own life and his wife's in order—separately. Tonight was done with as far as he was concerned. Tomorrow had not yet come. Between the two times there was now, tonight. He had not yet decided if he would invite her to his bed again. He wanted her, of course. He guessed it would take some time for his sexual craving for her to die. He would have to work on it. But he would just as soon resist the temptation to have her tonight. If he had her once, he would want her again, and each time he would be in danger of impregnating her.

He wanted something different out of tonight. Something— he could not think of a word to describe what he wanted. Actually there was a word but he was unwilling to use it even in his own mind. He wanted some warmth, some human closeness, some tenderness, some—romance. There, the word had come unbidden. He wanted a little romance. He mocked himself with both the word and the feeling it evoked in him. But it was what he wanted.

And so he invited her to walk to the lake with him after their waltz. He saw in her eyes that she understood him perfectly. He found it somewhat disturbing that within just a few days she had developed the uncanny knack of getting into his head with him as no one else had since the days when Will had been his closest crony. And even Will had not been so unerring in his understanding. He also saw in her eyes, of course, the mirror of his own feelings. She too wanted some romance tonight. It was an alarming realization. He should have run a mile from it. He should have danced with someone else and turned her over to another partner. He should have decided quite firmly to go to his bedchamber at the end of the ball and lock his door.

Instead he led her out through the French doors into the coolness of the evening, where several couples were strolling. He took her away from the terrace and the lights of the house, across the lawn toward the lake. He took her hand and linked his fingers with hers. Her hand was warm and smooth and curled firmly about his. When they were beyond the sight of anyone who might have been watching, he released her hand, twined his arm about her waist, and drew her against his side. After a moment's hesitation she set her arm about his waist. Her head came to rest against his shoulder. They had not said a word to each other since leaving the ballroom.

It could not have been a more perfect night for such a stroll. The air was cool but not at all cold. There was hardly a breeze. The sky was clear and star-studded. The moon was shining in a broad band across the water of the lake. They stopped walking when they were close to the bank.

"Have you ever seen anything more beautiful?" she asked with a sigh after a lengthy, perfectly comfortable silence.

"Yes," he said. "I have only to turn my head to see it." He turned his head and his mouth brushed against her hair.

"Where did you learn such foolish gallantries?" she asked, amusement rather than censure in her voice.

"Here at Enfield," he said. "Today and yesterday and the day before." *Steady,* he told himself. *Say nothing you will forever regret. Steady.*

She said nothing.

"Will and I used to sneak out sometimes at night," he said. "I can remember swimming here on at least one occasion. Even now I dread to think what would have happened to us if we had been caught."

"Or if you had had cramps," she said.

"I suppose," he said, "rules like the one forbidding children to go out alone at night are made for their own good, are they not?"

"Usually," she said.

"And I suppose I will be as drearily prohibitive with my own children," he said.

She did not answer him.

He winced inwardly. "If having children of my own were in my plans," he said. "But childhood can be a golden age despite prohibitions and punishments. I am sorry you had no brothers and sisters of your own."

"I had companions," she said. "I had a happy childhood."

"I am glad of it," he said, tightening his arm a little. "I would not like to think of you being lonely."

And then he felt lonely himself. He was here with her, co-cooned against present loneliness, but there was a strong awareness that tomorrow everything would be different. They would be traveling back to London. And after that their separate lives would begin. He would be married to her for the rest of his life, but he would probably never be with her like this again, just standing quietly in the moonlight, gazing across a calm lake. In harmony with another living person.

There was only tonight.

The anticipation of loneliness washed over him.

When he turned her in his arms, she tipped back her head and looked up at him with those very large blue eyes of hers—though he could not really see their color in the moonlight. He did not kiss her—not immediately. He was afraid to kiss her. He did not know what lay on the other side of a kiss. He was not sure he would be able to regain command of himself and his life once he had kissed her, though he could not quite make sense of his fear.

He held her against him with one arm and ran the knuckles of the other hand softly along her cheek and down beneath her chin to hold it up.

"Why did you not let me see on that day that you are beautiful?" he asked her.

"I have never been called beautiful before," she said. "I wanted the position."

"My quiet brown mouse," he said. He was rubbing the pad of his thumb very gently over her lips. He heard her swallow. "Have you ever been kissed, little mouse?"

"No." It was just a whisper of sound.

She had been bedded, but she had never been kissed. He had bedded, but he had rarely kissed. He moved his lips so close to hers that he could feel the warmth from them.

"Is this a lovely enough setting for the first?" he asked her. "Is the moment right? Is it the right man?"

"Yes." When she spoke the word, her lips brushed his.

He touched her with his lips—barely touched. He felt warmth and softness and sweet invitation. He felt her breath on his cheek. He moved his lips, parted them slightly, feeling her, feeling what she did to him. Not to his body. He expected his body to react predictably, but it did not do so. He felt what she did to his heart, or whatever unknown part of him was denoted by the name of a mere organ.

He wrapped his free arm about her shoulders, pushed his lips more firmly against hers, tasted her, was warmed by her, soothed by her, healed by her.

He knew all about tongue play. There had been a time when he had practiced it, enjoyed it. He did not touch her with his tongue or open his mouth. She parted her own lips only sufficiently to give him the softness and the warmth of her very essence. This was not a sexual encounter. He was right to have feared it. He raised his head and looked down at her.

"Thank you," he heard himself say.

He watched her eyes fill with tears and knew instinctively that they were not tears of grief or of anger or of disappointment. He drew her head to his shoulder and held it there for several minutes while she relaxed against him.

He was not after all in love with her, he thought, and he felt terror clutch at him. That was not it at all. He wished it were.

Being in love was a youthful, essentially shallow thing. He was not in love with his wife.

He loved her.

"I had better take you back to the ballroom," he said.

"Yes." She drew away from him and looked at him speculatively. The tears were long gone. "Will you do something for me? Please?"

"Yes," he said.

"Will you come to the library with me," she said, "and wait there while I—until I come back?"

He searched her eyes but she offered no explanation. He would ask for none. He had said yes.

"Yes," he said again, "I will."

She frowned for a moment, but when he took her hand she twined her fingers about his and walked by his side toward the house and the library.

Tonight he would do anything in the world for her.

Tomorrow he would begin to set her free.

Chapter 15

Charity was beginning to realize the enormity of the mistake she had made. She had agreed quite cold-bloodedly to a marriage that was not really a marriage just for the sake of money and security. It was a horrible sin she had committed. *I thought you were a fortune hunter*—Charles's words had haunted her all day. She had married on the very foolish assumption that her feelings would be no more engaged during a few weeks of a temporary marriage than they would have been during a brief period of employment as a governess. But her feelings had become involved with almost everyone at Enfield.

And now she knew that she was to suffer the ultimate punishment for her sin and for her foolishness. Her feelings were very deeply engaged in a much more personal way than just a concern for a family that was living in its own self-made hell.

She had experienced the ultimate embrace on her wedding night and again last night. But she had perhaps been too involved in the wonder of physical sensation on those occasions to feel the full impact of what was happening to her heart. She had understood with blinding clarity during that kiss at the lake. It had been exquisitely sweet, totally different from what she had expected. She had expected passion and had found tenderness. Tenderness was not something she would have associated with the Marquess of Staunton if she had not experienced it there in his arms and felt it in his lips. His lips had even trembled against her own.

She was not in a dream as they walked back up the lawn toward the house. She knew what was ahead for her, and the prospect was daunting to say the least. But there was tonight. And tonight all things seemed possible. It was a magical night, set apart from real time. And so she had suggested, quite impulsively, that he come to the library with her and wait there.

But there was magic elsewhere too.

She stopped walking suddenly, squeezing her husband's hand a little tighter as she did so.

"Look," she whispered. Perhaps she ought not to have drawn his attention to what she saw, but she sensed that he too was in a mellow mood.

Not far from the house, but hidden from it by the particularly massive trunk of an oak tree, a man in dark evening clothes stood face-to-face with a woman in a delicate white dress, his hands at her waist, her body arched toward his. Even as Charity watched, they drew closer together and kissed. Charles and Marie.

"They are bound only for heartache," the marquess said softly, drawing her firmly onward again. "He may be a duke's son, but he is only a younger son—hardly a worthy substitute for the heir, for whom she has been groomed. Her father will never allow it." He sounded more sad than cynical.

"Perhaps he can be persuaded," she said. "Charles is such a wonderful young man. My guess is that they have been friends all their lives and that they have loved each other for a year or more. Maybe all will turn out well for them."

"You must be a person who believes implicitly in the happily-ever-afters at the end of fairy tales," he said, though there was no censure in his voice.

"No," she said. "Oh no, I do not." She wished she could.

They walked the rest of the way in silence. The library was in darkness when they arrived there. He lit a branch of candles and turned to look at her, his eyebrows raised.

"I will not be long," she said. "You will wait?"

"I will wait," he said. His eyes, she saw—oh, his eyes almost frightened her. She could see right into their depths.

The Duke of Withingsby was strolling about the ballroom between sets, being graciously sociable. Charity stepped up to

his side while he was speaking with a group of neighbors—
there were so few names she remembered though she had paid
careful attention in the receiving line. She slipped an arm
through his, smiled at him and at them, and waited for the conversation to be completed.

"Well, my dear," he said then. "Your success seems assured."

"Father," she said, "come to the library with me?"

He raised haughty eyebrows.

"Please?" she said. "It is important."

"Is it indeed?" he said. "Important enough to take me from
my guests, ma'am? But very well. I shall not be sorely missed,
I suppose."

Her heart thumped as they walked from the ballroom to the
library. She had always had a tendency to meet problems
head-on and to try to maneuver other people to do the same
thing. Sometimes she had been successful, sometimes decidedly not. But she did not believe she had ever tackled anything
quite as huge as this. What if she was doing entirely the wrong
thing? What if she was precipitating disaster? But she did not
believe things could be much more disastrous than they already were. She could hardly make them worse.

Her husband was standing by the window, his back to it. He
did not move or say anything when she came in with his father. He merely pursed his lips. The duke also said nothing and
showed no sign of surprise beyond coming to a halt for a moment in the doorway.

"Father," she said, "will you have a seat? This one, by the
fireplace? It is more comfortable, I believe, than the one behind the desk. May I fetch you something? A drink?"

He seated himself in the chair she indicated, looked steadily
at his son and then at her. "Nothing," he said. "You may proceed to explain what this matter of importance is."

She stood by his chair and rested a hand lightly on his
shoulder. "Anthony," she said, "you brought me here two days
ago with the sole intention of hurting your father and destroy-
ing all his hopes and plans. You deliberately married a woman

far beneath you in rank and with the demeaning stigma of having worked for her living."

"I did not deceive you about my intentions," he said.

"And, Father," she said, "you have shown me affection yesterday and today with the sole purpose of annoying Anthony. Your plan culminated this evening in the gift of the topaz necklet, which you gave me to incense your son."

"The gift is still yours," he said. "I have not withdrawn it."

"You have both succeeded admirably," she said. "I have been hurt too in the process, but it is not my purpose here to complain of that fact. You have both succeeded in what you set out to do. You are both deeply hurt."

"You have judged the situation from the perspective of your own tender heart, my love," the marquess said. "His grace and I do not have tender hearts. I doubt we have hearts at all."

"Why did you choose your particular method of revenge?" she asked him. "You had alternatives. You could have refused to return to Enfield when summoned. You could have come and refused to marry Lady Marie. Either would have effectively shown Father that he was not to be allowed to control your life. Why did you choose such a drastic method?"

He did not answer for a long time. His eyes moved from her to his father and back again. A curious little half smile lifted the corners of his mouth.

"Because marrying the right woman has always been the single most important duty of the Dukes of Enfield and their heirs," he said. "Regardless of the personal inclinations of either the bride or the groom. If his bride has been chosen for him from birth, he marries her even if she feels the strongest aversion to him, even if her feelings are deeply engaged elsewhere. The right marriage, the right lineage for one's heirs, are everything. And so I married you, my lady, a woman who had answered my advertisement for a governess. Oh yes, sir. That is exactly the way it happened."

Charity had felt the duke's shoulder stiffen beneath her touch even before the end of his son's speech.

"And you, Father," she said. "Why did you choose to give

me the topaz necklet, of all the jewels that must be in your possession?"

Like his son, he did not answer quickly. There was a lengthy silence. "It was my wedding gift to her," he said at last. But the silence that succeeded his words was almost as long as the first. "My *love* gift to her. She spurned my love for over twenty years. She offered cold duty, and gave all her warmth, all her weakness, all her unhappiness to her children—most notably to her eldest son. She gave my gift to him before her death, and I whipped him for it, my lady, because I had never whipped her. Nor would have done so if she had lived as the ice in my veins for another twenty years. I whipped him for it again tonight by giving the gift to the wife with whom he had shown his contempt for me."

"You never knew the meaning of the word *love*," the marquess said.

"As you wish," his father said. "And so, my dear, you have contrived to bring us together here, my son and me, so that we may humbly beg each other's pardon and live in loving harmony for the few days that remain to me."

Yes, that had been her hope. It sounded silly expressed in the duke's cold, haughty voice.

"I told you we could not be expected to kiss and make up," the marquess said. "You are too tenderhearted, my love."

"The duchess is at the root of all this," she said. "You both loved her. And as a consequence you hate each other—or believe you do."

The marquess laughed. "He did not love her," he said. "All he did was keep her here when she would have enjoyed visits to London and the spas. All he did was burden her with yearly confinements, though she would cry to me in her anguish. She was nothing to him but a woman of the right rank and lineage to be bred until she could breed no more. My apologies, ma'am, for such plain speaking."

The duke's chin had lifted and his eyes had half closed. "She took your childhood and your youth away from you," he said. "She made a millstone of her own unwillingness or inability to adjust to a dynastic marriage and hung it about the neck of her eldest son. Her marriage and what happened within it were her concern—and mine. They should not have been the concern of any of her children, but she made them your concern. Your life has been shadowed by the demands she made on your love."

"It is a sad state of affairs," the marquess said, "when a woman can turn for love and understanding only to her children."

"It is sad for her children," the duke agreed. "But I have never spoken one word of criticism of her grace until tonight and will never utter another. She was my duchess, my wife— and there is no more private relationship than that, Staunton. If you ever again speak critically of your own wife—as you did tonight in your description of the way you obtained her hand—then you are not only a fool, but also a man without honor."

They gazed at each other, stiff, cold, unyielding.

"I think," Charity said, "that we must return to the ball. I can see that nothing more can be achieved here. I am sorry for it. And your lives are the poorer for it. But perhaps you will each remember the other's pain and the other's love."

"I believe, sir," the marquess said, "that you should withdraw to your bed rather than to the ballroom. My wife and I will see to the duties of host and hostess there. May I take you up myself?"

His father looked coldly at him. "You may ring for my valet," he said.

The marquess did so and they all waited in silence until the servant arrived to bear his master off to bed. The duke looked drawn and weary, leaning heavily on his man's shoulder. Charity kissed his cheek before he left.

"Sleep well, Father," she said.

Her husband did not immediately escort her back to the ballroom. When she turned to him after his father had left, he surprised her by catching her up in a fierce hug that squeezed all the air out of her. And then he found her mouth with his and kissed her with some of the passion she had expected at the lake.

"A crusading little mouse," he said, relaxing his hold on her. "With her head in the clouds and her feet in quicksand."

His face was stern and pale, but there was a certain tenderness in his voice. She had half expected a furious tirade.

"We have guests to entertain," she said.

"Yes, we do." He offered his arm and made her a courtly bow that had no discernible element of mockery in it.

Now more than ever he had to get away from Enfield. Tomorrow. Early. It was already early tomorrow. Yet he had not directed either his valet or his wife's maid to pack their things. It had just been too late after the ball to make such a cruel demand on his servants. Anyway, he supposed a very early start was out of the question. He would want to take his leave—of Charles and Marianne and Augusta, of Will. He would not run away this time without a word. He would want to take his leave of his father too.

He had been pacing the floor of his bedchamber. He stopped and closed his eyes. Perhaps they would remember each other's pain and each other's love, she had said. *My love gift to her,* his father had said of the topaz necklet. His mother had always claimed that his grace was cold through to the center of his heart. She had spoken openly of her husband thus to her son. Had she been mistaken? Had she *known* she was mistaken?

He had decided to spend the night alone. But his need for his wife gnawed at him. He did not believe he would be able to get through the night without her. Once they were back in London, once he had her settled in a new life, he would have to do without her for the rest of a lifetime. But tonight was different. After tonight, once he was away from Enfield, he would be able to cope alone again.

He could feel his resolution slip. Perhaps he would have held to it, he thought, if the need had been a sexual one. But it was not.

He tapped very gently on the door of her bedchamber and
eased it open carefully. If she was asleep, he decided, he
would leave her be. There was a long journey ahead. She
needed to sleep.

At first he did not see her. He could see only that the bed-
covers were thrown back from her bed and she was not there.
She was over by the window, the shawl about her shoulders
obscuring the white of her nightgown. She was looking back
over her shoulder at him.

"You cannot sleep?" he asked, walking toward her.

She shook her head. "Did I do the wrong thing?" she asked
him.

"No." He took her hands in his and warmed them with his
own. They were like blocks of ice. "And you must not blame
yourself for your lack of success. It was no simple or single
quarrel, as you have discovered. Our differences have been a
lifetime in the making. You tried. You had no obligation to
feel gentle emotions for anyone in this family, least of all for
my father and me, who have both used you ill. But you tried
anyway. I thank you. I will always remember your gentleness.
I believe his grace will too."

"He is so very ill," she said.

"Yes."

"You love him."

"Leave it," he said. "You are cold. Come to bed with me?"

"Yes," she said. "Yes, please." And she moved against him,
turned her head to rest on his shoulder, and relaxed with a
sigh. She was weary beyond the ability to sleep, he could tell.

If he had not felt her weariness, he would have made love to
her when he had taken her to his bed. It would not have occurred to him not to do so even though he had admitted to
himself that his need for her tonight was not sexual. But he
had felt her tiredness, and suddenly he was overwhelmed by
the need to give her something in return for what she had tried
to do for him this evening.

He drew her into his arms and against his body, wrapped the
bedclothes snugly about her, and kissed the side of her face.

"Sleep," he said. "I will have you warm in a moment. Just sleep. I forbid you to so much as think of sheep or their legs."

"Sheep," she murmured sleepily. "Who are they?"

She was asleep almost instantly—and so was he, he realized only a couple of hours later when his father's butler awoke him by appearing unannounced in his room.

He came awake with a start, and by sheer instinct pulled the covers up over his wife's shoulders. He remembered with some relief even as he did so that she was not naked.

"What is it?" he asked harshly and felt her jump in his arms.

"I did knock, my lord," the butler said. He was dressed, the marquess saw in the light of early dawn, but not with his usual immaculate precision. "It is his grace, my lord."

The marquess was out of bed without knowing how he had got out. "Ill?" he asked sharply. "He is ill?" He grabbed for his dressing gown, which he had tossed over the back of a chair before getting into bed.

"Yes, my lord," the butler said. "Brixton thought you should come, my lord." Brixton was his grace's valet.

"Has the physician been sent for?" the marquess asked, tying the sash of the dressing gown and moving purposefully toward the door as he did so. "Send for him immediately—and for Lord William. Have Lady Twynham and Lord Charles summoned. Lady Augusta may be left in her bed for now."

"Yes, my lord." The butler sounded uncharacteristically relieved to have responsibility lifted from his shoulders.

The marquess hurried from the room without a thought to his wife, who was lying awake in his bed.

His father had had a heart attack. There would be no recovery from this one. He was dying. That much was clear to his son the moment he hurried into his bedchamber. He lay on the bed, gasping for air. Every breath was labored. Brixton was flapping a large cloth in front of his face, trying to make more air available to him. The marquess chafed the duke's hands in a futile attempt to do something though he knew himself to be utterly helpless.

Time passed without his being aware of it. Marianne was in

the room, closely followed by Charles. Then Twynham was
there too, and Will and Claudia and Charity. Finally the physician appeared and they all stood back at the edges of the room
watching while he made his examination and straightened up
to give them the inevitable message simply by looking at them
and slightly shaking his head.

The Duke of Withingsby was dying.

"Fetch Lady Augusta," the marquess said, looking at Mrs.
Aylward, who was standing in the doorway.

"I will go," Charity said quietly. "I will bring her."

The duke was still breathing in audible gasps. But he was
conscious. His eyes were open.

"It is time to say good-bye," the marquess said, the fact reg-
istering on his mind that they were all—family, servants,
physician—looking to him for guidance. The duke was dying.
He was already the acting head of the family. "William? Claudia?"

They stepped up to the bed, Claudia chalk white, Will
scarcely less so. And then Marianne and Twynham, and after
them, Charles. The butler and housekeeper were nodded forward to say their farewells. Even through the numbness of
his mind, the marquess realized that this was the leave-taking
his father would want—something strictly formal and correct, his death like a well-orchestrated state occasion.

Charity had returned with a pale and clearly frightened Augusta. She clung to Charity's hand and shrank against her and
hid her face when Marianne would have taken her. And so it
was Charity who led her to the side of the bed.

"You must say good-bye to your father," Charity said gently. "He is looking at you, you see."

"Good-bye, sir," the child whispered.

But the marquess could see, and Charity could see, that his
grace's hand was pulling feebly at the bedcover.

"He would like you to kiss him," Charity said. "He would
like you to know that he loves you and that he leaves you in
the safe care of Anthony."

Augusta had to stand on her toes to lean far enough across

the bed to kiss her father on the cheek. "I will be a good girl for Anthony, sir," she said. "And I will work harder at my lessons." She hid her face against Charity's skirt.

"Father." Charity had taken that feeble hand in her own. "You have been kind to me. I thank you for your kindness. I will always remember it and you." And she bent over him, kissed his forehead, and smiled into his eyes. "With love," she added.

And then she bent down, picked Augusta up in her arms, and moved with her out into the anteroom of the bedchamber.

The marquess stepped forward and stood, his hands clasped at his back, gazing down at his father.

"Clear the room." The words were whispered and hoarse and breathless, but they were perfectly clear.

"Perhaps you would all wait outside for a few moments," the marquess said without looking away from his father's face.

They all left uncomplaining except for Marianne, who was muttering to Twynham that she was his grace's daughter and was being treated like a servant by her own brother.

The Duke of Withingsby was not a person one touched uninvited, and the invitation was rarely given. But the Marquess of Staunton looked down at the pale, limp hand on the covers and took his hands from his back so that he could gather it up in both his own. It was cold despite all his efforts to warm it a few minutes before.

"Father," he said, remembering even as he spoke the idea of a sentimental deathbed scene with which he had mocked his wife, "I have always loved you. Far too deeply for words. If I had not loved you, I could not have hated you. And I have hated you. I love you." He raised the hand briefly to his lips.

His grace's penetrating, haughty eyes, startlingly alive, regarded him out of the gray face and from beneath heavy lids. "You are my son," he managed to say. "Always my favorite son, as you were hers. You will have children of your own, my son. Your duchess will be a good mother and a good wife. You have made a fortunate choice. There will be mutual love in your marriage. I envy you. You have not succeeded in annoying me."

He could say no more. He closed his eyes. His son watched him for a while and then went down on his knees and rested his face on the bed close to his father's hand and wept. He felt foolish weeping for a man he had hated—and loved, but he was powerless to stop the painful sobs that tore at him. And then the hand lifted and came to rest on his head. It moved once, twice, and then lay still while the rasping breathing continued.

It felt like forgiveness, absolution, a blessing, a benediction, a healing touch. A father's touch. It felt like love. The marquess despised the feelings at the same time as he allowed them to wash over him. His father had touched him with love.

The nature of the breathing changed. He got to his feet and crossed to the door. It was time to summon the family back into the room. It was their right to witness the end. And the end was no more than minutes away.

Chapter 16

She sat on a chair in the anteroom with Augusta curled up on her lap. The child was not sleeping, but Charity had not taken her with everyone else back into the duke's room. It had been necessary for her to say good-bye to her father, to understand what was happening, but it was not necessary for her to witness the death. Charity smoothed her hand over the child's head and occasionally kissed her forehead.

Her husband was the first to come back out of the room. He came to stand in front of the chair and his eyes met Charity's. He looked pale, weary. He had been crying, she thought. She was glad he had cried. He came down on his haunches and set a hand on Augusta's head.

"He is gone, dear," he said in a voice of such gentleness that tears sprang to Charity's eyes. "He was peaceful. He will be happy now. He will be—with Mother."

Augusta opened her eyes, but she did not move or say anything.

"But you will still be safe," he said. "I will be here with you—always—and Will and Claudia and the boys will be close by. We will be a family. I held you, you know, when you were a baby. I was the first to hold you after you were born. I did not know it was possible to love anyone as much as I loved you. I had to go away soon after and stay away for a long time. But I always loved you. And now I am home again. We are brother and sister, but fortunately I am old enough to look after you and keep you safe almost like a father."

She gazed mutely at him, but Charity could feel that there

was less tension in her than there had been. In a few more minutes she would be sleeping.

"His grace knew he would have to leave you," the marquess continued. "He called me home so that I could look after you for him. Because he loved you, Augusta, and because he loved me. Because we were his children. Everything will be all right, dear. You may go back to sleep now. I will carry you to your bed and Charity will come with us." He looked at her and raised his eyebrows. She understood the silent communication and nodded. "She will stay with you and when you wake she will be there to bring you to me or to Will or Marianne or Charles. You are quite safe."

But as he got to his feet, the butler came out of the bedchamber. He cleared his throat.

"Your grace—" he began.

Charity watched her husband flinch before turning his head.

"The physician wishes to consult with you, your grace," the butler said.

"He will wait for five minutes," the Duke of Withingsby said, "until I have carried Lady Augusta to the nursery."

He lifted the half-sleeping child into his arms and waited while Charity got to her feet. This morning, she realized for the first time since the sound of her husband's voice had woken her with a start from a deep sleep, they were supposed to be on their way back to London. Today was to have marked the end of the charade, the beginning of the secure and wonderful life with her own family that she had dreamed of ever since her own father's death.

But today there was still a part to play—not even really a part. Augusta was going to need her today. There could be no more momentous event in a child's life than the death of a parent. Augusta's needs were going to have to take precedence over all else for today, and perhaps for longer than today. For some reason it seemed that the child was turning to her for comfort rather than to Marianne or Claudia.

And Anthony was going to need her today and perhaps for a few days beyond today. He had lost his father under difficult

circumstances. She suspected—and hoped—that he might
have realized his love for his father before it was too late. She
hoped that his father had been able to show some sign of his
own love. How foolish they had been, holding out until the
very end and perhaps even beyond the end. But there was a
look in his face, even apart from the evidence of tears, that
told her father and son had understood each other before they
were separated by eternity. They had been alone together for
all of five minutes.

He set Augusta down carefully on her bed, while both her
nurse and her governess hovered in the doorway. The nurse
was red-eyed from weeping—news traveled fast in a large
house. Augusta was already sleeping. He covered her snugly
with the blankets, and Charity was reminded of how he had
covered *her* just a few hours before and held her while she
slipped into an exhausted sleep. He straightened up and turned
to her. The servants had disappeared.

"You will stay with her?" he asked.

"Of course," she said.

She took an impulsive step forward and brushed back the
upside-down question mark of hair from his forehead. It fell
back almost immediately. She framed his face with her hands.

"I am sorry," she whispered. "I am so sorry, Anthony." And
she stood on her toes and kissed his lips.

He touched his hands to the backs of hers, held them against
his face for a moment, and then removed them, squeezing
them slightly as he did so.

"I am needed," he said and left the room.

It was only after he had left and she sat in the quiet room,
watching the sleeping child, that she began to be plagued by
terrible feelings of guilt.

It was an incredibly busy and wearying day. He had lived
his own independent life for eight years and was accustomed
to responsibilities. But finding himself suddenly the Duke of
Withingsby a mere three days after returning to Enfield, with
seemingly dozens of people turning to him for direction, was

stressful to say the least. There were the funeral arrangements to be made, letters to be written, arrangements for the guests who would arrive from some distance away for the funeral to be set in motion, early visits of condolence to be received, ordinary, unavoidable matters of household and estate business to be dealt with, the Earl of Tillden and his family to assure that of course they were perfectly welcome to stay on—and endless other tasks.

There was the shock of grief to be dealt with—his own grief and that of his brothers and sisters. Charles was perhaps the most inconsolable. The duke found his brother during the afternoon sitting in the conservatory, sobbing into his hands. But there was not the obligation to expend emotional energy on comforting him. Lady Marie Lucas sat beside him, patting his back with one small hand while the other clutched a lace handkerchief and dabbed at the tears on her own cheeks.

Augusta, released from both the nursery and the schoolroom, stayed close to Charity all day, though she came to sit on his lap during a brief spell of relaxation after a visit from the rector and his wife.

"Are you really going to stay with me?" she asked.

"Mmm." He wrapped his arms about her.

"And are you really going to be like a papa?" she asked. "Like William is with Anthony and Harry?"

"Do you want a papa?" he asked her. "Or would you prefer a big brother?"

She did not hesitate. "I want a papa," she said.

"Then I am he," he said. His mind flashed back briefly to the life he had been living and the attitudes he had held with great firmness just the week before. But that life was dead. He accepted the fact. This was not something he could fight against. He was not even sure that he *wanted* to fight. Some realities were too stark to be denied.

"And will Charity be like my mama?" she asked.

He closed his eyes. Ah. How did one cocoon a child against what would seem like cruelty? How could she ever understand?

"Do you want her as a mama?" he asked.

"Jane and Louisa and Martin have Marianne," she said, "and Anthony and Harry have Claudia. Now I have someone too. She is all my own."

"She will keep you safe," he said, kissing her forehead. "She loves you."

"Yes, I know," she said. "She told me. His grace loved me too. He never said so, but Charity says that some people cannot say it or even show it, though that does not mean they do not feel it. He always looked after me and he brought you home to look after me and be like a papa to me after he was gone. I could see this morning that he loved me. He wanted me to kiss him. His face was cold."

"He loved you, dear," he said. "You were his own little girl. And now you are mine."

He wondered how much time his father had spent with her, this child who had killed his wife. Not much, he guessed. She envied Will's children because they had a papa. But she would not remember their father with bitterness. Charity had seen to that.

It was a brief encounter. There were people and details to occupy every moment of his time until well after dinner. He wondered vaguely during the meal how it was that everyone except Augusta and his wife had been able to lay hands on black clothes so easily. They were all in deep mourning. Charity wore one of her brown dresses and looked endearingly shabby and pretty. Claudia's modiste, he heard as part of the dinner conversation, was busy making his wife a black dress to wear tomorrow.

He sat at the head of the table and looked about him. Oh yes, a week had wrought enormous changes. It amazed him now that he had imagined—only a few days before—that he could return here and be untouched by it all. A part of him had known. Something deep within had known that he needed to bring Charity with him if he was to stand even a chance of retaining his own identity. But what he had not understood—or what he had not admitted—was what that identity was. He had not known who he was. He knew now. He was Anthony Earheart, an inextricable part of this family. He always had been, even during the eight years of his self-imposed exile.

He had never been free of them. Yet strangely, now on the day when all freedom, all choices had been taken from him beyond recall, he felt freer than he had ever felt in his life. And it was not, he reflected, because his father was gone and could no longer exercise power over him. It was quite the opposite. It was because he had now become both himself and his father's son. His father, he realized, as he had realized this morning, had set him free to live with both those identities. His father had given him love at the last and had set him free.

Your duchess will be a good mother and a good wife. You have made a fortunate choice. There will be mutual love in your marriage.

He gazed down the table to his wife, his duchess, who was speaking kindly to a teary-eyed Countess of Tillden. Yes. Oh yes. But she would have to be wooed, not commanded. If he loved her—and he did—then he must set her free, as he had agreed to do. And he must hope that she would freely choose to remain with him, to be his wife, to bear his children, to share a mutual love with him for the rest of their days.

He was not without hope. She possessed more warmth, more charm, more love than anyone else he had known—how first impressions could deceive! He could still feel the warmth of her hands framing his face and the look of deep sorrow— for him—in her eyes and the soft kiss she had placed on his lips. No, he was not without hope. But he had lost some of his arrogant self-assurance in the past few days, among other things. He was by no means certain of her. There was anxiety to temper the hope.

Finally, well after dinner, he was free. He had been sitting with his father, who had been laid out in his bed and looked as if he slept peacefully. But Will had come and clasped his shoulder firmly and warmly and told him he would keep watch for a while.

"Go and relax, Tony," he said. "You look as if you are ready to collapse."

The duke nodded and got to his feet—and impulsively hugged his brother, who returned the embrace.

Augusta was in bed, he was told, closely watched over by her nurse. But Charity was not in the drawing room with everyone else. She had gone outside for a walk, he was informed.

"She did not want company," Charles said, "though I offered to go with her, Tony. She looked exhausted. She has been very good to Augusta all day."

"But she will want your company," Claudia said with a smile. "She has been watching you anxiously all day long. And you look as tired as she. I believe she said she was going to wander down by the lake."

"Yes, she did," Marianne said. "And she has indeed been very good to Augusta, Tony. Her experience as a governess must have helped her, of course."

Marianne had thawed, he thought as he left the house. But she had been unable to resist that final little jibe.

He found his wife down by the lake. It was an evening very similar to the last, though she wore a shawl about her shoulders. She was sitting on the bank, gazing out across the moonlit water. He sat beside her after she had looked up and recognized him, and took one of her hands in his.

"Tired?" he asked.

"A little." Despite the peaceful picture she had presented, sitting there on the bank, she was not relaxed.

"This is all too much for you," he said. "I am sorry. It was not part of our bargain, was it?"

But she only stiffened further. "It was all my fault," she said, her voice flat.

"What?" He dipped his head so that he could look into her face.

"I killed him," she said. "Have you not realized that? With my crusading zeal, as you put it. I forced him to the library last night. I forced him to that scene of bitterness and futility. It

was none of my business. As you just said, we have a bargain.
I am not really your wife. This is not really my family. But I
interfered anyway. I put him under that stress. And a few
hours later he was dead."

Oh God! "No." He squeezed her hand very tightly. "No,
Charity. No. You are in no way responsible for his death. I
was summoned here because he was dying. His physician told
me two days ago that he could go at any time. He had a perilously bad heart. It failed him early this morning. He died. His
death had nothing whatsoever to do with you."

"He had been told to rest," she said.

"Advice he constantly ignored," he reminded her. "He knew
he was dying, Charity. That is why he swallowed his pride and
called me home. But he would not die in weakness. He wanted
to die as he had lived, and his wish was granted. You did not
precipitate his death. But you did do something very wonderful."

"I killed him," she said.

"I told him I loved him," he said, "that I always had. And of
course I spoke the truth, though even I had not fully understood that until you forced me to face it. He spoke to me. He
did not tell me that he loved me—not in so many words. But
he called me his son, his favorite son. And he set his hand on
my head, Charity. It may seem a slight thing, but I cannot describe what it meant to me, feeling his hand there. He tried to
stroke my head but he was too weak. He might have shouted
out that he loved me and it would not have had the effect on
me that the touch of his hand had. He touched me because you
had made him admit something to himself. He was so very
nearly too late—we both were—but he was not. Because you
forced that confrontation last evening. You did it only just in
time."

She gazed out across the water and said nothing. But he
could feel from the touch of her hand that some of the tension
had gone.

"He was right, you know," he said after a few minutes of silence. "I loved my mother and resented her. I felt forced to

love her. She leaned heavily on me—even when I was just a young lad. I was only twenty when she died. She was very unhappy. She told me about the man she had loved and wished to marry. She told me how she was forced to marry my father. She even told me how he forced his attentions on her whenever she was not increasing. She used to cry to me and tell me that soon she would be increasing again because he was coming to her room each night."

He paused. He felt disloyal saying this aloud, even thinking it. But perhaps he owed his father something too. "He was right," he said. "She ought not to have burdened her own child with her unhappiness. She ought not to have spoken of the intimacies of her marriage with her son. Her confidences, the necessity of comforting her, of hating him, were a heavy burden to me. I did not even realize it until last night."

"Your mother demanded too much of your love," his wife said, "and your father demanded too little. Unfortunately we find it difficult to see our parents as people. We expect perfection of them. He did love her. That was very clear last evening."

"Perhaps she was as much at fault as he in their marriage," he said. "Perhaps even more so. She punished him all her married life for having been forced into an arranged marriage. She made no effort to make a workable match of it. Do you think that is what she did?"

"Be careful not to allow your feelings to swing to the opposite extreme," she said. "She was unhappy, Anthony. And despite what she told you, you cannot know what happened in the privacy of your parents' marriage. No one can know except the two of them, and they are both gone."

"I believe," he said, "she might have kept us from him. He was reserved and he was stern and—he said it last evening—he would never retaliate by saying anything against her. He never did, you know. She taught us to fear him and hate him, to think of him as a man cold to the heart."

"Anthony," she said, "you loved her. Remember that you loved her. She had a hard life. All those children, all those losses."

"I wonder," he said, "if you have ever taken anything from life. Have you always been a giver? You have given my family extraordinary gifts."

But she pulled her hand from his and jumped to her feet. She brushed the grass from her skirt. "Of course I am a taker," she said. "I am going to take a home and a carriage and servants and six thousand pounds a year from you for the rest of my life—for doing nothing but enjoying myself and basking in an unexpected security. I can scarcely wait."

He got to his feet too. "You are my wife," he said. "You will be kept in comfort for the rest of your life by virtue of that fact. That is not taking. It is the nature of marriage."

She was tense again and quite noticeably weary. It was no time to woo her in the way he planned to woo her once these difficult days were past, once the funeral was over.

"You are tired," he said, "and so am I. Let me take you to bed."

"With you?" she said. "Like last night?"

"Yes," he said, "if you wish. Or to make love first if you wish. It would not be disrespectful to my father. Life always needs to be reaffirmed in the face of death."

"You have a comfortable shoulder," she said, half smiling, "and safe arms. I slept so peacefully last night. You did too. Just for tonight again, then, if you will."

"Come." He set an arm about her waist and she relaxed readily against him as they made their way back to the house.

But after all, when they were in bed together, they made love by unspoken assent before they slept—he had never experienced silent communication with any other woman, but with her it seemed unerring. They loved slowly, warmly, deeply. She sighed into relaxation when she was finished, and he pressed himself deep and for the first time in his life quite consciously let his seed flow into the woman with whom he mated.

He had relieved what was undoubtedly her chief anxiety. It had seemed to her as clear as the nose on her face that she had killed her father-in-law. But of course she had not. Her husband had quite put her mind at rest on that issue.

The other anxiety gnawed at her less urgently. But it was not one she could share and not one she could talk herself out of. Quite the contrary. Her sense of guilt grew by the hour, it seemed, and there were constant reminders.

I thought you were a fortune hunter.

That had started it. She *was* a fortune hunter. She had committed a dreadful sin—oh, more than one. They multiplied with alarming speed. She had made a mockery of one of the most sacred institutions of civilization. She had married and had repeated all the marriage vows, knowing very well that she had no intention whatsoever of keeping most of them. She had done it all for money. Oh, she could try to rationalize what she had done by telling herself that she had done it for Phil and Penny and the children. But when it came to calling a spade simply a spade, then she must admit that she had done it for money.

And so the one great sin had led her into a whole series of deceptions. Her father-in-law had guessed much of the truth, but he had not realized that the marriage was only a temporary one. He had probably died in the belief that soon there would be a new heir to the dukedom. Perhaps too he had died in the comfort of the belief that Augusta would have both a mother figure and a father figure to watch over her as she grew to womanhood.

She hated to think of the deception she had perpetrated against Augusta. Augusta, she realized within a day of the old duke's death, *loved* her. It had happened suddenly but quite, quite thoroughly. Augusta was unwilling to leave her side. She would do so only to spend a little time with Anthony. Irreparable harm might come to Augusta when the truth came out.

And then there was Charles, who treated her with the easy affection of a brother, and Claudia and William, who were almost as affectionate. Even Marianne had begun to treat her with civility. Marianne's children and Claudia's always brightened considerably whenever she came in sight.

She felt a total fraud. She *was* a fraud. And all the servants called her *your grace* and treated her with marked respect, and all the neighbors who called on them with condolences addressed her by her title and looked upon her with almost awed respect.

She was a fraud.

She was a fortune hunter.

And since she was in the business of calling spades spades, then she might as well simply admit that she was a sinner.

There was only one thing she could do. The realization came to her gradually in the days leading up to the funeral, but finally it was firm in her mind. There was only one thing. It would not right all the wrongs—she thought in particular of Augusta. But it would show her sorrow for what she had done. It was the only honorable thing to do, the only thing that might in time give her a quiet conscience.

And so late on the afternoon of the funeral itself, when many of the guests had left and the few remaining ones sat in the drawing room, while Augusta slept in the nursery after the emotions of the morning, while the duke was riding with Charles for some relaxation, Charity walked down the driveway to the village, a small valise in her hand. There was a stagecoach leaving from the inn—she had checked the time.

She was going home—alone. She had left behind a note for her husband, but she had not named her destination. If she had, he would have sent her money—six thousand pounds a year. If she had, he would have sent his man of business to make sure that she had a suitable home and all the trappings that had been mentioned in the agreement. He would have insisted on paying for everything. And perhaps she would have found it impossible to resist. Perhaps she would have been tempted not to resist as much as she was able.

She had married and performed all the duties of her marriage while it lasted. Perhaps in time she would be able to forgive herself for marrying in the full knowledge that she would be called upon to fulfill those duties for only a short while. But she would never be able to forgive herself or live with herself if she accepted payment for what she had done.

Marriage was not employment.

Marriage was involvement and caring and loving. Marriage was—commitment.

She had thought him wrong when he had said she was a giver and not a taker. But perhaps after all he was right. She could not become a taker. She would lose her own soul.

Perhaps in time she would be able to forgive herself.

Chapter 17

It seemed incredible to the Duke of Withingsby when he thought about it later that his wife had left him during the afternoon of his father's funeral, yet he did not discover it until the following morning.

He returned from a long ride and a lengthy talk with Charles, feeling somewhat refreshed. But he understood that it had been a stressful few days for all his family. Charity had retired to her room for a rest, he was told. He hoped she would sleep and feel the better for it. He was busy with the remaining guests for the rest of the day. He did not call at his wife's dressing room to escort her down to dinner. When she had not appeared in the drawing room by the time dinner was announced, he sent a servant to inquire. Her maid had been told, he was informed, that her grace would not need her for the rest of the day, that she did not wish to be disturbed.

He did not disturb her. He made her excuses to his guests. She had given tirelessly of herself ever since her arrival at Enfield. They had all made demands on her energies, most notably Augusta and himself. She must be exhausted. He did not go up to check on her himself—he was afraid of disturbing her rest. And for the same reason he did not disturb her when he went to bed, though he did let himself quietly into her dressing room and noted that there was no light beneath the door of her bedchamber.

It was only when he went for a rather late breakfast the following morning, after attending to some other business first and discovered that she had not yet been down that he went to investigate. And then, of course, he discovered the letter she had left on her pillow. Not that it was on her pillow when he first saw it. Her maid was coming from her rooms with it in her hand, a look of fright in her eyes. She curtsied and handed it to him after telling him where she had found it, and obeyed his nod of dismissal with alacrity.

"Your grace," his wife had written, "I will be leaving on the stagecoach from the village inn this afternoon. I hope you do not discover this soon enough to come after me. I know you will wish to because we signed an agreement and being an honorable gentleman, you will wish to honor it. But please do not come. And please do not try to find me. I release you from your part of our agreement. I do not wish to receive payment for what I have done. It would be distasteful and distressful to me."

He closed his eyes and drew a slow breath. He was still standing in the hallway outside her dressing room.

"I am taking with me as many of my own belongings as I can carry," he read when he looked back at the letter. "I cannot resist taking my ballgown too. I know you will not mind. And my pearls. They were a wedding gift, I believe, and there was a wedding. I will not feel guilty about taking them, then. They are so very beautiful. I am also taking some of the money I found in the top drawer of the desk in your study. I will need to pay for a ticket to where I am going and for food during the journey. Again, I do not believe you will mind. It is all I will ever take from you. Please tell Augusta that I love her. She will not believe you, but please, please find some way to persuade her to accept that it is true. I am, your grace, your obedient servant, Charity Duncan."

Charity *Duncan*. It was like a resounding slap across the face. He crumpled the letter in one hand and really felt for one alarmed moment that he was about to faint. She was Charity Earheart, Duchess of Withingsby. She was his wife—his to protect and support for the rest of his life and even beyond that if she survived him. Whether she chose to live with him or live separately from him, she would always be his. She had written of honor. How did she expect him to retain his honor when she had done this to him?

Where would she have gone? His mind scrambled about in confusion for her probable destination. He was alarmed when he realized that he would not know where in England to begin looking for her. There were only her old lodgings in London. She would have given them up. It was very unlikely she would go back there. No one there would know where she had gone. He doubted she had even told them about Enfield. She had left on yesterday afternoon's coach. The devil! Had no one seen her leave Enfield—on foot at a guess—and thought to comment to anyone else on that fact or on her failure to return?

His first instinct was to have a bag packed, to call out his carriage, and to set out after her. It seemed not to matter in that first panicked moment that he would not know where he was headed. He would stop at the inn. Perhaps the innkeeper would know her destination—though it might not be her final destination, of course. Somehow he would follow her trail.

But instinct, he realized, closing his eyes and drawing steadying breaths again—he was *still* standing outside her dressing room—could not always be followed. He could not rush off into the horizon. There were things to be done. A few guests were leaving after breakfast. He must see them on their way. Tillden and his wife and daughter were to leave later. He had promised Charles that he would have a word with Tillden first. He had arranged to have a conference with Will later in the day so that they might set up a working relationship concerning the running of the estates. He had agreed to talk with him at the dower house so that Augusta would have a chance to play with the boys. He had been planning to invite Charity to go with him. There was—ah, there were a thousand and one things that must be attended to today.

Besides, she did not want him to go after her. She did not want to accept his support. She wanted to sever all ties with him. He did not know how much money he had slipped into that drawer in his desk. But he would wager that she had carefully counted out only just enough to purchase her ticket and the most meager of meals. She had taken her pearls, but he knew beyond a doubt that she would not have taken the topaz necklet, which was lying, somewhat incautiously perhaps, in a box on top of that same desk in his study. He had been intending to give it back to her during a private moment—as a gift from both his father and himself.

She did not want him. She preferred freedom and independence and poverty and the life of a governess to the alternative of being in some way beholden to him. He felt blinded by hurt.

Ah yes, he had been right in his assessment of her the evening after his father's death. She was a giver. She gave of herself with cheerful, warm generosity. She was not in any way a taker. But did she not understand that there could be a degree of selfishness in being all give and no take? Did she not understand how he would feel at the moment of reading her letter? Did she imagine that he would sag with relief? That he would cheerfully forget her and get on with the rest of his life?

He hated her suddenly.

He saw his guests on their way. He explained to them that his wife was indisposed and sent her apologies. He invited the Earl of Tillden into the library, explained to him that Lord Charles Earheart was to receive a sizable settlement according to the terms of his father's will and that he himself was preparing to gift his brother with one of his estates, considerably smaller than Enfield, but consistently prosperous. Lord Charles had just the day before expressed his intention of selling his commission and of living as a gentleman, administering his own estate. Lord Charles had asked of his eldest brother—and been granted—permission to pay his addresses to Lady Marie Lucas. He asked permission now through his brother to address himself to the lady's father.

Charles, the duke did not deem it necessary or even wise to explain to the earl, had had a fondness for Lady Marie all his life, and a deep passion for her for at least the past two years— a love that was reciprocated. His belief in the hopelessness of that love, since she had been intended for the Marquess of

Staunton, had precipitated his decision to take a commission in the cavalry.

The Earl of Tillden blustered and bristled and was clearly offended at the offer of a younger son when he had expected the eldest. But Lord Charles *was* the son and brother of a duke, and he was a wealthy man and was to be a considerable landowner. The boy might talk to him, he agreed at last. He remained in the library while the duke went in personal search of his brother. He was not hard to find. He was pacing, pale-faced and stubborn-jawed and anxious-eyed within sight of the library door.

"He will listen to you," the duke told him and watched his brother draw in a deep breath and hold it. "Remember who you are, Charles. You are no man's inferior. You are our father's son. Good luck."

Charles walked purposefully toward the library, looking as grimly courageous as he might have looked if he had known for certain that an axman complete with ax and chopping block was awaiting him on the other side of the door.

Augusta could not simply be told that Charity was indisposed. She had to be told at least some of the truth. Charity had had to go away in a hurry, he told his sister while he was sitting on a low chair in the nursery holding her in the crook of his arm as she stood beside him. There was an aunt who was sick and needed her help. He was going to go too as soon as he was able to find out for himself how long the aunt would need her. If at all possible he would bring her back with him. But sometimes sicknesses could go on for a tediously long time.

He despised himself for not telling the full truth. If he could not find Charity, if he could not persuade her to come home with him and be his wife in total defiance of their agreement, then he was going to have difficulties indeed with Augusta. There would have to be further lies or the confession that he had lied today. But he could not bring himself to tell the truth, to let Augusta know that Charity had never had any intention of staying at Enfield and being a permanent sort of mother to her. It would be unfair to Charity to tell the truth. It would make her sound heartless—and that would be an enormous lie.

Sometimes truth and falsehood were hopelessly confusing things.

Two days passed before he left Enfield in pursuit of his wife. The earl and his family had left—Tillden had come to an agreement with Charles, and the young couple had been permitted fifteen minutes alone together, during which time it had been agreed they might come to an understanding, though of course there could be no formal betrothal until the year of Lord Charles's mourning was at an end. Lord and Lady Twynham had returned home with their children. Augusta had been granted an extended holiday from the schoolroom in order to stay at the dower house with Will and Claudia. He had merely told everyone that his wife had had to go somewhere in a hurry and he was going to escort her home. No one probed more deeply—he guessed that for those two days he had looked about as approachable as his father had always looked.

Finally the Duke of Withingsby set out on his journey, following a cold trail to nowhere.

Charity trudged the three miles home from the coach stop and walked unheralded through the open front door of the house and into the parlor, where the children were just finishing their tea and were clamoring at Penelope to be allowed back outside to play. David was promising with loud insincerity not to get dirty again and Howard was declaring that his breeches had been torn quite by accident—he had been being very careful. Mary was proclaiming the fact that *she* had not got dirty *or* torn her breeches and so there was no reason why Penny should insist on her staying inside. Howard was just in the midst of pointing out the irrefutable fact that Mary did not even wear breeches when Mary spotted Charity standing in the doorway. She shrieked.

And then they were all shrieking or whooping and exclaiming and laughing and talking and hugging and yelling. No one in the Duncan family had ever learned the lesson that talking simultaneously with several other people resulted in little or no communication taking place.

"Well," Charity said at last, "here I am home again to stay, and you have all grown at least one inch, and if I may just sit down and be allowed a quiet bawl, I shall be myself again in no time at all."

She proceeded to do just that while Penelope rushed for the teapot and an empty cup and Mary dashed for the plate of scones—or what was left of them—and Howard told Charity how he had torn his breeches quite by accident and had then been falsely accused of being careless. David handed his sister his clean but much crumpled handkerchief.

It felt good beyond belief to be home. She did not tell the truth, of course. But she consoled herself with the thought that there would be no need of any more lies after today—or very few anyway. She told them she had not liked her new employment and so had left it. She told them that she had come home to stay, which would please Phil even if now he would have to bear the burden of their support all alone.

She was not quite sure yet if she really would stay. Perhaps after a while she would try again to find employment, but for a time at least she would be quite happy to stay where she was, licking her wounds, trying to persuade herself that doing the right thing was a virtue in itself and would eventually bring peace and contentment. She had undoubtedly done the right thing.

Penelope was openly relieved to see her. She loved the children and cared well for them, but she did not have quite the firm motherly touch that Charity possessed. Besides, she had a beau—the same gentleman who had offered for Charity once upon a time. Penny was clearly eager to accept his addresses. She was only anxious for assurance that Charity did not want him for herself.

"Of course I do not," Charity said quite firmly. "If I had wanted him, Penny, I would have had him when he was interested in me—before you grew up enough that he would see you are the prettier."

"Oh, I am not," Penny protested, blushing. "But perhaps you refused only because you were needed here, Charity."

It was partly the truth. But her feelings had not been deeply engaged either.

"I have no intention of marrying," she said. "I am going to stay here while the children grow up and then I am going to settle in to the congenial life of spinster aunt." She wondered if she was with child. But that was a complication that would have to be confronted if it proved to be so.

And so she settled back to life at home. She wrote to Philip, who would be happy, she knew. *She* was not happy about their situation, but miracles when they happened, she had discovered, were not really desirable things after all. Somehow they would manage. Somehow Phil would reach a point at which he would feel able to marry Agnes and begin a life of his own.

She tried not to think of Enfield or of any of the people there. In particular she tried not to think about *him*. It was impossible, of course. She felt sometimes as if he were actually a part of her, as if the physical oneness she had known with him in his bed had somehow passed into her soul. But she did succeed somehow in keeping him just below the level of conscious thought—for several minutes at a time and several times each day. The nights were a different matter, of course.

She kept herself busy. There was always plenty to do at home, and there was much to do beyond home too. There were friends and neighbors to be visited. She had been away for almost a year, after all. It felt very good to be back.

It was amazing how many ladies in brown had traveled on the stagecoach and left it at various destinations to disappear either on foot or in dogcarts or private carriages or other public vehicles in every direction of the compass. He wasted several days pursuing the most promising of the leads only to find that they led nowhere. Finally it seemed he had only two places left to go—back to Enfield or forward to London. She would certainly not have returned to Enfield. Yet if she had gone to London, his chances of finding her were slim indeed. He did have one moment of inspiration when he remembered the letter of recommendation that had been written by the rector of her former parish. But try as he could he was unable to remember the name of the place in Hampshire. The letter with all the applications had been destroyed. Besides, she had left that place because she no longer had a home there. It was unlikely she would go back there now.

He went to London. And since he had to begin his search somewhere, no matter how hopeless he felt, he went to the place where she had had lodgings before she married him. Even doing that was not easy. He could not remember exactly where it was. Fortunately his coachman was a little more sure. He drove to the wrong street at the first try, but they both recognized the second street and the building.

No, Miss Duncan no longer lived there, the landlord informed the duke when he asked, and no, he did not know where she had gone. No, she had not come there within the last week. They were the answers the duke had fully expected, but until he heard them he did not realize how much he had been hoping that he was wrong. Where would he look now? There was a frightening emptiness before him. There was nowhere else to look except all of England, starting perhaps with Hampshire.

"But *Mr.* Duncan might know 'er whereabouts, guv," the landlord said after he had turned to leave. "Hif you cares to come back tonight when 'e's finished 'is work."

Mr. Duncan? The duke stared blankly at the man. Her father? He was dead. Her husband? Her brother? She had no brothers. *Her husband!* He felt his hands at his sides ball into fists. He felt his mouth go dry.

"I shall do that," he heard himself say. "Thank you." He handed the man a sovereign.

But, he thought as he was clambering back into his carriage, plotting murder, *she had been a virgin.*

One thing was very clear to him. Charity Earheart, Duchess of Withingsby, had been telling him a lie or two from the start. Not only was she not a quiet brown mouse, she was also not—

Damn it, he thought, he knew nothing about her. Nothing at all. Except that she was his wife. Except that he loved her.

The day seemed endless. It seemed a fortnight long. But finally he was back at the rooming house and was informed that Mr. Duncan had returned from work no more than five minutes before. The duke climbed the stairs and knocked with the head of his cane on the door the landlord had indicated.

A rather tired-looking young man opened the door and looked at him inquiringly—a young man who bore an unmistakable resemblance to Charity. His eyes took in the elegant appearance of his visitor.

"Yes?" he said.

"Mr. Duncan?"

"Yes." The young man looked wary.

"You have a—sister, I believe," the duke said. "Charity."

A frown was added to the wary look. "And if I do, sir?" he said. "What business would you have with my sister?"

The duke sighed. "She happens to be my wife," he said. "May I come inside?"

He did not wait for an invitation. He stepped past the young man, who was staring blankly at him.

"I suppose," he said, turning, "there are a dozen other brothers and sisters too. It would explain a few things." The adept way in which she had managed them all and sorted out all their lives, for example.

"Who are you?" Mr. Duncan asked.

"Anthony Earheart—"

"Her former employer," the young man said, his brows snapping together again. "You are a married man, sir, with four young children. If I see before me the reason she felt constrained to leave her employment in such haste, then—"

"Yes, I am indeed a married man," the duke said. "I married your sister the day after interviewing her in Upper Grosvenor Street. We do not yet have four children or even one, but I have hopes. Much depends upon whether I can run her to earth. She appears to be under the illusion that by hiding herself away she can nullify our marriage."

Mr. Duncan was staring at him as if he had just dropped off some remote heavenly body. "You *married* her?" he said faintly. "And she has *left* you? She is *hiding* from you? What the devil—"

"I feel constrained to add," his grace said, "that I love my wife. I trust you know where she is. Managing the lives of the other dozen of you, I suppose."

"You *love* her? Yet she has run off from you after a mere few weeks?" the other man said. "I confess to total bewilderment, sir. And to a total unwillingness to give you any information that might put my sister in danger."

The duke sighed. "You have good fraternal instincts," he said. "I would have despised you heartily if you had fallen upon my neck without further ado and embraced me as a brother. I have Lord Rowling sitting in my carriage outside in the street, doubtless bored to incoherence at the lengthy wait. He was a witness at my marriage. My marriage papers are also in the carriage. I shall fetch both if you will promise not to bolt the door as soon as my back is turned. I mean to find my wife."

"*Lord* Rowling?" The young man's eyes had widened.

"Lord Rowling," his grace repeated. "I shall pull rank on you if all else fails, Duncan. In addition to being Anthony Earheart, you see, I am the Duke of Withingsby. Your sister, my dear sir, is my duchess. I shall fetch my proofs and then proceed to tell all. If you have always suspected your sister of an inclination to madness, it will be my pleasure to confirm your worst fears."

He left the room while Philip Duncan was still staring at him in fascinated shock.

Chapter 18

The children were playing on the lawn in front of the house—at least, the boys were playing an energetic game of war while Mary swung idly from the tree swing, fanning herself with a book she had been planning to read. It was a warm day.

They all saw the carriage at roughly the same moment. They stared in mingled awe and admiration at the grand conveyance with its crested door and its liveried coachman and footman. Their eyes widened simultaneously when they saw that it was slowing and turning in at the gates to drive up about the curved driveway to the front doors of their own home.

But they did not wait to watch it complete its journey. They dashed into the house as fast as they could scurry, each eager to be the one to tell the astounding news to their elder sisters. But only Penelope was in the parlor, stitching at her embroidery—Charity was out in the back garden cutting flowers to replace the slightly drooping ones that adorned each downstairs room. Penelope would have to do. A chorus of voices preceded the children as they dashed across the room toward her, all pointing backward in the direction of the door.

"Mercy!" Penelope said. "One at a time, please. *What* did you see? *Who* is coming? Mr. Miller?" she asked hopefully, her hands straying upward to check her golden curls.

But the noise ceased abruptly at the sound of another voice calling from the front doorway—they had left the door wide open during their inward dash, of course. It was a male voice. A familiar voice. They all stared wildly at one another—Penelope included.

"Phil?"

"Philip?"

"That's Phil."

"I don't believe it. It can't be."

They all spoke simultaneously.

But before they could all dash back in the direction of the hall and the front doors, their brother appeared in the parlor doorway, grinning at them.

"I thought the whole neighborhood at the very least must be gathered in here," he said. "What a noise!"

But before they could fill their lungs with sufficient air to enable them to launch into the only type of greeting worthy of a long-absent brother, someone else appeared behind him, and when Philip stepped inside the room, that someone else was fully visible in the doorway. He was an elegant, handsome, haughty-looking gentleman, clad austerely but extremely fashionably in black. His long fingers were playing with the handle of a quizzing glass. His eyebrows were raised and his lips pursed. He looked about the room unhurriedly, gazing at each of them in turn.

The Duncans for once in their lives stood perfectly still and perfectly mute. For all they knew it might be Satan himself who had decided to pay them a visit.

"Penny," their brother said, "David, Howard, Mary—goodness, how you have all grown!—may I present the Duke of Withingsby?"

If it were possible to be stiller than still and muter than mute, the Duncans were both for a few seconds. Then Penelope recovered her manners and sank into a curtsy. Mary followed suit and the boys, noticing the movement, bobbed their heads to the truly awesome figure of a real, live duke.

"We have traveled down from London," Philip said. "His grace has important business here. Where is Charity?"

His grace had strolled across the room and was looking from the window, his hands clasped at his back.

"She is—"

But Penelope did not need to complete her sentence. Charity

herself, arms loaded with flowers, had appeared in the doorway. She saw her brother immediately, and her eyes lit up.

"Phil!" she cried. "Oh, Phil, what a wonderful surprise. You did not let us know, you wretch! You are the last person I expected to see. What on earth are you doing here? Oh, let me set these flowers down so that I may hug you."

"I think maybe not the last person, Charity," he said, looking decidedly uncomfortable. "Maybe there is someone you expect less."

She looked at him in incomprehension for a moment until a movement close to the window alerted her. Her head jerked about and she looked across the room and became very still. He had only half turned toward the room. He looked steadily at her over his shoulder, his eyebrows raised.

"Charity," Penelope said into the tense and uncomfortable silence, "do you know the Duke of Withingsby? He has come with Phil on important—"

"He is my husband," Charity said quietly.

The Duncans might never be the same again. Marble statues might have considered them worth emulating.

"Perhaps," his grace said equally quietly, "I might be allowed a short while alone with my wife."

"We will step outside and admire the gardens," Philip suggested and mobilized his brothers and sisters into action. They filed past him meekly enough. But there was a chorus of sound the moment he closed the door behind him. The sounds receded in the direction of the back door.

"Well, Charity."

Curiously, he looked like a stranger again. He looked alien in the surroundings of her own home. He looked again like the man who had interviewed her for a governess's position. He looked satanic. He looked—very male.

"As you can see, your grace," she said, setting down her armful of flowers on the nearest table and folding her hands in front of her, "I live in a perfectly comfortable home and enjoy the company of numerous brothers and sisters. We are not wealthy. Neither are we destitute. You really do not need to concern yourself with me at all." She wanted to shower him with questions—how was Augusta? Had he missed her? How were Anthony and Harry and Claudia and William? Had he missed her? Had Charles been heartbroken when Lady Marie went home? Was there hope for them? *Had he missed her?*

"I need not concern myself with you," he said quietly. "With my own wife."

"I am not really your wife," she said. "It was only a temporary arrangement. Its purpose was completed. I came home. You did not need to come after me."

"You are not really my wife?" he said. "Yet there was a wedding. There is a church register that records our marriage. There was a ring, which you are no longer wearing, I see. You lived in my home and were received by my family. You shared a marriage bed with me on numerous occasions. What is a real wife, pray, ma'am?"

"You are being unfair," she said. "It was our agreement—"

"It was our agreement," he said, "that you would perform a service for me, in return for which you would forever be my wife, supported by me in a manner appropriate to your rank."

"But I cannot accept that support," she said. "The payment is in excess of the service, your grace. And I cannot accept payment for being your wife. It seems to me perilously close to accepting payment as your wh—as your whore."

His eyes kindled then so that she was truly frightened. When he took a step toward her, she had to exercise all her willpower to stand her ground.

"My whore?" he whispered—the whisper made her lick her lips in terror. "My whore, ma'am? A whore would perform her best tricks for me in bed, ma'am, and would be paid for giving satisfaction there. A whore would not be given my name. A whore would not be taken to meet my father and my family. A whore would not find herself in my own bed in my own home. A whore would not find herself supported in a manner appropriate to a duchess for the rest of her life. You are not my whore, *your grace*. You are not skilled enough to be my whore. You are my wife."

She could feel herself blushing hotly. And feeling stupidly humiliated. She had not pleased him? She spoke before she had time to think.

"I am sorry if I did not please you, your grace," she said stiffly.

He stared at her. And then his eyes changed. She almost jumped with alarm when he threw back his head and laughed. She had never seen him laugh like that before.

"I am glad that I amuse you at least," she said, on her dignity.

"If you did not please me!" he said. "In bed do you mean, Charity? You are still very much the innocent, my love, else you would know beyond any doubt that you pleased me there very well indeed."

And now she despised the smug feeling of gladness that she concentrated on keeping out of her face.

"I will not take payment from you," she said. "I thank you for showing enough concern to find me. But you need not worry. You must go back home. Augusta needs you."

He had been coming closer as she spoke. He stopped when he was within grabbing distance, increasing her nervousness. But she would not give him the satisfaction of stepping back.

"Augusta needs *you*, Charity," he said. "She needs you very badly."

Ah, this was unfair. This was grossly unfair. "My younger brothers and sister need me too, your grace," she said. "Besides, a house and servants and a carriage and six thousand a year will not serve Augusta's needs."

"Enfield needs you," he said. "It needs a duchess. It has been without one for too long."

Oh. The great stabbing of longing took her unawares and she feared it might have shown in her face. She frowned.

"And it needs an heir," he said. "An heir of the direct line."

She glared indignantly at him. "So *that* is it," she said. "You think to add to the original agreement. That was no part of it, your grace. You said—"

"And *I* need you, my love," he said. "I need you so much that I panic when I think that perhaps I will not be able to persuade you to come back with me to Enfield. I need you so much that I cannot quite contemplate the rest of my life if it must be lived without you. I need you so much that— Well, the words speak for themselves. I need you."

"To look after Augusta?" she said. She dared not hear what he was surely saying. She dared not hope. "To look after Enfield? To provide you with an heir?"

"Yes," he said, and her heart sank like a stone to be squashed somewhere between her slippers and the parlor carpet. "And to be my friend and my confidant and my comfort. And to be my lover."

"It was not part of our agreement." She must fight or she would go all to pieces. She watched someone's hands smoothing over the lapels of his coat as if to remove lint, though there was none to remove. They were her hands. But she could not snatch them away. His own had come up to cover them and hold them in place.

"No, it was not," he said quietly. "But you played unfair, Charity. You did not tell me you were not a quiet mouse. You did not tell me you were beautiful or charming or warm with concern for others or courageous or—wonderful in bed." She jerked at her hands, but he would not let her have them back. "You did not tell me you were a thief. I had to come after you to recover my stolen property."

"But the pearls—" She would have died of shame if she could. She had thought the pearls were a gift.

"Are yours, my love," he said. "They were a wedding gift. What you stole, Charity, was my heart. I have come to get it back if all else fails. But I would rather you kept it and brought it back to Enfield with you."

"Oh." Her sigh was almost an agony.

"And I am playing unfair too," he said. "I cannot deny the terms of our agreement. They are written down and signed by each of us. I will keep my side of the bargain if I must. But then you must allow me to keep it. I would far prefer to tear up the document. I have brought it with me—it is in the carriage. We will tear it up together, I hope. But I will agree to do so on only one condition. If you will be my wife in truth, then we will scrap the blasted thing. If you will not, then it must stand in its entirety. The choice is yours."

He held her hands flat against his chest. He held her eyes with his. What chance did she have?

"I am needed here," she said.

"No," he said, "not necessarily here. You are needed by your younger brothers and sister. They would perhaps like Enfield. They would perhaps like Augusta, who would adore them. Your older sister might like Enfield too."

"Penny likes Mr. Miller," she said.

"And if Mr. Miller likes Penelope," he said, "then I will concede that Enfield might be a far less attractive prospect than Mr. Miller's home. I assume he is eligible? But that is for your brother to decide. As for your brother, he and I have had a long talk. He is as stubborn as a mule and as proud as—what is the proudest thing you can think of? No matter. But he is no match for the Duke of Withingsby, my love. I am not my father's son for nothing. I can be marvelously toplofty when I wish to be. There are those who would say, indeed, that I never stop being toplofty. However it is, your brother will return here where he belongs and the debts which have kept him away working at menial drudgery will be paid off—he has not confessed to the debts, but I was not born yesterday. I gather that there is a certain paragon of beauty and charm? A Miss Gladstone?"

"Agnes," she said.

"I daresay she will be Mrs. Duncan before too long," he said, "so I will not bother remembering anything but her first name. I have everything taken care of, you see, my love. Are you with child?"

Her cheeks were instantly scarlet. She needed no looking glass to verify the fact. "No," she said.

"Ah." He smiled. "I must confess to some disappointment. But rectifying that situation will give us something to work on when we return to Enfield. Not that I intend to subject you to yearly confinements for the next twenty years. We will contrive a way to keep that from happening. But—" He stopped suddenly, dropped his hands from hers, took a step back, and turned to face away from her. "But I am babbling. I am so nervous I do not know what I am saying. Am I making any sense at all? Am I bullying you? Charity? Charity, will you be my wife?"

"It is not just, then," she said, "that you feel an obligation? That you have realized the distasteful nature of that agreement?"

He made a sound that was suspiciously like a moan.

"You really love me?" she asked wistfully.

"The devil!" he exclaimed, looking over his shoulder. "Did I forget to say it? The thing I came to say?"

"I love you too," she said. "I love you so much that it has felt to me since I came home that you are here all the time." She tapped her chest just above her heart.

"I told you you had stolen it," he said, and he smiled at her with such sudden warmth that she lost her knees and almost staggered. He turned and caught her in his arms.

"Anthony." She hid her face against his chest. "Oh, Anthony, what am I trying to say?"

"I have no idea," he said. "Has it not all been said? I would settle for a kiss in exchange for whatever we have missed. If you would just lift your face."

She did so and smiled at him while she slid her arms up about his neck. "You had better do it while we still have a moment to ourselves, then," she said. "I have never seen my brothers and sisters stunned into silence as they were when I came into the room. They have never been within a county's breadth of a duke before—especially one who looks so very toplofty. A few minutes ago they discovered that *their sister* is a duchess. But we are made of stern stuff, we Duncans. The shock is going to wear off any minute now and they are going to be bursting in here to ask a million questions each—of each of us. Be warned. It is no light task you have just talked yourself into undertaking."

"Dear me," the Duke of Withingsby said with a haughty lift of his brows. "We had better proceed with that kiss then, your grace. Clearly I need something with which to bolster my fortitude."

"Exactly what I was trying to say," she said while she could. She was certainly prevented from saying anything else for a good long while.

After a good long while there was the sound of voices all talking simultaneously approaching from the direction of the back door.